CORRIDORS OF HEALING

W⸻n
G⸻s
of⸻
m⸻n
En⸻d
M⸻A
fri⸻l
pa⸻a
de⸻a
an⸻e
an⸻s
are⸻a
M⸻l
lor

CORRIDORS OF HEALING

Walking the corridors of Brookhampton General are two young physicians, product of entirely different systems and environments. Hugh Ravelston, a member of an English medical family, and his friend Maxwell Okiya, son of an African chief. A friend too is Jock Calderwood, the hospital pathologist, who shares with Hugh a devotion not only to medicine but to the sea and sailing. But no friend is David Lyell, the ambitious house physician whose actions are to threaten Hugh's future through Linda Masterson, only six years old, terrified and lonely in the children's ward.

CORRIDORS OF HEALING

by

Elizabeth Harrison

Dales Large Print Books
Long Preston, North Yorkshire,
BD23 4ND, England.

British Library Cataloguing in Publication Data.

Harrison, Elizabeth
    Corridors of healing.

A catalogue record of this book is
available from the British Library

ISBN   978-1-84262-898-0 pbk

First published in Great Britain in 1968 by Ward Lock & Co Ltd.

Copyright © Elizabeth Harrison 1968

Cover illustration © David Thrower by arrangement with
Arcangel Images

The moral right of the author has been asserted

Published in Large Print 2012 by arrangement with
Watson, Little Ltd.

Dales Large Print is an imprint of Library Magna Books Ltd.

Printed and bound in Great Britain by
T.J. (International) Ltd., Cornwall, PL28 8RW

CHAPTER ONE

The two men pushed their way down the ward, through hurtling bodies demanding rides, hanging on to their legs, climbing up them, voices shrieking for attention, eyes that followed them hopefully from cots. Hugh Ravelston and Maxwell Okiya were popular in the children's ward.

But Linda Masterson made no overtures. She lay silently and watched them. She prayed that they weren't coming to see her. What she wanted was to go home, or if that were not possible, at least to be left in peace by the doctors in their white coats. They were all-powerful, and they terrified her. She was particularly terrified by Dr Okiya. She was unable to understand what he said, and she had never seen a black doctor before. His approach was the opening of a nightmare. She stiffened into a rigid paralysis of fear. He pretended always to be friendly, of course. But Linda knew better. His friendliness was false.

They had arrived. They had stopped at her bed. Now they both stood at the foot of the bed, with Sister, and turned over the papers where everything about her was written down. Then the other one came and sat down beside her, and began talking to her. She looked at him and said nothing. It was best simply to say nothing – then they might grow tired of her and leave her alone. In any case, she didn't know what to say. They always expected cheerful answers, brisk repartee, they made little jokes and smiled, while they pushed her about, peered down her mouth, put cold things on her chest and her back, said, 'Now cough', 'again', 'once more, *that's* a good girl'. But it was all false, all the joking and the way they looked at you and smiled. They were after something quite different, had some dangerous secret plan of their own, which they would go away and talk about. Then they would come back and do frightful things. She had seen a child wheeled away on an iron trolley, still and silent. No one saw her again. She never returned. The doctors were dangerous. And powerful.

Look at what they had done to her. She had been all right until she came here. Certainly Auntie Beryl had fussed, saying she didn't eat enough and she ought to be fatter, not so tired and pale, and there she was running that temperature again, but in fact she had felt well enough until she came here. Then they put her to bed and suddenly she was ill. Too ill to leave. Auntie Beryl came to see her and said she must stay in hospital, she was ill. She tried to explain that she was only ill because she was here; if she could leave this place she'd be well again. But it was no use.

Now this man was going to make her sick. He put that flat thing into her mouth, on her tongue, and pressed. That always made her sick.

She was sick. That would show him. She couldn't help it, she didn't do it on purpose, but that would show him, all the same.

Hugh Ravelston caught the fleeting gleam of triumph almost lost in the anguished rigidity, and tried to capture it before it fled beyond recall – the sole sign of a living child behind the terror.

He grinned at the spark in the fearful eyes that glared up at him and said, 'All right. You win. I won't do that again if you don't like it.'

She stared at him in amazement. Could she actually stop him doing anything he wanted to?

He added hastily, seeing what was in her mind, 'No need to be sick, though. You could just tell me, couldn't you?'

'You wouldn't take any notice,' she retorted disagreeably.

She had been in the ward five days now, and this was the first time she had spoken.

'I might, or I might not,' he said. 'It would depend. But you could try it and see.'

At least he wasn't always trying to be funny, like the others.

'I want to go home,' she said exploratively.

He looked unhappy, but only said rather briskly, 'Well, you can't, because we don't know what's wrong with you.'

'If you find out, can I go then?'

'Yes.'

She digested this. It was a new idea. 'How do you know there is anything wrong with me?' she demanded.

'Don't you think there is?'

'I was all right until I came here,' she pointed out.

Hugh sighed, and took her hand. 'You don't like it here, do you?' he asked.

She shook her head.

On impulse, he picked her out of bed and sat down with her on his knee. She at once put her thumb in her mouth and curled up against him, burrowing her head beneath his white coat. He patted her thoughtfully and wondered what might be wrong with her. She ought, he thought hopelessly, to be in the sort of children's unit where they had up-to-date buildings and admitted the mothers with the children into separate cubicles. Being alone and frightened in a strange echoing ward was doing her no good at all.

She took her thumb out of her mouth, pushed herself upright with firm hands on his chest, and said imperatively, 'Tell me a story.'

Hugh smiled wryly. Children were always amazing him with their resilience, their spontaneous recoveries, spiritual or physical. Right up and down inside five seconds flat. 'Not now,' he said firmly. 'I'm busy. Nurse will tell you a story.'

'Mavis will read her a story,' Max said, materialising suddenly. 'Mavis likes reading to people. Mavis!'

Mavis was a ten-year-old, small, red-headed, freckled, with an appealing grin and an excellent opinion of herself. She had been admitted six weeks earlier with acute rheumatism – a condition seldom seen in children's wards nowadays, though common twenty years ago. She had apparently recovered, and spent her days bouncing round the ward in high spirits, ready for home and school and a normal life. They were keeping her in, though, waiting to see whether her heart had been affected by the illness. She had time on her hands, and was extremely proud of her ability to read aloud, with enormous expression and elocutionary fervour.

Now she beamed cheerfully at a suspicious Linda, and said, 'O.K. I'll read to you. What'd you like? Batman?'

Hugh and Max left the two of them to sort themselves out, and went off down the ward. 'At least you got through to the child,'

11

Max remarked. 'That's more than anyone else has been able to do.'

'Poor little scrap. She wants her mother.' Hugh sighed. He had never grown accustomed to the deficiencies of this general hospital which had once been a poor-law infirmary, and whose buildings dated from the previous century. 'We ought to have cubicles and admit the mothers too.' He knew it was useless, but he could not prevent himself saying it.

'Not her mother. Her aunt. She lives with her aunt,' Max said. 'To be strictly accurate.'

'Oh? Why?'

Max shrugged. 'No idea,' he said. To Max Okiya, brought up in Nigeria, there was nothing unusual or demanding investigation in the fact that a child lived with her aunt rather than with the mother who bore her.

He and Hugh Ravelston were an interesting contrast. Both tall and lean, they were products of entirely different systems and environments. Maxwell Okiya, dark-skinned and dark-eyed, flat-nosed, with close-cropped fuzzy hair and a wide mouth that laughed easily and infectiously, was the son of an African chief whose local authority remained absolute today. Hugh Ravelston, blue-eyed and tanned, with the beaky nose of all the Ravelstons, came from a medical family of eminence. If the family had a black sheep, he was it. Public school, Cambridge and his teaching hospital had moulded him (though there were those who thought they had failed in their task). Mission school and the university at Ibadan had made Okiya. Resident Medical Officer and paediatric registrar respectively at Brookhampton General Hospital, they had been friends for some years, and often consulted one another over difficult or awkward cases.

'Mind if I have a talk to the aunt some time?' Hugh asked now.

'Go ahead. Wish you would. I can't get anywhere with either of them.'

Hugh made a note in his book, and looked at his watch. 'I must get a move on,' he said. 'I've a patient in Cartwright to see before I go, and I'm due at the Calderwoods for dinner. I'll talk to the aunt tomorrow, if I get a chance, and then have a word with you.' He ran quickly up the stone stairs (relic of the poor-law infirmary) to Cartwright, and saw his patient there. He was holding his own, and would do nicely until his return in the evening, he decided. He went to his room and changed, and then drove along the lanes to Marsh Farm, the Calderwoods' rambling old house overlooking the estuary. It was the turn of the season, spring moving buoyantly into summer, the grass was lush on the verges, the hedges a vivid green. The reeds swayed in the wind from the sea, and when he turned into the drive at Marsh

13

Farm he saw the cherry blossom was over, petals scattered still on the grass. In a week the lilac would be in bloom and the scent would come drifting through the windows into the old house. Already the flowers showed dark purple in the evening sunlight. Hugh's eyes saw all this, but his mind was still pondering the problem of Linda Masterson. Medically, she was interesting, and her unhappiness gave urgency to his speculations.

Jock Calderwood, a square pugnacious man in his late fifties with a mop of white hair, heard the car and came round the side of the house from the garden to greet him. He was the hospital pathologist, and Hugh began talking at once about the result of the tests on the child. 'Max feels he's missing something obvious,' he said. 'He's worried about her.'

Calderwood chuckled. 'I'd hardly say he was missing anything obvious,' he said. 'Forms of every hue have been pouring in at five-minute intervals from him. He's just about thrown the book at that child.'

'She's petrified,' Hugh remarked. This was the knowledge that refused to leave him alone. 'I wish to God we had an adequate children's unit, with cubicles for the mothers to stay.'

'Can't have everything, m'boy.' Jock Calderwood was unmoved. 'The intensive

14

care unit's coming along well. One thing at a time. In any case, even if we had any funds for rebuilding, that project would be doomed. Can you honestly visualise dear old Sister Addiscombe suffering mums all over her wards?'

'No, I suppose not. And she's not a bad old stick.'

'We can't afford to lose her,' Jock agreed. 'And while we have her, we needn't dissipate our energies in proposing modern methods of child care, because we won't get anywhere. They're still tussling with her about visiting hours, you know. Each year – after a protracted battle with Matron, the House Governor and umpteen different committees – Sister grudgingly concedes half an hour extra. And I can tell you it's touch and go. She thinks the rot's set in. So, as a matter of fact, does Harrington.' Harrington was the paediatrician, Max Okiya's chief. 'He's against open-visiting and too many mums, I can tell you.' Jock Calderwood, in addition to being a member of the hospital management committee, was chairman of the medical committee. 'We must work with the staff we have, you know, Hugh, not with the paragons we should like to engage if we had the money and knew where to look for them. Personally I rather doubt if we'd find anyone half up to Sister Addiscombe. She's devoted to children, she

15

works like a Trojan – she'll turn her hand to anything – she can keep her staff, and she's been with us for thirty years. She's entitled to her little ways.' He patted Hugh encouragingly on the shoulder, though quite what he meant by this he would have been at a loss to say. 'Sufficient for the day,' he added vaguely. 'Come along, you've time for a drink before we eat. We're all in the garden still. Claire's down, and Hermione's here too.' He led the way round to the lawns, where deck-chairs were out and a tray of drinks stood on the teak table that had weathered to silver-grey. Below the lawn stretched the sea, where *Sea Spray*, Jock's rakish thirty-five-foot ocean racer, rode to the tide. Closer inshore was Hugh's own Flying Fifteen *ffantasy*, while drawn up on the shingle were their dinghies. Hugh and Jock shared a devotion not only to medicine, but to the sea and sailing. Marsh Farm was bordered on three sides by the estuary, and from his study window Jock watched *Sea Spray* on her mooring.

Of the three women who awaited them, Margaret Calderwood looked exactly what she was – a brisk, kindly, managing and somewhat limited woman, with a trim figure, short grey curling hair and a complexion of the most expensive softest brown leather, criss-crossed with innumerable tiny lines. She served on a number of

16

local committees and ran her home without fuss. Marsh Farm, outwardly mellow, rambling, tranquilly beautiful, inwardly reflected Margaret's busy and pre-occupied daily life. The rooms had been furnished thirty years earlier, and in the intervening decades Margaret and Jock had played general post with the furniture. Pieces had been moved from one room to another to suit the exigencies of the moment, so that now no sofa matched a chair, no sideboard a dining table (the sideboard held drinks in Jock's study, while Margaret's dressing table stood in for it in the dining-room. Jock's first desk had become Margaret's dressing table). Even the loose covers made for the drawing-room had found their way into the study and Margaret's bedroom. It was a comfortable house, but it tended to re-semble a heterogeneous collection of goods hastily assembled from an auction room.

Hermione Dunn, Margaret's sister-in-law, longed always to *do something,* as she put it, about the interior of Marsh Farm. A dreamily beautiful girl, Hermione had become a dreamily elegant woman, with an air of far-away places. She ran nothing, not even her own home and certainly not her daughter, though once she had tried to do this.

Clare Dunn, down for the week-end from her secretarial job in London, had flopped exhausted into her deck-chair, and was looking all bones and angles in the way that so much worried Hermione. Her daughter, to her eyes, had no elegance and no beauty. Clare was sallow, and her dark hair was cropped like a boy's close to her skull, making her face all eyes and mouth. Poor little orphan Annie in person, Hermione thought, with a pang of tenderness accompanied by a spurt of irritation, hopelessly dressed in that brief straight sack of dark blue linen that did nothing at all for her, and with enormous – and surely quite unnecessary – dark glasses completely hiding her one good point, her great brown eyes.

Hugh, though, was delighted to see Clare. He was very fond of her, treating her as he might have done the younger sister he had never had, and after he had greeted Margaret and Hermione he ruffled her short hair affectionately, and remarked 'So here you are. How's London?'

'All right,' she said briefly.

'Sail tomorrow?'

'All right.'

Hermione frowned. Why couldn't the girl make an effort with this extremely good-looking – and, she had been given to understand, well-born and moneyed – young man?

Jock gave Hugh a dry martini and ice, and in his turn looked at his niece, remembering the battle there had been three years ago.

CHAPTER TWO

One summer day Hermione had telephoned Margaret from Fordham, the London suburb where she and Clare lived in the house in which both of them had been born. The telephone call in itself was a harbinger of crisis, since at that time Hermione went her own way and lived her own life, or what passed for life.

'Margaret,' she said in dramatic tones (Hermione was apt to indulge in drama, usually in dreams, but occasionally in reality) 'I simply do not know what to do about Clare.'

'What's wrong?'

'I can't do anything with her. I can make no impression on her at all.' Hermione sounded amazed, as well she might, Margaret thought. She and Jock had always deprecated the fact that Clare appeared to be little more than her mother's shadow.

'She refuses to take her A levels,' Hermione announced in a voice of doom.

Anticlimax, Margaret considered. But she knew better than to say so. 'What does she want to do?' she asked.

'My *dear*,' Hermione panted in a series of

drawling gasps heavily overcharged with emotion, 'my *dear,* she says – she says she *wants* – to do – to do a – a *secretarial* course.' She halted, on a note that implied total disaster.

'Yes, well, a lot of them do,' Margaret said peaceably, stifling laughter. She could see that in Hermione's scale of values a secretarial course would be the ultimate heresy.

'My dear,' Hermione resumed in the same drawling gasp, 'the *waste,* the unutterable waste. I simply can't *allow* it, and I've told her so.'

'What does she say?' Margaret asked with interest.

'I can simply make no impression. No impression at all. I don't know what to do. She's never *been* like this before. *Never.* I can't understand what can possibly have come over her. She's always been such a *comfort* to me,' she wailed.

The outcome of all this had been that for once Hermione had agreed to abandon her cosy little life and Fordham, and had come with Clare to stay at Marsh Farm for the summer holidays. Clare had been seventeen.

'Life,' she had announced to Margaret, as dramatically as her mother might have done, 'life is passing me by.' She had looked past her aunt to the ebbing tide, her chin lifted, an air of incipient tragedy ostentatiously maintained.

Margaret's lips had twitched. Later she had had her laugh out with Jock. 'Life,' she told him that night, 'is passing Clare by. That appears to be the trouble.'

They had both chuckled tolerantly.

'All the same,' Jock added unexpectedly, 'she's right, you know. It is. And it will continue to do so, unless we take some action. We mustn't simply shrug this off as a silly whim of a temperamental schoolgirl. She has put her finger right on the spot. Good thing she's capable of it. After all, life has passed Hermione by, you'll admit?'

Margaret did admit this. It was the most obvious fact about Hermione Dunn.

'No doubt about it,' Jock went on. 'Clare is in considerable danger of the same fate.'

'But A levels – such a ridiculous point at which to take a stand,' Margaret protested. 'I mean, we would never have allowed any of the children to dictate to us about their A levels.'

'No. But basically the girl is right. We must take her seriously, and I think we ought to help her to assert herself before it's too late. I'm delighted to know she has it in her. I'd always supposed she was completely under Hermione's thumb.'

'Hermione doesn't have thumbs,' Margaret said idiotically. 'Only little fingers, to wind people round.'

21

'I see what you mean,' Jock agreed. 'And that's why she can be dangerous. Let me talk to Clare,' he added somewhat grandiloquently.

For the first time he tried to get to know his niece. He found it heavy going. Clare was not a girl with whom he found it easy to sympathise. He found her dull as ditchwater.

No worse than that. Simply dull. But the dead weight of her dullness stupefied him, as he faced her daily at meals. He had to make a continuous effort to reach her, to understand her, to cross the barrier of her silences.

Clare, at seventeen, had no claim to beauty other than her huge eyes, none of her mother's blonde fragility and elegance. In fact she took after her father, and Tom Dunn's appearance when reproduced in a young girl was not an outstanding success. Her manner and clothes did nothing to help her. Her manner was abrupt. Utterly sincere, but curt to the point of rudeness, and extremely down to earth, two qualities that again had appeared to better advantage in Tom Dunn than in his daughter. She was subject to long silences and brief monosyllables, and was anything but ingratiating. Jock sometimes felt that when she did open her mouth she had the knack of reducing any conversation to imbecilic awkwardness.

Her clothes were supervised by Hermione, and failed to suit her, the gentle pastels and soft Liberty prints serving only to emphasise her lack of distinction. Hermione, of course, never actually saw Clare herself. She saw the child she had wanted to have, long-limbed and beautiful, with clothes out of a fairy story and looks to match. *La princesse lointaine*. All she had once imagined herself to be, once imagined Tom found in her. She knew that Clare could not fulfil this image, but she hoped she might at least approximate. There could be, she misguidedly thought, no harm in trying. She had never looked at her daughter with eyes clear of dreams and her own egotism, never seen her as she in reality was, or tried to come to terms with the living being who struggled and suffered and strove to exist.

At seventeen, Clare wore her hair in a plait. Her complexion was colourless and inclined to spots, her expression without vivacity. She treated her clothes – with some reason – with boredom and contempt. Her skirts sagged and her stockings wrinkled. What, she felt, was the good of trying? She could never be the sort of person her mother wanted her to be, so what the hell?

Hermione began to despair of her. 'If you'd only make some attempt to look clean and tidy, at least,' she urged her constantly. 'And pull your stockings up. Straighten your skirt, for heaven's sake. And why are you wearing that dreadful old pullover with it, when you have your pretty Tana lawn blouse?'

Clare loathed her pretty Tana lawn blouse.

'You're nothing but a *frump*,' Hermione wailed.

Clare knew this. It added to her sense of failure, but it was among the reasons for her final rebellion. To dress to please herself might seem a tiny ambition, and certainly could hardly be mentioned to critical and enquiring adults, but to Clare it was a vital symbol of emancipation. Not that she knew what she would, if independent, choose to wear. To be free to try, to make her own mistakes, was what she asked.

She wanted to make a clean sweep – of her clothes, her books, her entire life up to date. Failing this, she could see herself, plodding on for her A levels, a solitary senior at St Ursula's (where it was in the nature of a triumph to have a pupil taking A levels at all). Then three years at London University, travelling up and down daily from Fordham, working alone in her room each evening, becoming more and more like poor old Miss Farquharson every day. Miss Farquharson was her head-mistress, and Clare knew she hoped that her most brilliant pupil *(ugh)* would return to St Ursula's to teach. A life sentence. Nothing but writing essays and examinations for years and years, and at the end of it another lifetime of teaching English and correcting other people's essays. With every year that passed she would be turning more fatally away from life.

She had been cut off from her contemporaries throughout her schooldays. Now the time had come to break out. This was it. Her future hung in the balance.

Although she knew this, felt it in every fibre, she became dumb when asked to explain it. Part of the trouble, of course, was the presence of Hermione. Clare was too fond of her mother to fling at her before outsiders the furious cry that so often threatened to explode from her, 'I've got to get away from you.' Clare had secretly longed for independence since she was about twelve, but Hermione had no one to share her life but her daughter. This had always been the difficulty. Clare loved her mother and she was compelled publicly to stand by her. No one suspected that she often raged in her room, when she should have been writing one of her essays.

How far did devotion go? For the past few years Clare had given herself an answer that made compliance bearable, because temporary. 'Just while I am at school. After that–'

Now 'after that' was staring her in the

face. It showed every sign of being the same old story.

Clare had grown up in the quiet and spacious house at Fordham that belonged to her grandfather. Charles Seabrook, a quiet, scholarly man, conscientious and pain-staking, had been a general practitioner in the suburb for most of his life. He had followed his father into the family practice, and when the old man died he had moved into the big Edwardian house where he had spent his own childhood, and from which the practice had always been run. He had continued in the old style. When the Health Service came into existence in 1948 – the same year that Clare was born – he knew he was already elderly and set in his ways. He decided not to enter it, but to remain in private practice. By the time Clare was going to kindergarten, he had retired. By this time, too, Clare had accepted the fact that there was Mummy and Grandpa, but no longer Daddy. She could not remember her father, though she was faintly conscious of a time when a third figure had played a part in their lives, coming and going. Finally he had gone to somewhere referred to as the States, to do something called research, and there, Clare eventually gathered, he had died in some sort of accident. It was difficult to establish much about her father, for if she mentioned him there were odd silences, her mother's face became stony with attempted control. Grandpa looked worried and harassed. Her mother always made an attempt to answer fairly anything that she asked, but the attempts radiated an odd sort of cold disapproval of Clare for her temerity in raising what she ought to recognise was a momentous subject. Soon Clare's own mouth would involuntarily turn down at the corners, her throat would tighten, a sob would irresistibly push its way up. Then she would be on Grandpa's knee, and he would be comforting her.

She soon learned to avoid these scenes, so that by the time she was seven her father's name was never mentioned. She knew nothing about him, except that he too had been a doctor like Grandpa.

When Grandpa had retired from practice he had turned the rambling old Edwardian family house into flats. He had retained the ground floor, and had let the upper floors, making a separate entrance for them, and building a wall across one end of the garden to retain his own privacy.

Life there had been tranquil, a quiet routine of days. Clare had been taken to and from the kindergarten, then the first form, at St Ursula's. Very occasionally other children had been invited to tea, or she had paid a visit, but these outings were a source of much consideration in the family.

Grandpa would ask her what she was going to wear for her visit, she would parade before him in the latest Liberty print Hermione had made her, she would kiss him good-bye affectionately, and on her return she would tell him exactly what they had eaten for tea (and, of course, where they had eaten it. He was distressed to discover how many families of quite good background appeared to have their meals in the kitchen these days. He often wondered what Fordham was coming to, and discussed this with Hermione at some length).

At home they never ate in the kitchen. They had breakfast, lunch and supper (that the meal was now unmistakably supper and not dinner was sufficient concession to slack modernity and the servant problem, Grandpa considered) in the dining-room, and tea in the drawing-room off the big old silver tray, though Hermione no longer made it, as her mother had done, from a silver kettle over a spirit lamp. It was made, now, in the kitchen with an electric kettle. This alone showed that they moved with the times, Grandpa asserted.

In the kitchen was Mrs Wood – Woodie – who was the mainstay of the household. She did all the cooking and housekeeping, and supervised the daily woman who cleaned and old Moffat who did the garden and washed the car. Woodie was not, unfortunately, a very good cook. She had come to them as a parlourmaid in the nineteen thirties, but she was the practical member of the household, and they all knew her to be invaluable, and irreplaceable. Clare took her presence for granted. As far as she was concerned, Woodie was a member of the family.

Grandpa died when Clare was thirteen. She missed him, particularly missed his masculine presence, for with his death the household became entirely feminine, and its essence spinsterish. The routine of life went on as before. A year or two earlier Grandpa had argued Hermione into taking a job. While he had been out of touch with modern ways, he had never lost contact with people. He saw that his daughter had. In the old days she had helped him a little with the practice, she had done his letters for him, sent out his accounts, made out his lists. She had never answered the telephone; Woodie had done that in her old-fashioned parlourmaid style. But for many years now there had been none of these duties, and Grandpa had watched Hermione become increasingly isolated and lost in her prolonged day-dreams, as he called them, to her considerable annoyance. Rather to his surprise, he had succeeded in his efforts to persuade her to find a part-time post in the neighbourhood. That he had done so was the result of the intervention of one of Hermione's few friends, Mary Farquharson, the headmistress of St Ursula's. She had been the English mistress there when Hermione herself had been a pupil. Together they had explored Shakespeare and the great English poets. Hermione, Mary Farquharson had considered, had a poetic imagination. Mary herself, innocent, inexperienced, was romantic and still searching for the perfect relationship, longing both to worship and be worshipped. Then came Hermione, with her blonde beauty and her creative imagination – the long-sought student who gave meaning to her vocation. Hermione, Mary was sure, had it in her to become a modern poet of distinction.

This had not so far come to anything. Mary had deplored Hermione's marriage at only seventeen to that very ordinary young doctor. Her talent would, like that of too many girls, be submerged in nappies, cooking, shopping and ferrying children here and there. She thought it could only be for the best when Hermione found herself alone again after five brief interrupted years of marriage.

Hermione continued, Mary knew, to keep up with modern literature and to read her old favourites. The two of them often enjoyed delicious discussions about Tennyson's imagery or George Eliot's delineation of character. But Hermione had written nothing herself. The time might still come.

When she announced that her father was urging her to take a job, Mary had snapped her up for St Ursula's. There she would be under her own influence. She thought that the reason Hermione had not yet written had been that, first of all, she was lazy, and secondly, that she had lacked the stimulus of congenial companionship. Now it would be Mary's privilege to nurture her imagination, to encourage her, even to drive her. The prospect was enchanting.

In any case, it would be disastrous for Hermione to find the wrong sort of post. Some routine job would be soul-destroying. (For a specialist in English language and literature Mary Farquharson was surprisingly addicted to cliché. It was perhaps hardly to be wondered that she found originality in Hermione Dunn.)

Mary had recently taken over the headship of St Ursula's from old Miss Smallpiece, who had finally retired, almost dotty and, so they said, well into her nineties. She asked Hermione to join her, nominally as the bursar, a new and grandiose title which she hoped would lend tone to the establishment and compensate locally for Miss Smallpiece's departure. Miss Smallpiece had been eccentric and beloved in the district, and of unimpeachable standing. Mary was correct in imagining that some gesture was needed to offset her retirement, but whether

31

Hermione's appointment met this need was dubious. Though, as Mary never failed to realise, Hermione had a material worth in addition to her somewhat problematic value as the Fordham poet. She was indubitably old Dr Seabrook's daughter.

'The post will be entirely what you make of it, my dear,' Mary had declared, hope shining optimistically through the thick lenses of her spectacles.

Hermione had not made a great deal of it. She continued to dream through her days, so that her few routine duties were usually behind schedule, and she did not, as Mary had hoped she might, direct brilliant productions in the drama field (St Ursula's was a school where poetry, drama, music and painting had pride of place), or encourage *avant garde* poetry readings among the upper forms. She rearranged the furniture here and there, and did lovely bowls of flowers in the hall and dining-room, always much admired by visiting parents. Otherwise her presence in the school was unnoticeable.

Not unnoticeable, of course, to Clare. She had been only eight when Hermione had first joined the staff, and at that age she had taken it for granted that her mother should accompany her to and from school. But when the children in her form grew older, she suddenly found herself the only child to be escorted by her mother. She had to go and find her every day (in Miss Farquharson's study, of all places) and walk home with her. Otherwise Hermione was dreadfully hurt. Clare tried to escape from this dragging routine, saying 'I'll see you at home, Mummy, I want to go with the others to the Johnsons and see their new games room,' or 'I'm going home with Betty to look at her guinea pig,' but it didn't work. There were arguments, discussions with Miss Farquharson about the families in question, detailed investigations and enquiries as to whether Hermione had been introduced, ever, to this Mrs Johnson, she didn't think she had been, and in that case, darling, or what time would Clare be leaving Betty's, perhaps Hermione might pick her up there? All this followed by tragic accounts at teatime of Hermione's utter loneliness as she had wound her isolated path homewards (all five hundred yards of it) over the paving stones hallowed in the past by their joint excursions. The strain was too much for Clare. She gave in. Each day at the end of school she went along to Miss Farquharson's study to find her mother.

Not surprisingly, this practice cut her off from her contemporaries, from the rowdy groups that were often in trouble, from the casual invitations that led to friendships and outings with other children's families.

Instead she joined Hermione, and often Miss Farquharson too, who spoke kindly to her, tried to 'draw her out' as she described it, one of her favourite activities with the hopeful young in her care.

Hermione told her father that she would not be sorry if Clare made no close friendships at St Ursula. 'They don't have the same type of girl there now, Father. It isn't at all what it was when I was there. If it wasn't that Mary would be so hurt – and she takes such an interest in Clare, too – I would really think we ought to consider taking her away.'

'Where would you send her, my dear?' Dr Seabrook asked pertinently.

'Oh dear, that's just the point,' Hermione admitted with a sigh. 'Where would I? She could hardly go to the grammar school.'

'Of course not.' They were both distinctly out of date – about two hundred years, Clare often thought.

'The only alternative would be to send her to boarding school, and I don't want to do that.'

'Can't send a girl away to school,' Dr Seabrook agreed with certainty.

'Perhaps if Mary gives her special coaching, as she has promised me she will, and if Clare doesn't see too much of the type of girl they are getting there now – fortunately she doesn't show much sign of wanting to invite them home or anything. Or at least not often.' Hermione was reminded of one or two awkward occasions when she had been forced to tell Clare 'not to invite Rachel – Sandra – Pauline – here again, if you don't mind, darling, she isn't at all our sort of person, I'm afraid. When you're older you'll understand what I mean.'

'Mary Farquharson has let that school go down,' Dr Seabrook announced. 'It wasn't like this in Beatrice Smallpiece's time, when your mother and I sent you there.'

'It simply can't be helped, Father,' Hermione rallied at once to Mary's defence. 'It's the new Education Act that has changed everything. A lot of girls from quite nice families are going to the grammar school, apparently. I can't imagine allowing Clare to go there, of course, but still. If they pass their eleven plus they seem to go there, or else to boarding school, nowadays. They leave St Ursula's and go on to the grammar school. That never used to happen. Mary only keeps the ones who fail their eleven plus.'

'I don't know what things are coming to,' Dr Seabrook grumbled. 'The cult of the second-rate, that's what we have in this country now.'

This conversation, which took place several times a month, often occurred in Clare's presence. Once or twice she asked, though she knew it was hopeless, why they didn't send her to the grammar school or to boarding school? Nothing ever came of these suggestions, other than a hurt declamation from Hermione that surely she didn't *want* to leave home, and surely she was grateful to Mary Farquharson for all the extra coaching she gave her? Clare would have traded this in for even one term at what she privately thought of as a proper school.

Her longing was never to be fulfilled. Throughout her schooldays she was to remain, in effect, on the outside looking in. Watching the groups of girls who, in her eyes, led real lives. Who played in matches, who belonged to debating societies, who had houses at school, with colours, house meetings, house matches, going to Cambridge for Greek plays, to Stratford-on-Avon to see Shakespeare, and to the Aldwych to see the French theatre. Clare knew all this because Rachel Bloomfield told her. The Bloomfields were one of the families of whom Hermione disapproved, but Clare and Rachel had been at St Ursula's together until they were nearly twelve, and somehow they maintained a precarious friendship still. The Bloomfields had exciting holidays, ski-ing in vast parties at Christmas, sailing on the Norfolk Broads one summer, caravanning in Scotland, catching fresh trout from the loch for supper, then going even farther afield, taking their caravan to the French Riviera, then to Italy, then on to the Adriatic.

Hermione and Clare went with Grandpa for three weeks in September to the hotel in Frinton he had favoured for the past forty years, where he knew he could get his game of golf, and be undisturbed in the writing-room in the evening as he read his way through Gibbon – his personal holiday treat. 'Nice sands, too, for children,' he added enticingly every year. It was not clear whether he envisaged these as a joy for Hermione or Clare, both of whom had long considered themselves past the sandcastle stage.

At seventeen, with this uneventful, circumscribed childhood behind her, Clare was determined to break free, to join the vast army of her contemporaries before they left her behind for ever. The method she proposed was to go to secretarial college in London, to live in a hostel, and then to take a job.

'After all, Mother, you were married at seventeen,' she pointed out. 'Surely I can take a secretarial course?'

'It's not at all the same thing,' Hermione said huffily, remembering the high romance of her marriage, and comparing it with what she considered the sordid reality of secretarial life. 'How can she possibly suppose there's the least connection between taking a secretarial course and my marriage to Tom?' she asked Margaret Calderwood despairingly.

'I suppose the secretarial course looms large on her horizon,' Margaret suggested vaguely. She had just returned from one of her committee meetings, and was pre-occupied with the plight of the old and sick. Hermione's complaints were an interruption.

Jock Calderwood, though, was not feeling vague. He expressed himself forcibly on the subject to Margaret out of Hermione's hearing. 'The difference,' he pointed out irritably, 'is the opposite of what Hermione imagines. She was much too young at seventeen for marriage, whereas Clare is not too young for a secretarial course. Do her all the good in the world.' He repeated this to Clare, who turned glowing eyes on him, her face alight with anticipation.

'Then you agree?' she breathed. 'You'll actually tell Mother you think it's a good idea?' She hardly dared trust her good fortune. Jock was touched, and found himself committed.

It had not been easy. But Jock had enormous patience, and Hermione was no match for him. When the battle was fought, his attitude to Clare changed. He began to be irritated by her apparent neutrality, her dowdiness. These, he now saw, did not represent the girl underneath. He watched for the sudden lifting of her sad and drooping mouth, for the light in her eyes as he won some advantage for her. He could see the possibilities of freeing her from Hermione; he began to have an inkling of the girl she might become.

Jock's daughters were married and had homes of their own, one in Canada, the other in Hong Kong. He missed them often, and he was ready to respond like a father to Clare's faith in him. He felt his own power to mould her, and he basked in her esteem. He began to take her sailing with him – always a sign of acceptance. Clare was terrified, and Hermione furious. Jock watched the unspoken struggle between mother and daughter before Clare, in a pair of Margaret's jeans, walked at his side for the first time to the dinghy drawn up on the foreshore. He had been prepared to intervene, but this had not been necessary. Clare had won her own victory, though it had left her miserable and on edge.

Jock had been angry. Hermione, however unconsciously, was spoiling her daughter's life. He had been right. They must be separated.

CHAPTER THREE

As a result of Jock's support, Clare was entered at a secretarial college and had a place found for her at a hostel in Kensington – the same college and the same hostel that Rachel Bloomfield was to enter, though Clare succeeded in keeping this information from Hermione until she was safely launched into her new life.

Rachel continued what Jock had begun. After a summer at Marsh Farm and a winter in London, Clare could hardly have been recognised as the morose and apparently sullen girl who had sat, pasty-faced and unsmiling, heavy-eyed, returning brusque answers to all Margaret and Jock's probing.

Her appearance had changed for the better even before she had moved to London. After her first few sails wearing clothes borrowed from Margaret, she had insisted on buying jeans, shirts and a thick polo-necked sweater for herself. She wore this outfit for the remainder of the holidays, and it suited her much better than Hermione's charming prints – though Hermione of course was unable to see this, and continued to deplore her appearance. She began wearing her hair in a pony tail, and secretly cut inches off it. The sea wind and the sun tanned her skin, her spots disappeared. Above all she had life in her. She herself had hardly known how apathetic she had become in the dull days at Fordham, bored, sheltered, protected. Not naturally introspective, without stimulus or competition, she had allowed lethargy to rule her, so that days – weeks – months – passed as a pattern of meals interspersed with coaching and the writing of detailed essays on subjects that hardly raised a flicker of interest in her mind, though she was competent enough to be able to turn out the material Mary Farquharson demanded.

When she first sailed with Jock she had been terrified. She had never been afloat in her life. The entire proceeding seemed fool-hardy in the extreme. She found that her fear was accompanied by exhilaration. When they returned to Marsh Farm for tea (they had been for a gentle two-hour tack in a Force 3 breeze) she was exhausted physically and emotionally, and longed to repeat the experience.

Jock sailed *Sea Spray* throughout the season, using as crew Hugh Ravelston, who was almost as experienced as Jock himself, and staff from the laboratory at the hospital who were anxious to sail and willing to pull their weight. Over the years he had built up a considerable group whom he was able to call on for his different needs. There was what Hugh termed his rugger team for racing, or less dedicated enthusiasts for the leisurely cruising that he enjoyed as much. It was then that he took Clare along, and to her, with memories only of the holidays at Frinton, cruising in *Sea Spray* was unimaginable excitement. Sleeping on board, the early morning starts, slipping down the estuary in the grey light before sunrise, breakfast at sea, mugs of coffee and slices of toast and marmalade in the cockpit, then sailing down the Channel, heeled over with the bow cutting through the green water, all the changes in the weather, from squalls to brilliant sunlight on a blue sea. Oilskins and a drenching downpour, or sunlight and, as the men put it, 'birds in bikinis'.

Then the arrival. Mooring for the night, shopping in an unknown village for stores, drinks in the cockpit as the sun went down and then the hot meal and the talk under the oil lamp in the cabin. Finally, a last look round on deck, silence and darkness, the gleam of the water and the slap of the tide – and the knowledge that she would wake to another day of this intoxicating life.

Lonely and cut off at school, she had longed above all for companionship, longed to be part of a group. She had no wish to shine. This was Hermione's dream for her. Clare herself desired only to belong. Now she found herself an accepted member of a group of sailing enthusiasts with a common background of medicine. She heard again the medical gossip that had once been part of life at Fordham, but which had ceased with her grandfather's death, and had been succeeded by English Literature and dress-making. Sailing and medicine. This was the world for Clare. By the end of that summer, she knew almost as much about the proposed intensive care unit at Brookhampton as Jock himself.

When she went to secretarial college in the autumn she was bursting with confidence and optimism. Life was on the move. At once she was absorbed into another group, the crowd Rachel had known at school. They all exclaimed at Clare's clothes. She was reluctantly back in Hermione's choice, until during the evening she changed with relief into her now faded jeans and her polo-necked sweater.

'There,' they cried at once when she appeared at supper, 'how different you look. You simply can't go on wearing those frumpish dresses your mother bought you. No one wears that sort of thing these days. Even if you shortened the hems by a foot – no, it's hopeless. You can't do anything with them.'

'But–'

'Let's see exactly what she's got,' they

declared. They all trooped in and sprawled on her bed that evening, while Clare hauled all her clothes out, and paraded apologetically. They surveyed her dejectedly. 'They're all so *pretty*,' they wailed disapprovingly.

'How much *money* have you got?' they demanded. Clare enumerated her allowance – not ungenerous. But it was not designed to provide her with a complete wardrobe, merely with her lunches, fares and postage stamps (for letters to Hermione).

They sighed.

'What is she to *do?*' they asked one another despairingly.

They donated her some of their least favourite garments. Soon she had some hideous clothes which suited her no better than Hermione's choice, but in which she felt acceptable. Hermione, the following week-end, was horrified, Margaret Calderwood tolerant. 'The girls were exactly the same,' she assured her sister-in-law. 'Of course she looks awful, my dear, but so do they all.'

Hermione was far too cross to be approached for an increased allowance, but Jock Calderwood, confided in on Sunday morning as he tinkered with the engine of *Sea Spray* while Clare did whippings on rope-ends, came across generously. Clare returned cock-a-hoop to the hostel and a renewed onslaught on her wardrobe.

Among her set the fashion just then was for brief sleeveless tunics that they ran up out of furnishing material, worn with sludge-coloured sweaters and stockings, and Clare was soon indistinguishable from them all. At last she was properly dressed. Improperly, Hermione considered. The girl was showing her knickers and suspenders half the time. 'I need tights,' Clare agreed. 'Everyone has them, but they do work out expensive.'

Hermione tutted irritably, and complained to Woodie. 'She's just young, that's all it is,' Woodie said. 'She's happy, that's all that matters.'

'I don't know what's come over her,' Hermione protested. 'I never thought she'd turn out like this.'

'It's all these young people she knows now,' Woodie said comfortably. 'She wants to be like them. It's only natural.'

Sighing, Hermione disgorged the money for tights. 'I don't approve, and I'm not going to pretend I do. But I simply cannot let you go round looking totally indecent.'

'Thank you, you're an angel,' Clare said, and hugged her. 'I know you can't see it, but it's quite different from in your day, Mother.'

Hermione, at the decrepit age of thirty-seven, might have been forgiven her indignation. 'I think she imagines I've one foot in the grave,' she said in exasperation to

Margaret. 'I'm beginning to feel I must have. I give up.' Not before time, Margaret and Jock considered.

Clare did well at the secretarial college, since she had a good memory, neat fingers, application (the legacy of all those dull years at St Ursula's) and common sense. The course itself was surprisingly boring, but at least it was the gateway to the future.

The time came when they were all looking for jobs. Out came Hermione's soft expensive prints, and they sallied out for demure interviews, their hair lacquered into position instead of flopping alongside their noses in the fashion they preferred.

First job proved amazingly different from secretarial college, there was no doubt about that. At last real life, they told one another. They began to leave the hostel in droves, after furious arguments at home with exhausted parents, and shared flats in groups of three or four, so that they could invite men in for meals and to listen to pop music. It wasn't, of course, the meals and the pop music that worried the parents. 'But surely you *trust* me?' the children cried heart-rendingly, confident themselves, though their parents remained amazingly sceptical. What *had* it been like in their day?

Clare shared a flat in a quiet square off the Earls Court Road with Rachel, a friend of hers from the grammar school, called

Jennifer, and an Australian called Kate who refused to share with other Australians. Not, she asserted, what she had come to London for, though she filled the flat with them night after night.

It was all gay and exciting and hard work. There were young men to take Clare out, swinging London round her. There was Uncle Jock to go home to, down at Marsh Farm, *Sea Spray,* and of course Hugh Ravelston. Every man Clare met had to stand comparison with him. Men found her cool, aloof, scrutinising. They tried hard to make some impression on this slick chick, with her cropped head, her huge eyes and her sparrow's body in its brief gaudy garments (the sludge-coloured phase was over. Vivid green, purple and orange were in now).

The cropped head came as a result of her first job. Until then Clare had worn her hair long, straight, and loose, with the heavy fringe they all favoured. In London it was exactly right, and she ironed it before parties at the same time as her dress. Down at Brookhampton, though, her hair was a nuisance. Not only did Hermione never cease complaining, but – more serious – it was in the way when she went sailing, and she felt she looked her worst. This was not at all what she intended. Confiding this one day in the office to her immediate senior, Diana Thornton, a svelte blonde of twenty-five, she was despatched at once to the hair-dresser.

'Go to Paul. I'll make an appointment for you. Go in the lunch hour today.'

Clare returned cropped, and apparently skinnier than ever. The new look was a tremendous success with everyone in London, less so – predictably – with Hermione. It was a success, too, with Diana, who took to inviting Clare home to her flat.

Diana lived in Chelsea. Her husband was a Canadian airline pilot, and when he was at home Diana laid in great stocks of food and liked to leave the office punctually to entertain half the airline. Now there were Canadian aircrew to take Clare out, in addition to the Australians and all the Bloomfield cousins and friends.

The three years that went by between Clare at seventeen and Clare at twenty brought changes to Hermione too. To everyone's surprise she had acquiesced in a suggestion made by Margaret Calderwood that she should give up the flat in Fordham and settle in Brookhampton. Margaret had had little hope when she put the plan forward that Hermione would do anything but turn it down out of hand.

But Hermione had already made the tremendous effort of uprooting herself once from her safe retreat in Fordham to stay at Marsh Farm for the summer. This prospect had terrified her, and if she had not been at a loss to know how to deal with Clare she would never have embarked on the visit. However, she had survived.

Now she compared the beauty of the estuary at Brookhampton, the changing light on the water, the great expanse of sky and the glory of the sunset each evening of that amazing summer, with Fordham and its dull brickwork and conventional gardens.

In her dreams, all her life Hermione had sought beauty. But she was exceptionally timid, and had been afraid always to strike out on her own, to expose herself to new situations or strange people where she might be an outsider. The result had been that until now her search for beauty had been carried on mainly between the covers of books. But at last she saw it in the countryside round about her, and she was fascinated – fascinated enough even to overcome her terror of living in the midst of the busy Calderwood household, where the telephone constantly rang, there were committees to be attended, people dropping in for essential little talks before some event or other, Margaret had tea parties and coffee mornings, there were dinner parties several times a week, and Jock had colleagues for sherry before dinner to – as he often put it – 'hatch a plot, my dear,' or whisky afterwards for the same purpose. All in all, a new way of life Hermione had shunned. Until now, her overwhelming need for security and protection had cut her off from opportunity. She had never had to make a home for herself, because she had always, even during the years of her marriage, lived in her parents' house. Now she was enchanted not only by the light on the sea but by Marsh Farm and its lawns stretching down to the estuary. At this psychological moment Margaret took her to see Lavender Cottage, empty since Colin Warr's death and Judith's departure for the U.S.A.

Hermione fell in love with the cottage, and to everyone's astonishment, not least her own, within a month she had leased it, let the flat at Fordham, and moved herself and Woodie down to Brookhampton.

Woodie was ready for the change. Since old Dr Seabrook had died she had been bored. Her cooking improved noticeably, while Hermione threw herself into the joys of beautifying the cottage and its garden.

She found she was thankful to be away from Fordham and St Ursula's at last, and she suddenly understood what Clare had been talking about. She had been right, after all. They both needed to escape from St Ursula's and Mary Farquharson's domination. They would both, Hermione decided, flower in this new existence.

She was honest enough to decide that if

Clare had been right about this, she might be right about her secretarial course and her hostel, as Jock and Margaret had asserted. Hermione, in any case, would give her her chance. She herself owed her present life to her daughter, and she regarded her with new eyes. Clare had grown up.

Having decided this, she was often to doubt it, and to be irritated – as at one time she would never have been – when Clare showed a lack of maturity or sophistication. However, on the whole Jock and Margaret thought they could congratulate themselves on having done well by both Hermione and Clare. They were less happy in their minds about the effect of their actions on Hugh Ravelston.

CHAPTER FOUR

For years Hugh had been in love with Judith Warr. She had not given him an easy time. This had been inevitable. After the death of hr husband, she had been at a standstill, and Hugh had supported her loyally, asking nothing in return.

The trouble was that Judith had fallen into the habit of offering him nothing, yet counting on his support still. After two years in the United States, trying to summon her courage to take up life without Colin, she had returned to her flat in London, and had resumed her career as a musician. She had not returned to Brookhampton, filled with memories of Colin and his last illness. The Calderwoods were beginning to think that she never would, but sometimes they felt that they had been responsible for setting the seal on her absence, and consequently on Hugh's loneliness, by encouraging Hermione to take over Lavender Cottage.

Hugh, of course, was working hard at the hospital, and it was undeniable that this was what he had set his heart on doing. But at thirty, Jock thought, he appeared to have settled into a routine of medicine and sailing. Little gaiety, no real personal life, no wife, no girl friends, only Judith in London tormenting him.

In fact, this was how he looked at matters himself, when he had time to consider his own hidden feelings, which was not often. He was always busy, often tired, usually preoccupied, and there was little that mattered to him but work. Work and memory.

Once it had seemed that he would be satisfied for ever if only he could work again. This had been in the days when he had been unable to practise. They had all warned him that he would soon look farther than the hospital at Brookhampton. They had told him he was a fool to try to return to clinical medicine, where for someone with his history there would never be any future, merely the dull routine posts. Stay in the laboratory, they had all advised him (he had been working in Jock Calderwood's laboratory at that time), make a new career for yourself in biochemistry. He had refused to listen.

To begin with, it had been enough – to be back in the wards, in the clinics, in touch with humanity in all its unpredictability. The busy routine of the hospital wrapped him round with comforting, accustomed arms. This was what he had missed. This was how he wanted to spend his days. Not in the withdrawn, remote laboratory, but here, in the wards, in the midst of life and death, pain and humour, discord and petty irritations, inefficiency and shortages (not that these two characteristics were missing from the laboratory), the clash of people living and working together, and the occasional upsurge of the human spirit to heights of endurance and devotion that made the whole inglorious muddle worth while.

Was it enough? He supposed so. He seemed, though, to have left behind him all the excitement and striving, love and anguish and desire. Even his feeling for Judith, which had threatened to tear him apart in Colin's lifetime, was no more than a gentle enduring ache, a reminder of the past and a stab of hope for the future.

He lived in the lives of others. And about time too, he thought a little bitterly. There had been too much egotism for far too long in Hugh Ravelston, he knew. Now his ego had apparently slunk quietly away, his dreams too. He was a busy physician, immersed in his patients and the packed and ordered hospital day.

Saturday lunch was abominable. So-called minestrone, indistinguishable from washing-up water in appearance, and quite likely in taste, though he had never gone so far as to test this hypothesis personally, steak and kidney pie – one piece of kidney the size of sixpence, two pieces of gristle the size of golf balls, a glutinous brown mixture, and a rectangular portion of pastry, crisp and dry, cooked entirely separately. Two boiled potatoes shading gently from black to grey, and a spoonful of wet cabbage. After this, a suet pudding that smelt of dirty dishcloths. Then coffee with the indescribable taste of hospital coffee. Hugh wondered why he had stayed for the meal, when he could have bought a sandwich and eaten in on board *ffantasy*. Then he remembered why. He had to see Linda Masterson's aunt. He looked at his watch. The visitors would be arriving.

He went along to the children's ward. Sister Addiscombe had done her stuff and cornered Mrs Masterson for him, and she sat on a chair in the corridor.

'You can use my office, Dr Ravelston,' Sister said. Evidently he was in favour.

'Mrs Masterson – it is Mrs Masterson?' he asked, suddenly realising that this might not be her name at all.

'Oh yes, doctor. My husband and Linda's father are brothers,' she volunteered at once. 'Linda lives with us, you see, while her parents are away. Philip is a mining engineer and he–'

'Has Linda always been with you?'

'Oh no. Only recently. Because she's six now, and they thought – well, life's is so unsettled where they are. It used to be Northern Rhodesia, it's Zambia now. You

55

can't tell what's going to happen next. Philip wanted to Janet to come home too, but she said she was going to stay with him. As a matter of fact she likes it out there, in spite of everything. Philip doesn't like it, though. He doesn't like working for the blacks, you see. It's difficult for him, of course, I'm bound to say. My husband is in Shell, and so was Philip to begin with. But then he had this opportunity to go into a private firm out there. Much better prospects, he told us. And they wanted to settle there anyway. Fred warned him it was risky, but he was always one for a gamble, was Philip. Get rich quick, that's him all over. Now it all seems to have gone wrong, and they sent Linda back to us, to be on the safe side.' She sighed.

'Has Linda been upset by it?'

'Poor little thing, it's not her fault. She misses her Mummy and Daddy, and then she isn't used to the way we live here, or the climate. She's not been an easy child at all, but, poor lamb, you can't blame her, can you? That's what I say. And I've got two of my own, you see, while she's been an only. It's all very hard on her, and I must say I think it would have been better if Janet had come home with her, for the first few months at least, until she's settled down. But there, it's no good telling people what they ought to do, is it?'

'Not much,' Hugh agreed, with a grin. He

56

found himself warming to Mrs Masterson, despite her volubility and her flow of miscellaneous detail.

'No. Well I expect you know that better than I do, Doctor.'

'How long has Linda been with you?'

'Nearly two months, it must be by now. She came B.O.A.C., in charge of the air hostess, you know, and I had to go and meet her at London Airport. Poor little mite, she was terrified. I do think Janet might have — well, no good going on about it, and of course the fare *is* expensive.'

'What about get rich quick?' Hugh asked, intrigued.

'Oh, that's all gone by the board now. Get poor quick, more likely, if you ask me. And there they are, Janet and Philip, with all these posh ideas, and no lolly to keep them up. It is a laugh, really, if it wasn't so sad. Anyway, the outcome is I've got poor little rich girl (that's what my two call her, I'm sorry to say, young monkeys) on my hands, and that's a fact.'

'Does she know that they call her that?' He was engrossed, now, in the Masterson family.

'I hope not. I've told them what I think of them for speaking of her in that way, and I've forbidden them to do it. After all, it's not her fault she's so toffee-nosed, it's Janet's. I hope they haven't let her hear them referring to her like that. But I know they still do it, and that's a fact. You can't stop children, can you? And there's no doubt, she can be a bit of a young madam.'

'The first sign that she was unwell, apart from her homesickness, was when she began running this temperature, was it?'

'More or less. Mind you, it's hard to be sure. She's been off her food ever since she arrived. She may have eaten less lately, or she may not. And she's had headaches and been fretful, you know. I saw Dr Walker about her several times, but he said he thought it was just that she was finding it difficult to settle down, and it had sort of thrown her system out generally.'

'It may well be that. So far all the investigations we've done have been negative. It may simply be that we are dealing with an unhappy, uprooted child.' He was thinking aloud.

Mrs Masterson's face fell. 'Oh dear, I do feel a failure, Doctor.'

'Nonsense,' Hugh said briskly, coming to himself. 'Think of one of your own children, suddenly transplanted to – to Zambia, you said, didn't you? And having to settle in. Nobody's fault if they found it difficult, would it be?'

Mrs Masterson appeared relieved. Then she suddenly giggled, and remarked, 'I'd like to see Janet coping, I must say.'

Hugh smiled back. 'She doesn't sound exactly the type. Linda wants to go home, in any case, so you haven't done so badly.'

'Oh no, that means Lusaka. She never calls it home here.'

'Oh, I see. Pity. Do you know anything about her general health while she was out there? Has she been fit up to now, as far as you know?'

'She's been all right, yes. She had chicken-pox, I remember Janet writing about it.'

'Anything else? Any other infectious diseases?'

Mrs Masterson could remember none. Hugh cross-examined her as to the usual childhood ailments, but elicited nothing further.

'Of course,' Mrs Masterson added, 'when she arrived she was taking some tablets for malaria, but that was supposed to be just a precaution, Janet said.'

'How long did she take them?'

'Oh, for quite a while. Whatever the instructions said – would it be six weeks? Anyway, we saw she had them for the time it said, all right. Though Janet did mention it wasn't really necessary to bother. But I thought we ought to, and I was very particular about it.'

'Nothing else, that you know of?'

'I can't remember anything, Doctor. And according to Janet's letters, Linda's always

59

been a very active child. They always seem to be going for picnics and swimming parties, and off to stay with people at the week-end, or having people in, and I think I should have heard if Linda hadn't been well. It would have interfered with all that.'

The fact that Beryl Masterson had no time for her sister-in-law became increasingly clear.

'What about these swimming parties?' Hugh asked. 'Do you know where they took place?'

'Oh, they were always swimming. At the Club, I suppose. Does it matter?'

'It might, but it's a shot in the dark. If you think of anything else, let me know. We need any clue we can get as to what may be wrong with her. Very likely, of course, it *is* unhappiness and separation from her parents, rather than any specific infection. But we might be wrong. I didn't know before that she'd only been in this country for such a short time, or that she'd come from the tropics. That opens up a good many possibilities we hadn't thought of. We'll have to see. We'll keep her in for observation, and see how it goes – and we must see if we can't somehow cheer her up between us, eh?' False joviality, he thought disparagingly to himself. But what else was there to say? At least they ought to try to cheer the child, though he feared they were unlikely to succeed. What she needed was her own mother.

In any case, Mrs Masterson accepted his remark at its face value, thanked him and went off to see Linda. Sister came up to him. 'Did they tell you, Doctor, that Sandra Clifford's in again?'

Sandra was the only child of Hugh's one-time landlady in Malden Road, and he had taken an interest in her since she was ten. Pasty-faced and chesty, Sandra was always in and out of hospital, always ailing, and a constant embarrassment to her mother, who was trim, neat, driving, a perfectionist. Sandra had been a disappointment to Mrs Clifford from the day of her birth, when she had been bitterly ashamed of the puny creature she had produced. As Sandra grew up, Mrs Clifford's shame grew with her. She had expected an attractive, well-fed child, blooming and pink-cheeked, gay and full of fun. Instead she had Sandra, who snuffled and choked, who picked up every infection that was going, who looked undersized and pallid. In babyhood her nappies had always smelt abominably, and it had been this as much as any thing that had caused her mother's revulsion.

Now at fourteen Sandra was worse. She had no dramatic complaint, but a chronic condition that was slowly killing her. She suffered from an incurable disease, and any respiratory infection could lead to her death. The cause was to be found somewhere in her genes, and for this reason the Cliffords, who had been told that the chance that the same condition would be inherited by any other child of theirs was one in four, had only Sandra.

When Hugh had lodged with the Cliffords he had himself supervised Sandra's daily exercises. She did these morning and evening to clear her chest, and with his encouragement this had been regularly achieved, and her general condition had benefited. But since he had been living at the hospital, as he had done for the past few years, Sandra had grown slack. She missed the interest Hugh took in her even more than the exercises. She was bored with her dreary existence at home, miserable and lonely. She had missed so much schooling that she was behind the others of her own age and had few friends. Finally, she was afraid of her mother – though she admired her tremendously. She could never bear to face the fact, but she was somehow aware that she was a bitter disappointment, and recognised in her mother's hard impatient tones the concealed hatred she felt. Her father had a tender love for this miserable scrap that he had somehow managed to produce, but this was mingled inextricably with disillusion. He had married Irene in hope and joy, only to find he was tied to a shrew and had fathered a doomed child. He too recognised the concealed loathing Irene had for Sandra, and to hear the two of them together struck him to the heart. He was a railway worker, and for years now he had divided his life between the locomotive sheds and the public houses, returning to Malden Road only to sleep or to watch soccer on television.

Hugh was fond of Sandra. Her pigeon chest, pasty face and miserable whine for him were simply part of her condition. He saw only another sick child. If he found himself with a spare half hour between breakfast and a ward round or clinic, he called in at Malden Road and bullied Sandra into completing her exercises and draining her chest frequently. For him her eyes shone and her mouth curved into a tremulous smile, as she strove with all her will to do as he urged her with her increasingly ailing body. His visits to Sandra exasperated Mrs Clifford, secretly jealous of the attention Sandra received from this good-looking young doctor who had no eyes for anyone else. She banged doors and shouted, clattered in the kitchen, plugged in the Hoover, erupted into the room and muttered furiously, 'Bed not made yet, bed not made, can't get in to do it, how I'm expected to get round I don't know, some people don't know the meaning of time,'

63

and crashed out again, flinging the door shut behind her.

So Sandra had been admitted again.

'No, Sister, I didn't know,' he said.

'Yesterday evening. She's in the side ward.'

'I'll pop in and have a word with her. Dr Okiya's seen her, I suppose?'

'Yes, and he didn't like the look of her. And neither do I,' Sister said ominously.

Hugh sighed. Sandra was deteriorating before their eyes, and there was very little they could do about it. He went into the side ward now, and jollied her up while he read the notes. Max had put her on tetracycline again, of course. He had ordered fresh X-rays and liver function tests. There was an increasing bronchiectasis, and the outlook was not good. Soon her heart would show the strain of her badly impaired breathing capacity, he knew, and that would be the beginning of the end. Less than fifteen years of a sad and pathetic life that seemed to have been little good to anyone, least of all its owner. And there was nothing he or anyone could do about it. She had been born with the condition, and treatment could only be palliative. If they had known, when Sandra was a baby, as much as they knew today about the treatment of her condition, they might have been able to prevent the very extensive lung damage that would one day lead to *cor pulmonale* and kill

64

her. But it was all a very chancy business, and Sandra was one of the unlucky ones.

'That's a smart bed jacket you're wearing,' he said with a cheerfulness he did not feel. 'You're very grown up these days, Sandra.'

She was pleased, as he had known she would be.

'It's Mum's,' she said proudly. 'Like it?'

'Marvellous,' he said falsely. Its pink ruffles made her look more colourless and wizened than ever, and at the same time more childlike. But she fancied herself in it, this was clear, and Hugh realised he might have done Mrs Clifford an injustice. In her way she perhaps did her best for her daughter.

CHAPTER FIVE

In his room, Hugh changed rapidly into his sailing gear. He was late now, and unless he hurried they would miss the tide. He hoped Clare was on board already.

She was. She saw him arrive and rowed ashore for him, workmanlike in jeans and shirt and one of Jock's cadet lifejackets – a bright splash of orange, making her hair and eyes darker by contrast.

'Good,' he said. 'We want to catch the last of the ebb.'

'That's what I thought,' she agreed.

They worked together with the speed and co-operation of many sails, and were soon tacking down the estuary in a good stiff breeze. Clare, as usual, made an excellent crew, he thought, anticipating his movements and interpreting his orders almost before he had thought them, let alone voiced them. This was not all she anticipated.

'I brought you some sandwiches,' she remarked, as the water gurgled beneath the hull and they cut through the wide expanse where the river finally became one with the open sea. 'And also there's a flask of coffee.

I thought you might not have had a proper lunch.'

'How right you were, duckie. Lunch was unspeakable. Unmentionable. Don't let's mention it, in fact. And I am very hungry.'

Wordlessly, she handed across a poly-thene-wrapped package.

'Here, you take the helm,' Hugh said. He was soon munching with zest. 'Splendid girl. Marvellous sandwiches.'

'Those top ones are tongue, as you've discovered. Underneath is cream cheese and cucumber. Then I've brought some apples.'

'What an intelligent duck you are,' he said contentedly.

Clare could have hit him. It wasn't that she expected him to do anything dramatic, like falling in love with her. Everyone knew he was in love with Judith Warr, and had been for years. But she did wish he wouldn't treat her like his ten-year-old sister.

Or did she? When she thought the problem out (and Clare was constantly thinking out the problem of Hugh Ravelston. It was her chief spare-time activity) she knew that there was no other way of being so constantly in his company. Only because he never thought of taking her seriously, because he considered her a companionable child, did he take her sailing so often, accept her invitations to the cottage, and occasionally escort her to a slap-up meal at the Rose and Crown in Brookhampton. He scoffed at the Rose and Crown himself, saying it was pretentious and tasteless, in every sense. But Clare was young enough to enjoy the dressing up and the service from ostentatiously obsequious white-coated waiters, all the flummery over what Hugh declared was an indifferent bottle of rosé. He took her there indulgently, as though he were taking a child to the circus for a birthday treat, a benevolent uncle repaying her for her help in varnishing the dinghy. She knew that if these were the only terms on which she could enjoy his company, she would settle for them. Now she remarked, 'Mother said to invite you back for dinner, but I told her you'd probably have to be back at the hospital before that. The Calderwoods are coming.'

The invitation appeared unenthusiastic, if not ungracious, and Hermione would have been furious. But Hugh and Clare understood one another, and he knew that she meant simply that she had arranged it so that he could easily evade the invitation. On the other hand, the Calderwoods would be there. Hugh and Jock would be free to talk medicine together, while Margaret chatted to Hermione.

'Thanks very much,' he said. 'I'd like to – if she won't mind me in my sailing things. Or ought I to go back and change?'

'If we arrive late enough we can both have dinner in jeans and sweaters,' Clare said firmly. This was the attitude Hermione deplored. 'My dear,' she said to Mary Farquharson when she came for the following week-end, 'there is this absolutely charming young man – good family too – and she simply makes not the slightest effort.' Mary was heard to mutter that men were not the only aim in life. Hermione retorted at once, 'But she refused a university career, Mary. What other point can there possibly be in taking a job as a secretary except to meet men?' They agreed that this must, sadly, be the case. 'I'm afraid,' Mary added, 'that Clare is not fundamentally serious-minded. In spite of all our efforts.' Hermione ignored this, as having little importance. 'Then,' she wailed, 'she comes down here every week-end and spends the time pottering about in those awful old jeans and a boy's sweater that does *nothing* for her. I simply can't make her out.' They were able to unite in agreeing that neither of them could make her out. The subject was, as far as Hermione was concerned, inexhaustible, though Mary found it less fascinating. She hoped they might talk about one other – St Ursula's, perhaps, or Hermione's poetry.

Hugh and Clare sailed in silence, while Hugh munched his way through all the sandwiches and two apples, only remarking, as he threw the second core overboard, 'You're off the wind. Ease her.' Clare made a fractional adjustment. 'That's better,' he said. 'You must keep your luff just lifting.' His eyes, alert and concentrated, were fixed on the burgee fluttering at the masthead, and Clare experienced the surge of sheer physical devotion to him that so often came when they were together. She longed to throw her arms round him, to hold on to him for ever – or if necessary for the few moments that might be all life would allow her. She said, 'What about some coffee?'

'M-mm. Please. Go about, and then we can come in a bit and pick up that buoy.'

Clare put the helm over, and they went about.

'Right,' Hugh said. 'Give me the helm. That's it. Now, get the buoy as I come alongside. Now. Good. O.K.?'

'O.K.'

'Right. Where's this coffee?'

Clare reached for the Thermos.

'By the way,' Hugh remembered as he was drinking the excellent strong brew that was one of Clare's recent accomplishments, picked up from an Italian girl she had met at secretarial college and who now had a flat near her in Earls Court, 'do you want – magnificent coffee, duck – do you want to come round to East Callant next week-end

70

and help to bring *Sea Goose* round here?'

Clare turned shining eyes on him above her coffee mug.

'It means an early start on Saturday morning,' he warned her. 'Liverpool Street at dawn. I can't take the car, because there's no one to drive it back. Ben's coming. If you want to, you can meet us there.'

'I want to all right. Shall I bring any food?'

'Could do. Be useful if you did.'

'O.K. Will do. Thanks, Hugh.'

'Nice to have you,' he said in the smooth voice he sometimes adopted when his thoughts were far away. Clare looked at him with a moment of despair. 'Notice me, notice me,' she wanted to shout.

Hugh drove her, still in her jeans and sweater, to the station for the London train that evening. 'See you at crack of dawn at Liverpool Street Station on Saturday,' he said. 'You want the first Colchester train. I think it's five-thirty, but you'd better check. If the forecast's bad, you won't be able to come, of course. I'll ring you in that case. But if I don't ring it's on – all right?'

'Shall you and Ben go if the forecast's bad?'

'Probably. Depends. But Ben and I can bring her round in anything short of fog, more or less.'

'Then why can't I–'

'You're not coming if it's a bad forecast, so

don't argue about it.' She was prepared to do so, but their conversation was terminated by whistles and the departure of her train. Hugh raised his hand in salute as it drew out, and went off to telephone Ben.

Ben Calderwood was his oldest friend; they had been at Garside and Cambridge together, and then medical students at the Central London Hospital. Their friendship had remained unaffected by Ben's success and Hugh's relegation to what the Central considered to be provincial nonentity.

Ben was very much Jock Calderwood's son. They had the same stocky dependability, and the same square rugged features and black eyes. Jock had a mop of white hair and beetling white eyebrows that terrified junior members of the staff at the Brookhampton General. Ben had unruly black hair and jutting black eyebrows that were beginning to terrify junior members of the staff at the Central.

'Yes,' he said when Hugh rang him. 'I've had next week-end booked all right, and I've managed to defend it against all inroads. How are the tides?'

'Afraid it means an early start. First train from Liverpool Street. Five-thirty.'

'I could go down the night before, if you want to.'

'Can't manage it. I'm having dinner with Rodney and Emma on Friday, and I don't want to cut it, because I shan't see the old boy for a couple of years.'

'And it does just happen that *Sea Goose* is his property, eh?'

'Well, there is that, of course. But anyway I want to see him. As a matter of fact I offered to take a half-share in *Sea Goose,* because I seem to have at least as much use out of the boat as Rodney. But he wouldn't hear of it. He likes the feeling of ownership.'

'I can understand that. I wouldn't mind the feeling of ownership myself.'

'You can have *ffantasy* if the urge is that strong. I shan't have time to sail the two.'

'M-mm, not a bad idea. I'll think about it.'

'I've asked Clare to come on the trip. She won't be any trouble, and she can cook and so on.'

'What about asking Judith, then? She might like a week-end's sail.'

'Oh, I don't think so,' Hugh said quickly. 'Ring her up and ask her, if you feel like it. But she won't come.' He was sure of this. 'It'll interfere with her practising, for one thing, and she can't afford that.' He knew, too, that Judith was afraid to visit Brookhampton.

Ben decided to telephone her. He was unable to imagine that she would not jump at the opportunity of a week-end's sailing, and in any case he thought it was time Judith began to put herself out a little for Hugh.

Hugh would never suggest this himself, so he, Ben, would put a bit of pressure on.

But he failed. Judith refused, as Hugh had told him she would. She had an engagement on the Saturday evening. Not an important one, she admitted, but she could not default on it. Judith played with a quartet that was hoping to make a name, and they were booked to play for some suburban music club. She would see Hugh, though, she told Ben, on the Friday night, as Rodney and Emma had asked her to dinner. A pity, Ben thought, that Rodney was off to the Antarctic. Evidently he and Ben shared similar views on the subject of Hugh and Judith. Together they might have been able to make some impression. They should, he realised too late, have joined forces earlier.

Rodney, though, had little time at present to spare for Judith. She was simply that good-looking auburn-haired pianist his cousin Hugh went around with. He wanted to talk to Hugh about *Sea Goose*, the folk boat that he loved, Emma sometimes feared, more surely than herself or the children. Now they covered her, in their conversation, almost plank by plank and shackle by shackle.

In their childhood it had been Rodney who, seven years older than Hugh, had taught him to sail. They had been close friends ever since, and when Hugh had first gone to Brookhampton, Rodney had written from the Antarctic – against the wishes of the family – offering him the use of the boat during his own absence. This had been all he had been able to offer in the way of comfort to a young cousin in disgrace, and the old man, their grandfather, and Hugh's guardian, had been furious. He had no use for Hugh. 'I can't think what possessed you,' he had written angrily to Rodney, his favourite grandson. 'That careless boy is utterly irresponsible.' There had followed a long catalogue of the disasters the old man had been able to dream up, from dismasting to fire.

Hugh had been deeply touched by Rodney's gesture, coming as it did at a time when he thought his family had washed their hands of him. He was amazed, too. He could recognise, as easily as their grandfather, the risk Rodney was taking, and he knew how devoted he was to the boat. Hugh had determined then that he would look after *Sea Goose* as meticulously as Rodney himself might have done, and Rodney had been surprised and reassured on his return. Now, off to the Antarctic for the second time, he had no hesitation in leaving her in Hugh's care.

Nor was *Sea Goose* all he left to Hugh. It was with him, rather than with his brother Don or his parents, that he left the responsibility for Emma and his young family. 'Keep an eye on them for me, won't you?' he asked. 'By the way, you'd better see these.' He took Hugh to his desk and gave him solicitors' addresses, details of insurance policies and investments. 'You never know,' he said vaguely.

Then Emma joined them. The children were in bed, and the *au pair* girl had been sent to the theatre. They had drinks companionably together while they waited for Judith, who arrived flushed and late from a rehearsal, full of apologies. The meal had been keeping hot in the oven, and they sat down to it at once.

Rodney brandished the carving knife and fork, and remarked, 'Back to tins soon. The sole objection I have to my job is the dullness of the food. In the meantime, thank God for good roast meat.' He carved the saddle of lamb, Emma passed round her perfectly cooked roast potatoes, beans from Jean Ravelston's Cambridge garden, red currant jelly from Cambridge too, while Rodney poured claret.

Judith sat opposite Hugh in heartrending beauty. She had never put on the weight she had lost during Colin's illness and after his death, and today she had a fine-drawn loveliness that she had hardly shown in the past. When Hugh first met her, she had seemed a big, vital girl, with tawny hair and a wide mouth, brimming with affection and capability. Now she had fined down, her eyes had sunk in their sockets, and her wide mouth only emphasised the fragility of her white skin and hollowed cheeks. Even her hair seemed to have deepened in colour.

Hugh, as always, longed to take her away and somehow bring back happiness to her. Longed most of all, of course, to make love to her. But Judith could not yet bear a love that meant turning the key finally on her life with Colin, so that although they both recognised that her body responded readily to Hugh's desire, her spirit forbade this response and turned puritanically away. She was in conflict – and so, inescapably, was Hugh, though his struggle was simple and straightforward compared with Judith's.

Tonight he watched her across the candle-lit table. She was breathtaking in her loveliness, and the natural end to the evening would have been to take her home and make love to her, to begin a sharing that would develop through the rest of their lives. But he knew it would be useless, that to attempt any sort of physical approach would result in argument and misery for both of them. They had been through this so many times before. This was no occasion to repeat it. He had to leave the house at four in the morning to take *Sea Goose* round to Brookhampton, a hard forty-eight-hours sailing. Ten years earlier he would cheerfully have attempted this after a sleepless night, but not today.

So he watched Judith across the table, her auburn hair red gold in the candlelight, her long fingers clasping the stem of her wine-glass, turning it to catch the light as they talked, and kept a tight hold on himself. He was left, inevitably, with a sensation of love unfulfilled, of hope receding interminably and perhaps for ever, of frustration and loss. He saw her into a taxi outside the house, not offering to accompany her to her flat, and went back to the untidy sitting-room, where Emma was sewing last-minute oddments for Rodney, and where the signs of their four children could never be entirely eliminated, and felt desperate with loneliness.

Many of them at the Central – where Rodney worked in the research laboratories when he was not in the Antarctic – had been surprised when he had married Emma. She had no claim to beauty or allure, and she seldom bothered to dress fashionably – now, of course, she had no time for it. Hugh, though, knew why Rodney had married her. She was cuddly and loving, with round cheeks and full breasts and a neat little behind, and he would not at all have minded coming home to her himself and taking her into his arms the night through. Thinking this, he scowled. It was a long time since he had had a girl in his arms until the morning, and looked like being longer.

He missed the glance of startled interrogation that passed between Rodney and Emma, amazed at his rapid return. 'He can't have attempted to see her home,' Emma pointed out when they were in their bedroom. 'He must have just shoved her into the taxi and that was it.'

'He was edgy all evening, I thought,' Rodney said. 'She's playing him up, you know. I wish he'd never become involved with her. Just one damn thing after another that goes wrong for him.'

Judith was unaware of the trouble she caused. She was always taken by surprise when a memory of Colin suddenly banished the love she was sure she had for Hugh, and unless he brought her to this point she never doubted the fullness of her passion. Now she sat in her lonely taxi, hurt and abandoned, wondering what she had done to offend him. Surely he hadn't expected her to cancel a concert engagement to go sailing? Could he be angry with her about that? Was it possible?

Hugh, meanwhile, soaking in his bath, was asking himself what had possessed him to arrange to spend the week-end sailing when he could have spent it in London with Judith. If they had been together for the whole week-end they might have reached some haven of mutual understanding that would have sheltered the two of them and yet have found room for Judith's memories of Colin. If he had not committed himself like this – why did he have to be so busy, always, first one appointment and then another – they could have spent long un-interrupted hours deepening their love, strengthening their inner devotion. Too late now. He could not cancel the sailing plans at this stage. He smiled ironically at the thought of telephoning Ben and Clare, each no doubt safely tucked not bed, the one in Bloomsbury and the other in Earls Court, sleeping peacefully with their alarums set for four o'clock.

Too late to change all that. But Judith might have put herself out. He came out of the bath in a swirl of water ('What Hugh does in the bathroom, I can never imagine,' Emma complained. 'But he always leaves a flood as bad as if the children had been playing skin divers there.') He towelled him-self ferociously. No good blaming it all on Judith. She had her concert on Saturday night. She could no more decide suddenly to spend the week-end sailing round from East Callant to Brookhampton than he could abandon Ben and Clare and their plans.

What is the matter with us both, he wondered? We put everything and everyone first, except each other. Is it simply that we've acquired responsibilities and commitments, and can't drop everything for love, as we might have done at twenty? Or are we a pair of egotists?

He stalked out of the bathroom, leaving it in the unutterable chaos that Emma expected, and went to bed. In the early morning the alarum woke him, and he crept out of the sleeping house, lonely and despondent in the dawn, and caring nothing for the sail ahead, to which he had been looking forward for weeks.

Dawn at Liverpool Street was as dispiriting as it could be, but Ben and Clare were there, the one looking dependable as always, and the other shining with young excitement, and accompanied by a vast canvas grip. He hid his depression behind an avuncular teasing. 'What on earth have you got in that thing, duckie? Apart from the kitchen stove, I mean. If you're under the impression that you're going to make as many changes of outfit as that great Gladstonian pantechnicon suggests, you've a shock coming. It ain't going to be that sort of cruise.'

'Weighs a ton, too,' Ben contributed. He had carried it up the platform for her.

'How we're going to get it aboard is the next problem. I wonder if we could persuade Morrow to let us use his hoist? Leave it in the left luggage, there's a good girl. There's still time. Come as you are, we love

81

you for yourself, not your *haute couture*.'

'I'll put it in the left luggage if you like,' she agreed. 'Just as you say.' She was suspiciously meek.

'What's in it?' Hugh demanded alertly.

'Well ... there's a barbecue chicken, some lamb chops, and a tin of tongue. A lot of potato salad, and two loaves of bread and some rolls. Six eggs, half a pound of bacon, two pounds of tomatoes, some cans of Whitbread, and–'

'That's my girl,' Hugh said expansively, opening his arms. 'Come home to father, ducks, all is forgiven.' He folded her in a bearlike embrace, which she treasured for months.

'I must say, the child is learning,' Ben remarked approvingly. 'That's a very good stock.' He licked his lips appreciatively.

'Clare enjoys her food,' Hugh explained. 'Which is tremendously useful. She likes to eat well and she'll see to it that everyone else does too.'

'I must say, I think that's a bit thick,' Clare protested. 'It was for you two hulking brutes that I carted this lot across London. If you think I get through a chicken, six chops, a pound of tongue and two loaves of bread all by myself in a week-end on my own–'

'All right, no need to get excited,' Ben said with a grin. 'You've done it all for us, it's a great thought, and you're going to be in the galley cooking it, even in the teeth of a Force 8 gale. Keep your hair on.'

'Just what she hasn't done, as a matter of fact,' Hugh pointed out. 'Do you like her new hair-do? I think it's smashing.' He ruffled it amiably.

'It made Mother want to smash things, anyway,' Clare volunteered with a snort. '"Darling, what *have* you done to yourself?" The end, positively and finally the end. Into the dustbin with her dutiful daughter.'

'Good thing too. About time,' Ben said succinctly. He shared his father's views on the relationship between Hermione and Clare. 'Anyway, I like it. It suits you. Gamine is probably the word.'

'Guttersnipe,' Clare translated. 'Mother would be with you there.'

'Urchin cut,' Hugh suggested.

'That's exactly what it is, as a matter of fact,' Clare agreed, surprised.

'You can always trust the old devil to know all the ins and outs of feminine hair styles – and clothing,' Ben murmured, ostentatiously behind his hand to Clare. 'Remind me to deliver a few cousinly words of warning in the not too distant future re Hugh Ravelston, the secretaries' delight and the staff nurses' ruin. You should have seen him cutting a swathe through them when we were housemen. Of course, they say he's turned respectable now, but you want to watch out. Full of tricks.'

'Would you like me to move to another carriage, perhaps? Then you two could have a really cosy chat.'

'My dear chap, don't mention it – not embarrassing you, are we? By the way, talking of girl-friends, I couldn't get Judith. I expect she told you. She has a concert tonight.'

Clare knew a moment of concentrated fury, in which she metaphorically hurled her canvas bag of food out of the carriage window, and announced to Judith Warr, unsuitably clad for sailing in a full-length ball dress, 'You're his girl-friend, it's your job to do the catering. I'm just the child around here, I'm going to lie on the foredeck in the sun.'

CHAPTER SIX

When they arrived at East Callant station, it was seven o'clock on a grey morning. Hugh and Ben humped Clare's bag down the road to the quay, while she carried Hugh's oilskins (he was wearing the dark suit he had worn for dinner the night before), and the Brookhampton charts. Ben was already in his sailing clothes.

Clare began to think about cooking breakfast, but the two men put a stop to these plans.

'We're going to be a bit short of time,' Ben remarked.

'Yes. Have to put to sea at once, for a fair tide down the river.'

'Suppose I row you straight out, so that you can go aboard, get changed and make ready, while I row back for Clare and all the gear?'

'Good plan.' They had reached the quay now. 'Stay there, Clare. Wait.' They were in the dinghy and Ben was rowing strongly out to *Sea Goose*. Clare watched them, and stared at *Sea Goose*. So this was Rodney's folkboat, that Hugh and he loved so passionately. Hugh had had the boat for

85

nearly three years, Jock Calderwood had told her, in his early days at Brookhampton. He had all but lived aboard her then, though in fact he had had some dingy lodgings in Malden Road. Clare had discovered Malden Road for herself, one day when she had been shopping in the town centre, and she had stared amazed at the dreary row of Edwardian terraced houses that ran its depressing length. Amazing to think that Hugh had lived there once. Sometimes she could hardly bear to dwell on the unhappiness he must have known, though she never dared to raise the subject with him. He had never, in all their companionship, mentioned any aspect of his personal tragedy – his ruined career, his lost love Nicola, who had abandoned him, Ben said, when he had had to leave the Central. She was now married to his cousin Don, Rodney's brother, and one of the youngest consultants at the hospital, who apparently had all the Ravelston looks and the most caustic tongue in the family. Beautiful Nicola, who had come once to a party at the Calderwoods with Don, and had caused a sensation. And now, Ben said, another unhappy love for Hugh, Judith Warr, who was unable to forget her husband.

Colin Warr had been an outstanding man. The junior consultant in general medicine at Brookhampton, he had been Hugh's chief. He had died slowly of an incurable disease.

Hugh had worked for him throughout this time, and of course they had both known he was dying. Colin, though, had refused to allow Judith to be told his diagnosis, and after his death, Margaret Calderwood said, she had turned on Hugh and blamed him for keeping the truth from her. She had blamed Jock too, Margaret added. 'But then his shoulders are broader than Hugh's. In any case, he wasn't in love with the girl. He was simply sorry about everything, and dreadfully sad for poor Judith, as we all were. But Hugh was tormented by a conviction that he ought to have been able to do more. He couldn't have done more than he did.'

Clare watched Hugh clamber on board *Sea Goose*, and knew that he would carry some part of her heart with him for ever. He filled the emptiness occupied until now only by dreams and strange longings. For her, his bones, his flesh, the thoughts and feelings locked inside his skull which she could glimpse fleetingly in the set of his lips or the light in his eyes – these were destiny. To know him was worth every minute of the longing and even the pain of her knowledge that one day he would inexorably be gone from her, married to his Judith, and the days of their companionship ended. Meanwhile she stored every gesture, every turn of his head, to add to her memories.

Ben was back. 'Can you manage to hand

me the pantechnicon?' he asked.

'Of course,' she said with dignity. He took it from her and stowed it in the stern. 'Here are these,' she added, passing over the oilskins and a zip bag of Hugh's. 'And then there are the charts.'

'You'd better hang on to those. Step past me into the bow. Keep *down*. That's it. All right?'

'All right.'

'Good.' He pushed off.

On board *Sea Goose* Hugh had changed into sweater and jeans. He came and took the bags from Ben, and said, 'If you make the dinghy fast, and then stand by to cast off, I'll start the engine.'

'Shall I make some coffee?' Clare asked.

'No. No time. Check the stowage, if you want something to do. But don't start unpacking that thing, there isn't time.'

Within ten minutes they were going down the river under engine. Half-past seven on a grey morning with a spatter of rain in the air. They were soon in oilskins.

Hugh had been brought up on this river and the sea at its mouth. He knew every buoy – every bent twig, it appeared, that marked the deep-water channel.

Clare went on the foredeck with Ben and helped him with the Genoa. He was a careful and methodical sailor, and though he had not been on board *Sea Goose* for

88

several years, he made no mistakes. There was no panic as they found the jenny halyard foul round the crosstrees or the sheet inside the rigging. They were sailing in the open sea under main and Genoa, with a splendid bow wave and the sound of *Sea Goose* cutting her way joyfully through the seas. No more engine noise, only the sound of wind and water.

Clare was pink with exertion, and her hands were sore. She had not had time to find her gloves, lost somewhere beneath the chicken and the loaves of bread.

Hugh and Ben were pleased, adjusting the sails, putting her more into the wind so that she heeled over at what Clare would once have thought a terrifying angle.

'Now you can make coffee if you like,' Hugh said generously.

'O.K. Breakfast?'

'Splendid idea,' Ben agreed. 'Let me see … didn't I hear something about bacon and egg?'

'If you like.'

'No, she can't start cooking at this stage. Give the girl a chance, let her find her feet. We've a long day ahead. Coffee and toast and marmalade, duckie.'

'I don't mind making–'

'Well, you're not to. Go below and unpack your stuff. And stow it properly, for the Lord's sake.'

At eight o'clock they were drinking hot steaming coffee in the cockpit and eating slices of toast and butter and marmalade. A watery sun had appeared and the sea glittered to the east, while the land they had left was a blue strip in the distance.

After breakfast Ben went below to check the course Hugh had worked out one evening the previous week. After half an hour he reappeared to say it was all right.

'Just as well, as we're on it,' Hugh said. 'I wonder if we can pick up North Foreland yet for the nine o'clock forecast? You might try, because we haven't heard one since last night.'

Ben went below again and fiddled about on the trawler band. He succeeded in raising North Foreland, with a highly satisfactory forecast, which he duly wrote down. After that he allowed Clare into the cabin to wash up. The day had cleared, the sun shone brightly, visibility was good, wind and tide, still with them.

'She's fairly roaring along,' Hugh said, pleased. 'I'd like to see North Foreland under our stern before High Water Dover, though.'

They had the cold chicken for lunch, with potato salad, lettuce and tomato, and beer.

'This is the life,' Ben said, waving a leg of chicken happily in emphasis.

'Makes up for everything,' Hugh agreed,

his mouth full and his hair rumpled with the wind.

Was there so much wrong, Clare wondered, her eyes shadowing with pain.

'You're upsetting the infant,' Ben commented, watching her expression.

'M-mm? What?' Hugh was taken by surprise. He had in fact spoken lightly, no deep unhappiness in mind, referring only to the pleasant break in routine, the open sea, and their picnic meal, a vast improvement on the hospital diet.

'She thinks your life must be filled with grief and anguish, and this your fleeting solace,' Ben explained, with the uncanny and infuriating accuracy occasionally displayed by relatives at the least opportune moment.

Hugh looked at Clare, who was deeply embarrassed, and would have liked to have administered some excruciating torture to Ben, cheerfully munching his way through the chicken leg still. She turned her head away. Hugh put his arm round her and asked, 'You don't worry about *me*, do you?'

Clare wriggled. 'Not exactly,' she said crossly. Hermione would say she was handling this absolutely wrong, she thought, and, what's more, she would be dead right. Why can't you be feminine and loving, you moron, instead of twitching and scowling like a delinquent fourteen-year-old?

'My God, she does,' Hugh said. He looked

blankly at Ben.

'A Calderwood characteristic,' Ben said with the same uninhibited accuracy. Hugh reddened.

'I'm not a Calderwood,' Clare said baldly.

'For all practical purposes,' Ben said.

'You can stop worrying about me, the lot of you,' Hugh snapped, throwing the chicken bone into the sea.

'I see no occasion for that,' Ben retorted. 'You must allow your friends to worry about you from time to time. Don't be so bloody superior.'

'That's what Colin used to say,' Hugh remarked with a reminiscent sigh, not for himself, but for the absence of this loved friend, part only of the past.

Clare, though, thought otherwise.

'There, you've worried the infant again,' Ben pounced immediately. 'Heaving great sighs like that.'

'I was only wishing Colin was alive still,' Hugh explained. 'You mustn't take me over-seriously, you know.'

Not much, Clare thought angrily. She gathered the plates together, disappeared into the cabin.

'She adores you,' Ben stated.

'Eh? Me?'

'Yes. Surely you've noticed?'

'I don't think I have,' Hugh said slowly.

'Nonsense, you must have done.'

'Now you mention it, I can see I should have done. But it honestly never crossed my mind. She – she was just around, you know, and – and she's very companionable, of course – and – and I simply never thought about it. I'm afraid I've always sort of taken her for granted. Bit thick of me.'

'Be very good for her,' Ben asserted confidently. 'Part of growing up.'

'Oh, thanks. Thanks very much indeed.'

'Perfectly true. Unpleasant for her, but highly educative.' He grinned nastily.

Hugh found himself at a loss for words. Ben took pity on him, and began to relate the latest gossip from the Central. Vanstone, Hugh would be anything but sorry to hear, was passing through a period of unpopularity and apparent failure.

'Unthinkable.'

'Would have been once. But after Barham snatched the chair of medicine from under his nose – and his girl-friend at the same time (you remember?)–'

'I remember. I'm afraid I found it very comforting.'

'So did a lot of people. Supercilious so-and-so, Vanstone. He hadn't endeared himself to anyone much. Except Ramsay's daughter, and of course he married her in the end, as we all said he would. Much good it's done him, though. But it's since he lost the chair – and he was so damned certain he'd get it, too – that things seem to have gone wrong for him. He isn't what he was. No influence, you know. Of course a lucrative private practice. A smooth society practitioner with a carnation in his button-hole. You know the type. But at one time he promised to be much more than that.'

'I would have thought so, certainly. I'm afraid there *is* something I find pleasurable in the notion of Vanstone failing. But I wouldn't be surprised if the fault isn't mine rather than Vanstone's. Sheer nasty envy, in fact.'

'Oh, quite. I feel the same. One can't suc-ceed like Vanstone without being disliked.'

Hugh laughed. 'At least it looks as if I might after all be in for a career of consider-able popularity. But you – you'll have to watch it, Ben. You're doing far too well. Soon they're all going to be gathering round, waiting to see you fall flat on your kisser.'

'It's a pity one always has to do that in public. What's the news at Brookhampton?'

'Oh, we're chugging along.'

'How's the intensive care unit coming along? Dad's pride and joy?'

'The builders are in.'

'Good Lord, I didn't think it had come to that yet.'

'It was a surprise to me. I thought they were going on talking about it for another five years at least. In fact, I was confident that they'd sit round tables talking until the whole thing was cancelled by some new plan for a comprehensive school or a motorway on the site – long before the fuddy duddy old N.H.S. got round to rebuilding. Cars and the latest teaching gimmicks come a long way ahead of the dying in any politician's scale of values, as far as I can see. But I was wrong. Foundations are being laid, with enough noise, you'd think, for the laying down of a battleship on the Clyde. No doubt work in Out-patients – which is alongside, if you remember – is going to become progressively more intolerable for the next few years. What we're all wondering is how we're going to be able to staff the place after it's built.'

'Surely my dear old Dad has taken that into account – he's usually so realistic.'

'Oh, he swears there won't be any difficulty. Nurses like working in intensive care units, and they'll flock to it. His line is that possession of the unit will send up the standard of nursing, and improve the staffing position. Matron apparently agrees with him. I hope they're right. Of course, it remains to be seen whether there'll be any money in the budget to pay for the increased staff. Perhaps not – isn't there a new hospital somewhere in the Home Counties fully equipped to the most up-to-date standards, with only the out-patient department open, because they omitted to allocate any funds for staffing the place? Now they can't do it until next year – if then.'

'Bureaucracy leads to some weird decisions. I know a lot of doctors are mad, but bureaucrats are undoubtedly madder.'

'An odd lot, it seems to me.'

'Did you know that in one London teaching hospital there isn't room in the new single rooms in the intensive care unit for a theatre trolley? And to get to the other side of the bed, when it's pulled out from the wall for access to the patient's head – which, after all, it nearly always is – nurses have to get down on hands and knees and *crawl underneath?*'

'Good grief.'

'Perfectly true, I'm sorry to say. And it's the administrators who are at fault, not the architects. They were given the wrong specifications. No one suggested they should have a chat with a house surgeon, of course. Or even a staff nurse.'

'That's not the only tale I've heard about trolleys. They were in trouble with them at the county hospital. They've a new accident ward there (no piped oxygen and suction, incidentally – presumably they got lost somewhere in the committees.) But the lifts there are too small to take the trolleys. This seems to have been because the administrators saw an opportunity to save some money. They knew the lifts were smaller than originally planned, but they were pleased with the economy effected. They managed to fit in an extra room as well. It never occurred to them that they were now useless. None of them knew the size of a trolley, you see. Your father heard about this – I had the story from him – and like a flash he had Burrows, our Supplies Officer, round to dinner. He and Daniel Snelgrove kept plying him with drinks, apparently, and explaining the background to the intensive care unit to him. They're telling him it's going to make the name of the hospital, put us really on the map. Apparently they're managing to sell him the notion that it's a privilege to be associated with the project, and that career-wise he may make his name, if he plays his cards well.'

'And how is he meant to do this?'

'I gather by never making a move without consulting your father.'

'He's a wily old bird, my old man.'

'He gets results. No one else would.'

'He and Dan Snelgrove. They've always been hand in glove, as long as I can remember. Of course, you know what it is – it should be a lesson to both of us.'

'What?'

'An infinite capacity for taking pains.'

'Talking of pains, we nearly missed a child with schistosomiasis the other day, simply

97

because our incompetent young paediatric house physician failed to take a proper history. We thought that child had lived all her life in a housing estate in Brookhampton, whereas in fact she'd just been sent home from Zambia to her aunt.'

'Didn't the capable Max spot it?'

'Not to begin with,' Hugh said somewhat cagily.

Ben gave him a look. 'Oh, so you were the bright boy, were you? Even the highly efficient Max slipped up, did he? And over a tropical disease, too. His face must have been red.' He laughed.

Hugh grinned. 'I'm lying rather low about that aspect,' he said. 'But I admit I'm secretly rather pleased with myself.'

Schistosomiasis is a tropical disease usually contracted from bathing in pools infected with the Schistosoma, a parasite which begins life as an egg. If it reaches water it can hatch out into a free-swimming larva, which enters a fresh-water snail. In the snail, this larva produces in due course enormous numbers of offspring, cercariae, which escape back into the surrounding water. Here they have an independent life of about forty-eight hours, during which time they may gain access to a human being, by penetrating the unbroken skin. Then they pass into the bloodstream and reach the liver, where within about two months they develop into adult male and female worms, and produce spined eggs.

Troops in Africa are familiar with this disease, and sometimes have been found to be infected by it months after their return home. Young men, of course, often feel that the medical officer's injunctions about bathing are over-cautious and fussy. To refuse, in a hot and sticky climate, to enjoy the odd swim in a pleasant pool or the river, conveniently accessible during the day's march, simply because the M.O. would disapprove if he found out, would be unnatural. What the eye doesn't see, the heart doesn't grieve over. Eventually, though, the eye – through the microscope – does see, and they pay the price for their casual attitude, as Linda Masterson paid the price of her parents' scorn for what they considered to be old-fashioned rules of hygiene laid down by bureaucratic old women in offices in far-away London.

'I see now why I was so certain I ought to recognise what was wrong with her,' Max told Hugh with disgust. 'I ought to be shot. I must have seen hundreds of children with it. Bad history-taking. The classical fault, eh? It never crossed my mind to wonder if she had any tropical disease, until you got on to it. Calderwood and I both think the tests are positive, but they're complicated, of course, and we've sent specimens to the

Hospital for Tropical Diseases in London for a second opinion. I'm certain in my own mind, though.'

'Interesting. I've hardly seen a case. Certainly not since I was a student.'

'As I say, I've seen hundreds. But you were the one who spotted it. I ought to have my head examined.'

As soon as the results of the tests were through, Max started Linda on the drug used for this condition, which she had to take twice a day. Unfortunately the treatment was highly unpleasant, and each time Linda received her dose, she vomited. More important than the vomiting was the fact that she felt dreadful. As she was far from unintelligent, she at once linked the new medicine, which they had told her would cure her, with her sensations of acute distress. She was more frightened and distrustful than before of the doctors and nurses who were looking after her.

Hugh she continued to trust, and each time he saw her she begged him to let her go home. He explained to her that the medicine would make her better, and she gazed at him with betrayed eyes. He hated this, and was temped to stay away from the ward. After all, she was not his patient. But conscience drove him back. He knew she trusted him, and he learned from Max that she remained terrified of everyone else, and had lapsed again into her isolated silence, broken only when they gave her her treatment, when she would scream and refuse to take the drug.

'Sister has to force it down her each time,' Max said.

Hugh sighed. 'It is a frightening experience for a small child. A pity her mother isn't here. The aunt does her best, I know, but I don't think Linda trusts her any more than she does the rest of us.'

'I'm giving her Largactil to reduce the nausea and vomiting,' Max said. 'It does, to a certain extent. But I think it's depressing her even more. Although she's less excitable and edgy than she was, she seems to me to be more sunk into an apathetic misery, poor little wretch. She won't listen to Mavis when she tries to read to her, either. She turns away from everyone, rejects all overtures. All the nurses have tried hard to make contact with her. No good, though.'

'I'll go and talk to her,' Hugh said. He went down the ward and sat by Linda's bed. She ignored his arrival.

'Why don't you listen to the stories Mavis reads you?' he asked. He had soon discovered that sympathy and kindness, if offered at the outset of their conversation, only alienated her further. She was eaten up with suspicion and terror. The one method he had found of dealing with her was to

101

inveigle her into conversation by surprise tactics.

At least she answered him. 'Mavis?' she queried.

'Yes. She comes and reads to you. But you won't listen.'

She said nothing.

'It's rude,' he said.

'She's common,' Linda stated flatly.

Hugh wanted to laugh, though he knew a wave of fury at the same time. Her mother had taught her to behave like this. Mavis was common, so Linda Masterson in her loneliness and fear could not accept her helping hand. She was not the only human being, of course, to be walled about by self-imposed and absurd values. 'Poor little rich girl,' her aunt had called her. He began to see what she meant, to understand a little of what she must have had to contend with in assimilating Linda into her household. He knew the address where the Mastersons lived, as he knew, by now, most of the roads in Brookhampton. It was a road of semi-detached houses in a post-war estate. Those who lived there were probably all, in Linda's vocabulary, common. Cut off by fear and snobbery, he wondered, what can be done to help her?

'You could at least be polite,' he suggested.

Linda swivelled her eyes and looked at him. 'I don't feel well enough to be polite,' she retorted. An entirely understandable reaction, he had to admit. One he might have had himself.

He sighed. 'I see what you mean,' he agreed. 'But it's a bit hard on Mavis.'

Linda looked superior. 'I never asked her to come and read to me.'

'No, but Dr Okiya did.'

'He *would*,' Linda said devastatingly.

Hugh's lips twitched. 'He was trying to help you,' he suggested.

Linda sniffed. 'Well, he doesn't know much, I don't think.'

'You're wrong. He knows, for instance, a great deal about your illness. Far more than I do.'

Linda looked disbelieving, and obstinate.

'Far more than I do,' Hugh repeated firmly. 'I've only read about it in books, because it's not an illness you see much in England.' He had her full attention now, he saw. 'But Dr Okiya has treated hundreds of children with it, and made them better again. He is really a specialist in this particular disease you have, and you're extremely lucky to have him to look after you. He knows all about it.' Her face was closed and blank again, he realised. He felt he was battering unavailingly at her wilful disapproval of Max and anything he did. 'He has treated hundreds of children like you,' he said again.

She came to life and looked at him waspishly. 'Probably he's killed hundreds of children,' she said. 'Black savage.' She put on a smug and disapproving air, and watched Hugh covertly to see how he took the remark.

He took it badly. 'That's a childish and unintelligent thing to say.' He stood up. 'You're a very stupid, rude little girl, and I can't waste any more time talking to you. Dr Okiya is very clever, and if you think you can tell the size of people's brains by the colour of their skin, it's time you learnt how wrong you are. And he does not kill children, he makes them well, just as he's going to make you well, in spite of your silly and babyish behaviour.' He stalked away up the ward, not looking back. His heart bled for her. He knew she must be in tears.

Linda did cry. Loudly and clearly. Her wails pursued him down the ward, a bid to retrieve his attention. An unavailing bid. She saw his erect figure bump the swing doors open, and depart, white coat flying behind him. She ceased to roar, and wept quietly into her pillow. She longed for Hugh to come back. 'Please God, make him come back, make him come back. Please God, make him come back.' Presently her sobs quietened, only an occasional gulp shook her. 'Please God, make him come back.'

A figure passed the end of the bed. Her

eyes brightened. 'Mavis,' she called.

Mavis came suspiciously up to her.

'What is it?' she demanded.

'You can read me a story if you like,' Linda offered graciously.

Meanwhile Hugh sat opposite Max at lunch, eating Tuesday's badly cooked mince, boiled potatoes and marrow, with a lumpy sauce tasting like glue. All that could be said for the meal was that at least it was easily and rapidly scooped up and swallowed. No time need be wasted on refuelling, though little could be said for the quality of the food. Max, he saw, was adopting the same technique. He had an afternoon clinic with his chief, Dr Harrington.

Black savage, Hugh thought. An epithet very far from the truth. He wondered how often on his journey through university and hospital Max had had it flung at him. This time, at least, it had not reached his ears. Hugh intended to see that on the children's ward at the Brookhampton General it never would.

He would not have raised the subject of Linda at all, but Max did. 'She's not responding, you know,' he remarked, as he downed his coffee hurriedly. 'I'm getting Harrington to see her tomorrow, but it looks as though we'll have to take her off oral lucanthone and put her on to antimony intravenously.'

105

Hugh grinned. 'You're going to ask old Daddy Harrington, Brookhampton's leading specialist in tropical medicine, to decide this knotty point, are you?'

'I intend to get his blessing,' Max said with a wooden expression. He seldom responded to jokes against his chief, of whom he was fond. He had been educated at a mission school where they believed in old-fashioned loyalties.

'No doubt he'll give you that,' Hugh agreed.

'The trouble about tartar emetic is that it's highly toxic.' Max frowned. 'I'm not looking forward to adding that little chore to my daily round.'

'Poor little poppet.'

'At least she'll only need treatment every other day, instead of twice a day, as she does now. Just as well, for my sake, as well as hers. It's a difficult injection to give – I wouldn't leave it to young David, for instance. However, that's something we'll have to face in due course.' He shrugged. 'Sufficient unto the day,' he said, and went to his clinic.

CHAPTER SEVEN

With an effort, Hugh left *Sea Goose* on her
mooring in the estuary and joined Judith in
Switzerland for a week's holiday. After the
failure of their previous meeting, he had
determined that they should spend a period
alone together, to work out their relationship. Judith was already committed to this
month in Switzerland, and suggested that
he might meet her there. He, of course,
would have infinitely preferred to take her
for a cruise in *Sea Goose,* but he told himself
firmly that he must put himself out and
comply with her wishes. In any case, he felt
confident that once they were away from
their usual busy routine, with leisure to talk
and days to spend wandering the mountains
or lying in the sun at the lakeside, all their
problems could be solved.

It didn't turn out like this at all. Judith
seemed, during the previous three weeks of
her holiday, to have acquired as many
commitments in Brünnen as she had at
home in London. She and the friends she
was staying with had met Swiss musicians in
Lucerne, and they seemed to move about in
one vast group, talking music non-stop.

Judith, through an introduction from the new friends in Lucerne, had found a piano on which she could practise for four hours daily. This cut into her time with Hugh considerably, and in addition they all by now had their favourite time for swimming in the lake, their special places for drinking in the evening, their chosen walks, their own particular shops in Lucerne. He, it seemed, was to be permitted to tag along and fit in – if he wished. If not, perhaps he could amuse himself? Of course he could, and did. In any case, he had four hours to fill in while Judith was practising.

This all struck him as a lost opportunity, but he could not pretend that he was not enjoying himself. Brünnen and the lake were beautiful, he had time on his hands – sufficiently rare to be a deeply felt pleasure. He enjoyed the swimming and the walks that he went on with Judith's friends. He enjoyed his hours alone almost as much, when he explored Lucerne, took the bus up the mountains or to one of the villages along the lake. Only he lacked privacy with Judith, and their relationship stood still, unchanged from what it had been in London. He saw her at meals and with her friends. They were a cheerful party, and he liked their companionship, though he could not join in their interminable musical arguments. He felt himself an outsider, but he did not attempt to blame Judith for this. She must, after all, have taken the same difficulty in her stride on so many occasions when Colin was alive. She had sat then in groups of medical men discussing cases or techniques that were as much jargon to her as music was to him now. He realised for the first time that in those days she must often have been bored and lonely, and he vowed that he would see that she never had to be submerged in medical talk again.

At this point he had to laugh. The fact was that Judith was entirely capable of taking care of herself. Much more likely than that he would be in a position to save her from too much medicine was the possibility that she intended to remain aloof from medicine in the future, and he would have to defend himself constantly from too much music. He was beginning to understand, he thought wryly, what it was to be the unconsidered partner, to whom those engaged in fascinating discussion were absent-mindedly polite. A perfectly welcome member of the party, but one without any life of his own that they recognised, a mere appendage of Judith's. They were all friendly and well disposed to him, but often they forgot his existence, and he knew they considered him a bit of a bore.

'Medicine must be very *gruesome*,' one of them said kindly, attempting to make conversation. 'I expect you must be glad to get right away from it occasionally.'

It wasn't and he wasn't, but useless to try to explain to them what he felt about his profession. They didn't want to hear. Any attempts to interest them were met with polite tolerance.

This, he grasped suddenly, is what it must be like to be husband to the famous. If he married Judith, would he be 'Judith Warr's husband, you know, he's some sort of a doctor – terribly gruesome?' Somehow the word continued to sting, though he had retaliated by saying 'Music is so noisy. I expect you must be thankful for a bit of silence occasionally?' They had laughed, but they had not seen that the remark carried any implications as to his own feelings for medicine. After all, it was not an art, but a science, they would say. Not even a real science, more of a technique.

He began to wonder how he would feel, working in Brookhampton while Judith played at concerts in London or elsewhere. He supposed he would have to travel up to the London flat for weekends, when he could manage to get away. Judith would not have time – even if she learnt to face Brookhampton again – to travel down to him. Well, the girl was right to rebuild her career, and he respected her for it. She had thrown it over once for Colin, and he could only be thankful that she had the courage and resilience to take it up again and work at it. This was the sort of wife he wanted. Someone like Judith, with much more to her than merely her beauty, staggering as he continued to find that. If the situation had its inconveniences, this surely was a small price to pay for something infinitely valuable?

Not that Judith's friends seemed to think a great deal of her musical achievements. Their attitude to her career was sceptical in the extreme, and Hugh's new awareness of this brought him an understanding of her need to drive so relentlessly forward along her chosen path.

Judith's friends regarded her as an amateur. She was under constant pressure from them to display a more professional attitude. 'You're not,' she was told more than once in his hearing, 'a married woman living in a provincial town any longer, dabbling in music instead of dressmaking.'

Judith, who had never seen herself like this, would flush and protest. She was at these moments lovely and impassioned, and Hugh longed to be able to help her prove herself to them all. But he knew she alone could do this, over the long hard-working years.

'It's one thing to do a bit of teaching at the grammar school and be the mainstay of the local music society, and quite another to be a professional musician,' they pointed out.

'I don't think you have grasped yet what a tough fight anyone has to make a name as a musician,' she was told. 'It's hard enough if you start in childhood and spend your waking life locked on to it from then on. You can't play about, dropping it and picking it up again when you feel inclined, and still expect to be taken seriously by people who have always given up everything else. You threw up your career for your marriage. That was your decision. You can't behave now as though you had never done it. You lost over five years, and quite honestly I doubt if you can regain them.'

'I'm not sure there's even much point in trying,' another volunteered. 'After all, you did once give up the piano for marriage. I don't honestly think you could have done if you were the sort of person you need to be to have any chance of success. There are plenty of people as good as you are who will never make a name. You've got to have that extra quality, that intangible something in your personality that everyone who succeeds has. I don't know what it is, some extra drive, extra force, something that the average man or woman lacks. Without it you're wasting your time.'

'And you think I lack it?' Judith asked bravely.

'Most of us lack it. There's nothing surprising about *not* having it. The surprise is when it's there. I don't know if you have it. The chances are that you haven't. At any rate, you haven't displayed it yet, and time is getting on.'

Judith frowned, and played with her amber beads, her hair falling forwards across her cheeks.

'Partly it's a quality of ruthlessness. Very few women have that. They are far too much at the beck and call of all and sundry.'

'You think I am?'

'You were once. You can't be wife and housekeeper and run a musical career. You can have a very pleasant life, enjoying your music and your home. You can work very hard and impress all the other wives with your ability. But none of that has anything to do with a career, and if you think it's the same thing, that you can go on in the way you have been doing, then it's time you woke up, darling.'

'Like everyone else, sooner or later you have to make a choice,' they told her, in unison.

'Personally,' one added, 'I think you've already made it, only you haven't noticed. But one thing is certain. You can't have music and a streamlined, organised, well-run life, with family and friends and dinner parties and holidays. You can have music or all the other ingredients. Not and.'

'But–'

'Don't kid yourself. You must choose. Not that you'll necessarily succeed when you have chosen. There's no guarantee. But there's one absolute certainty. It's useless to *dabble*.'

Judith was furious. 'I don't dabble,' she shouted, pushing her chair back and walking angrily away. Hugh longed to go with her, but he felt that he had a duty not to influence her. If life with him was supposed to be part of dabbling, if it was to be a choice between music and him, then she must face her own decision, just as she would have to live her own life once her choice was made.

This was what she was thinking herself. I've got to face facts and make up my mind, she was telling herself. She was still angry at the accusation that she dabbled in music, yet she was aware that her anger was the furious reaction of a guilty heart to the unwelcome thrust of truth. Not only was she dabbling in music, she was dabbling in Hugh Ravelston.

What was she going to do about him? Should she give up her music for him, as she had once done for Colin? She was not ready to do this. Should she give him up for her music? She was not ready for this either.

When would she be ready? When she had succeeded in her career? Was he some sort of insurance policy? Did she expect him to hang around until she had proved to herself that she could make a career? Suppose he did – and there was no guarantee of that either, she reminded herself – and supposing, too, that she managed to grab success. What then? Would the career, once made, be any easier to give up?

She could not say. All she knew was that while, when Colin asked her to marry him, she had not counted the cost, now when she thought of marrying Hugh she counted out every fraction of what she would pay like an unwilling miser. If this meant that she should put her music first, and send Hugh away – then she could not do it. She depended on him, and she could not bear to let him go out of her life.

She kicked a stone along the path, under the trees by the lake, and scowled, then sighed. Perhaps it would all solve itself. Perhaps her music, as they all threatened, would come to nothing, and she would be glad to marry Hugh and settle down to raising a family. She supposed that very likely this would be how it would turn out. She half hoped so. But only half, of course.

She agreed, though, to go with Hugh to visit his mother, Annabel, at the summer chalet she and her husband had in the mountains. They spent three days there before returning to England, and Judith allowed Annabel to assume that she would be marrying Hugh within the year. She could see no way of denying this prospect without being disagreeable. It turned out to be the first time Hugh had taken a girl to stay with his mother. Annabel not unnaturally assumed, as she put it to Simon, that 'this was it'. She approved of Judith immediately, finding her beautiful and poised and artistic. 'Just the wife,' she announced, 'I would have chosen for him myself. Not a Ravelston type at all, thank heaven. I was always terrified he would marry one of those ghastly hearty physiotherapists, like poor Archie.' She was referring to Rodney's mother, Jean, with whom she had never been able to come to terms.

Annabel now, in her delight, offered Hugh the summer chalet for his honeymoon.

'Steady on,' he protested. 'You're going too fast. I don't know she'll marry me.'

'But of course she will, darling. And she's a charming girl, just the wife for you. She has imagination, and – and – well, she's out of the ordinary. Not one of those limited medical women like poor Jean.'

Hugh knew exactly what she meant, but he didn't feel inclined to give in to her. 'Jean is all right,' he said firmly. 'I'm very fond of her.'

'Of *course* you are, darling. So are we all. But I wouldn't want you to marry someone

116

like Jean.'

As a matter of fact, Hugh realised with a spurt of irritated amusement, he wouldn't want to himself. It was all very well to appreciate Jean, and to be annoyed with Annabel when she disparaged her, but he didn't want someone like Jean for a wife, loyal and competent and devoted as she was. His mother was right.

'So what are you waiting for?' she now demanded. 'If you haven't actually proposed to Judith, why not do it now?' She rose from her chair, as if about to summon Judith for this purpose.

'Sit down and relax,' Hugh said, grinning. 'Because she'd only turn me down, that's why.'

'What makes you think that?' Annabel asked at once. 'I see no sign of her turning you down. Quite the contrary. She seems to me quite settled in her mind. You can trust me, darling, I am not *unversed* in this sort of thing.'

He laughed helplessly. 'I'm sure you aren't *unversed*, Mother. *Au contraire,* no doubt.'

Annabel smirked.

'But Judith isn't ready to marry.'

'But, darling, she seems to me to take it all for granted.'

Hugh sighed. 'Well, you're quite right, she does. But what she takes for granted is that one day we'll do something about marriage.

She shies off it if I – if I actually–'

'Name the day?'

'Oh, long before that.'

'Silly girl.'

'She hasn't got over Colin yet.'

'I'll tell you what, I'll have a talk to her, shall I?' Annabel suggested delightedly.

'No, you won't,' Hugh retorted firmly. 'For the Lord's sake, don't meddle.'

'But–'

'No.'

'But darling, I'm quite sure I–'

'No.'

Annabel looked thoughtfully at Hugh, and decided to give in amiably, but to make an opportunity to have a cosy little chat with Judith alone before her return to England. This she succeeded in doing.

'Tell me, Judith darling,' she began with cunning, while they were sitting having tea together without Simon or Hugh, who had gone walking, 'all about Colin.'

'Well,' Judith said, startled, plaiting her fingers together until they cracked. She had not expected to have to talk to Hugh's mother about Colin. She paused helplessly.

'Hugh says he was rather a wonderful person,' Annabel added. She had a sure hand when it was a question of winning anyone's confidence.

'Oh, he was,' Judith agreed fervently. Suddenly the floodgates opened, and she found herself telling Annabel all that Colin had meant to her. Annabel was a responsive and understanding listener.

'People don't realise it,' she assured Judith, 'but it's years before you recover when you have lost your husband. Simply years. I remember how lost I was when darling Andrew was drowned.' She relived the days, a quarter of a century earlier, when Hugh's father had died at sea, and she had been left a young widow of twenty with Hugh a baby learning to walk. Judith was fascinated to hear about Hugh's childhood, and hardly realised how rapidly the conversation had been switched from herself and Colin to Annabel and Hugh. Annabel seldom thought of Andrew these days, but immediately she did he sprang into life for her, young, handsome, daring and, as she told Judith, 'so terribly like darling Hugh – except, of course, that Hugh has a great deal of *me* in him. He is very far, heaven be praised, from being all Ravelston. Oh my dear, I can't tell you how incredibly dreary they are as a family. All so dreadfully medical, and grand, in the most pompous fashion possible, and so correct it simply isn't true. Andrew and I used to joke about it – especially about his father, old Sir Donald Ravelston.' This statement was far from the truth, for Andrew had been very fond of his father. But Annabel had never had the slightest difficulty in believing whatever she chose. 'Did you ever meet him?' she asked Judith.

Judith had not, but remembered that he had died in Hugh's early days at Brook-hampton. Hugh had gone up to London to a memorial service.

'That's right,' Annabel agreed. 'That was the old man. A memorial service at All Souls, Langham Place. I'm afraid I didn't go. He was the bane of my life when Hugh was a little boy. Like a lot of these eminent specialists, he thought he was the Almighty in person, and expected to be followed about by a train of disciples, all ministering to his every whim. Life for him was a perpetual ward round. By the time he was old, he wasn't a real person at all, but a cardboard cut-out, the top consultant, Sir Somebody Something. A stereotype from a teaching hospital. I always wanted Hugh to escape that fate, and thanks to you, my dear, he may be able to do it. But I warn you, the Ravelston influence is strong. It's been too strong for me, ever since the old man insisted that Hugh went to that stuffy Gar-side at the age of twelve. Since then he's been more than half Ravelston, and it's been very bad for him. But you can save him, I know you can. It's a blessing, really, that he couldn't stay at the Central. That would have been the end of his independence, he would absolutely inevitably have turned into simply another machine, entirely predictable, nothing in his life but medicine and that horrid sailing. The Ravelstons are so boring. Now you can get him away from all that. Widen his horizons.'

Judith could not help but enjoy this picture. Her own wishes became acceptable, turned out to be for Hugh's good. She began to be more hopeful for the future. Annabel could see she was making an impression.

'Get him away from that dreary Brookhampton, to start with,' she urged. 'Why he had to bury himself down there I have never been able to understand. He's not made for life as a provincial nobody.' This was something Annabel had always been sure of – after all, Hugh was her own son. Judith was less sure. She had not known Hugh in his London days, and for her he had never carried the aura of worldly triumph and excitement that those who had known him in the days of his youthful success had accepted as part of his personality. Nor, to her, did the Ravelston name mean much. She was ready to take it at Annabel's valuation. This made everything simple. She need have no compunction in remaining in London, in weaning Hugh away from Brookhampton. She would be broadening his horizons. She saw herself taking Hugh into a brilliant world he would not otherwise be eligible to enter, changing his life, opening out vistas.

But what sort of job could he find in London? He had always maintained that he was lucky, with his history, to have landed the Brookhampton post. He had told her that Brookhampton was the only place now where he had any influence. Colin and Jock had organised him into his present post, he had declared, and without their backing he would never have been so much as short-lived. She related this to Annabel.

'Nonsense,' Annabel said briskly. 'He underrates himself. That's the Ravelstons again. He was the youngest, and he failed at their sort of life, so he thinks he's no good by any standards. Ridiculous. It's Ravelston standards that are at fault, not Hugh's ability. Who cares if the Central London Hospital won't open its doors to him?'

'Well, he does,' Judith pointed out. She was sure of that.

'Then you must get him out of that frame of mind. False values, my dear, as you and I see so clearly. But men are blind. You must show him that there are more things in heaven and earth than stuffy old teaching hospitals and Ravelston pomposity.'

'But,' Judith asked, forcing herself to stick to essentials, though in spirit she was entirely with Annabel, 'but what about a job? He can't live on air. He has to earn his living.'

'Earn his living?' Annabel echoed, in apparent astonishment. 'My dear, why should he? He has plenty of money. I only wish some of it had come to me. No need for him to be chained to a treadmill of dreary routine.'

'Plenty of money?' Judith in her turn echoed. In some ways she was wholly unworldly, and she had had no notion that Hugh was in any way affluent.

'But of course. Didn't you know? The Ravelstons are extremely well off, and since the old man died Hugh has a better income from capital than Simon has from his post here. His *important* post,' she added hastily. Annabel's husband and son had to reflect credit on her, and she did not want Judith to assume that Simon's occupation provided any sort of meagre return.

'No, I didn't know that,' Judith said slowly. How much difference did this make to their plans? It had never before crossed her mind that Hugh was not dependent on his salary. If he was so well off, why had he come to Brookhampton, taken a junior laboratory post and lived in squalid lodgings in the town? She asked Annabel.

'My dear,' Annabel replied at once on a huge sigh, 'I have never been able to understand it in the least. There was not the slightest necessity for him to behave like that. I wanted him to come here, he could have had such a pleasant time, and it would have been such fun for me. But he wouldn't hear of it. Insisted on working away, far too hard, at that *tedious* little job he managed to find for himself, turning his back on all my offers of help. I always thought it must be some sort of punishment he wanted to inflict on himself. But it's time he stopped hurting himself and began to enjoy life again. He used to be so gay and happy. I rely on you to prevent him being so hard working and puritanical. I'm afraid there's a large streak of Ravelston in him, but it's not good for him to give in to it.'

'But–' Judith began doubtfully. She had remembered Colin vividly, at that moment. He too had had what Annabel would have undoubtedly considered a dull job in a provincial hospital. But he had not been punishing himself. He had, as Judith knew, loved medicine. Until now she had assumed that Hugh shared the same devotion, which had never previously struck her as puritanical. For Colin, and she had thought for Hugh also, medicine gave meaning to existence. 'But I think,' she suggested faintly, 'medicine is important to him. He's not just punishing himself. He may have been once, but I don't think he is now.'

'Habit,' Annabel retorted airily. 'Simply habit, my dear. And the Ravelston influence. You must break him of it. He will be perfectly happy away from those horrid patients with all their complaints and their disgusting diseases. He only has to get used to the idea. He can do research,' she added, inspired.

'Research?' Judith repeated. Nearer to the medical world than Annabel, she suspected that one had to execute research for a purpose, or at least in a specific field of interest. 'Research into what?' she asked.

'Oh, I don't know,' Annabel said a little irritably. 'I can't dot the i's and cross the t's for you. I'm sure there must be plenty of opportunities. In fact, I know there are. Archie offered him a post at Cambridge several years ago, and he turned it down. Goodness knows why.' Annabel's information was accurate. Archie Ravelston, who was Professor of Physiology at Cambridge, and director of the well-known Forshaw Laboratories there, had offered Hugh a post as a biochemist three years earlier. Hugh had turned it down in favour of clinical medicine at Brookhampton. 'You see? There are masses of opportunities, if he would only take them. No need to stick to research, even, if he doesn't want to work under Archie. I wouldn't blame him for that. He could write medical scripts,' she added with zest. 'Or advise on some of those programmes about science. Why not? Simon has contacts – any number of them.

He could soon put him in the way of it.'

Judith hesitated. Hugh had seldom said much to her about his mother or his stepfather, but he had said enough for her to suspect that he might not relish being 'put in the way of it' by Simon. 'I don't think,' she suggested tentatively, 'that – um – that sort of thing would – um – strike him as a full-time job.'

'A full-time job? Of course not. He would have some time left to enjoy himself, that's what I've been saying.'

For Annabel, work had always been a dirty word. The supposition that anyone found enjoyment in the activity was entirely foreign to her, and Judith's suggestion that this might be the case with Hugh was instantly demolished. 'Of course not. He can't. I've told you, it's those wretched Ravelstons. He's simply pretending to be one of them heart and soul. No one could possibly enjoy the life he seems to lead at Brookhampton.'

'He enjoys medicine, though, and–'

'He thinks he enjoys medicine, because that's what the Ravelstons are supposed to do. In any case, medicine is different now from what it was in his grandfather's day. Then it might have been possible to enjoy it. A doctor had status then, and money, and there were servants and chauffeurs and so on to look after him. He was respected, and he had leisure too. Now it's all different. No one who wants any fun out of life would be such a fool as to go in for medicine these days. Get him away from it, my dear, and teach him how to enjoy himself again.'

CHAPTER EIGHT

Hugh returned to Brookhampton to find the hospital seething with discontent. There had been a horrifying row in the children's ward, and everyone had taken sides.

The trouble had started when Linda Masterson's mother, summoned in desperation by her aunt Beryl, had arrived. She had swept complaining into the ward.

'My poor darling,' she had exclaimed, gathering the pallid Linda into her arms, where she immediately began sobbing bitterly. 'My poor darling, what have they *done* to you?'

This was a remark guaranteed to antagonise Sister, who saw that Linda's mother was going to be even more troublesome than her daughter. She heartily wished her back in Africa, or wherever she had come from. She arranged, however, despite her disapproval, for her to see Dr Okiya.

The fat was in the fire. Linda, after all, had not invented the term black savage for herself. She had, along with many other phrases and attitudes, adopted it from her mother.

What Mrs Masterson had said to Max no

128

one knew for certain. Whatever it was, it had stung. Max had told Sister Addiscombe to see that Mrs Masterson came into the ward only at the official visiting hours. 'Then I can make certain that I never run into her,' he explained. 'Because if I do see that idiotic woman again I cannot guarantee that I shan't be extremely rude to her.'

This led to a brush between Mrs Masterson and Sister Addiscombe.

'Those are the official visiting hours,' Sister said firmly, enjoying herself.

'But that's outrageous, Nurse,' Mrs Masterson retorted (she had perfected the art of annoying the staff). 'I've flown home from Africa especially because of my little girl's illness. Of course I intend to be with her as much as possible. Nearly all day, in fact. She needs me, poor darling. And I've told my sister-in-law that I shall be spending all day here,' she added in offended tones, as if this ended the matter.

'I can't help what you've told your sister-in-law, Mrs Masterson,' Sister Addiscombe replied snappily. 'This hospital is not run for the benefit of your sister-in-law, I'm afraid.' Her voice expressed considerably more pleasure than fear. 'Those are the visiting hours and I must ask you to abide by them, as the other mothers do.'

Mrs Masterson did not care to be classed with the other mothers, and she began telling an unimpressed Sister Addiscombe that she was not used – and neither was her little girl – to the rules and regulations of a *public* ward. 'We have always been private patients, you know. And when Linda saw Dr Harrington for the first time she saw him *privately*. But he advised my sister-in-law that it would be all right for Linda to come in here.' She cast a disparaging glance round the ward. Sister Addiscombe thought that Mrs Masterson's sister-in-law, poor soul, was in for trouble, and hoped that Linda's mother, in her fury with the lot of them, would remove her daughter from the ward and put her into a private nursing home. She said as much to her staff nurse. 'But a pretty penny it would cost them,' she added. 'And I wouldn't trust those nurses at the Hollies an inch. Heaven knows what would become of the poor little mite. Not that I wouldn't be thankful to see the back of her, I must say. She's been more trouble than all the rest put together.'

She was to be more trouble yet. Mrs Masterson, in a state of near-hysteria which she had worked up during the remainder of the day, telephoned Dr Harrington at his home (he was in the midst of a dinner party, which did not please him), reminded him that she was really a private patient, and informed him that she was not at all satisfied with the care Linda was receiving at the hospital.

Wearily he made an appointment to see her during his clinic the following afternoon. By this time there had been more trouble.

Max had been particularly busy. He was half an hour late in giving Linda her injection. As a result Mrs Masterson had arrived for the official visiting hour before he had seen Linda. As soon as he came into the ward, he saw her mother there with Linda, and nearly turned back. He could let the houseman give the injection for once. Anything to avoid a scene.

But it was a difficult injection to give. Max thought that David Lyell was not yet sufficiently experienced, or sufficiently cautious, to be entrusted with this procedure. He ignored his own inclination to keep away from Mrs Masterson, asked for screens, and advanced on Linda.

Linda, as was usual, began screaming. Mrs Masterson lost her head, and the children's ward, with all its visitors, was treated to an unedifying scene, in which Linda's screams and tears were easily surmounted by Mrs Masterson's cries of 'black savage' and 'you niggers think you rule the world these days'.

Max kept his dignity and walked out of the ward in silence. In the appalled blankness that accompanied his exit, Sister Addiscombe could be heard remonstrating, while

Linda's sobs had entirely ceased. She was in fact tremendously impressed by the effect she had produced, and lay thoughtfully sucking her thumb.

Mrs Masterson continued her tirade, in the course of which she asserted that she had an appointment with Dr Harrington that afternoon, and that she intended to tell him 'every single thing that has happened'.

Sister saw her opportunity. 'An excellent plan,' she said decisively. 'He'll be in his clinic now. I think you should go down there and see him immediately. Nurse – take Mrs Masterson down to Dr Harrington's clinic and tell Sister she has an appointment.'

She watched them both depart, stumped purposefully down the fascinated ward and into her office, where she rang Out-patient Sister. 'I've sent you down a packet of trouble, dear,' she announced, and related what had taken place.

'Dr Okiya came in, looking like thunder, and slammed the door. I wondered what had happened,' Sister O'Sullivan told her. 'He's still talking to Dr Harrington. They haven't started the clinic yet. They're late now, of course. I sent Nurse in to hurry them up, but they threw her out.'

'Well, he'll have to deal with it,' Sister Addiscombe said firmly. 'I wash my hands. Linda hasn't had her injection yet, either,' she added irritably. 'Who's going to give it to her, that's what I want to know?'

'Perhaps Dr Harrington will give it himself,' Sister O'Sullivan suggested.

Her supposition was almost correct. Dr Harrington came up to the ward with Max, they both disappeared behind the screen, accompanied by Sister Addiscombe and followed by the eyes of a hushed and expectant ward. Linda began screaming again, and then they both came out, followed by Sister, who snapped her fingers at a nurse and retired again behind the screens. This was all the ward was to know.

Max had given the injection, though it was the last time he was to do so.

This was what annoyed the staff so intensely. Dr Harrington, they considered, had been hopelessly weak and had given in to Mrs Masterson in the most humiliating way.

He had had a very difficult interview with her, as he explained to Max. 'If I followed my own inclination,' he said, 'I should tell her to take her wretched child out of this hospital and go to hell by the quickest route possible.' He shrugged wearily. 'But the child's in the middle of this course of treatment.'

Max nodded.

'We shall just have to continue with it and put up with the difficult mother. It won't be the first time, or the last. However, it's you who will have to bear the brunt of it all, and

I'm sorry about it. Especially as she seems to have been rather unusually offensive to you personally.'

Max shrugged. 'She's a silly woman.'

'Oh, very. The worst type of memsahib, as they used to say. Before your time, my boy. The days of Imperial India.' He grinned, and Max grinned back.

'I expect,' he remarked, 'that quite likely she has had something to put up with in Zambia. I don't imagine that she has endeared herself to the authorities there, since Africanisation.'

'Anyway the Mastersons seem to have lost their money, and the husband's out of a job. If it wasn't for that I'd take her up on all this "I am a private patient" stuff and nonsense. But they can't afford it. According to the sister-in-law they have nothing.'

Max did not look unduly distressed at this information, Harrington noted. Who could blame him? He had stood more from Mrs Masterson than anyone could have expected. 'Anyway, for the time being,' he said, 'I think it would be better if we let David look after the child. You keep out of the way.'

'It's not an easy injection to give,' Max pointed out.

'Time he learnt,' Harrington retorted. 'You can't carry that young fool for ever.'

Max frowned. 'Do you think this is a good time–'

'No time like the present. I'll give him a talking to, and I'll supervise him myself on the first occasion. That ought to make him take it seriously. He's got to take on some responsibilities. Stop sliding out of everything at all difficult. If he doesn't begin he'll never learn. Let him handle mother and daughter. It'll be good experience for him. You can offer useful advice from the sidelines.'

Harrington felt he was doing his best by all concerned. He was relieving Max of the disagreeable duty of caring for a child whose mother was liable to appear and insult him, while retaining the child in the ward to complete her treatment, and at the same time giving the young houseman some useful experience.

This, however, was not how the hospital saw it. Here, opinion was that Harrington had failed deplorably.

'He ought to have sent the woman packing,' they insisted. 'If she doesn't like her daughter being looked after by Dr Okiya she can push off.'

'Instead of that old Daddy Harrington has simply given in to her in the weakest possible way. I do think he's hopeless.'

'All he's done is to tell Max to keep out of her way as much as possible, so that he doesn't upset her. I think it's outrageous. She was abominably rude to poor Max –

everyone heard her – and he ought to stand up for his own staff, instead of letting patients abuse them whenever they feel like it.'

'He should have told her to apologise or get out.'

'Well, you know why he hasn't, don't you? The Mastersons are *private patients*.'

'So poor Max has to be sacrificed. Doesn't it make you sick?'

All this in the nursing dining-room. In the medical mess they thought the same, only expressing their views in less printable form. The leader of the discontent, as it happened, as David Lyell, Dr Harrington's houseman. He had been snubbed by Dr Harrington, who thought him lazy and irresponsible, on a number of occasions, and he was delighted to be able to redress the balance in his own favour by accusing his chief of weakness of moral fibre and partiality towards paying patients.

David Lyell was a young man who liked the sound of his own voice, and he was unable to understand why his seniors failed to appreciate it. The trouble had begun in medical school, when lecturers seemed to have nothing better to do than to score off him. He had gone into medicine, he maintained still, full of idealism, but even before he had qualified he had been horrified by the pettiness of the medical establishment. He had been disgusted, also, by the practice of medicine, though this fact he disguised from his contemporaries and a good deal of the time even from himself. His ideals could not stand the test of reality, and he clung to them desperately, blaming humanity and existence for failing to fit them. Like a number of people unable to face life, he was constantly in retreat, though he labelled it advance. He had never been able to admit to himself that just as he found humanity in the raw disappointing and insanitary, so he found medicine and surgery messy and unsavoury. The result of his hidden dislike, though, of his daily tasks, was that he was a bad doctor.

Everyone but David himself knew this. He was aware of the disapproval of his seniors, and of the contempt of the nursing staff, but this awareness only fed his own poor opinion of his colleagues. No one but himself cared for the higher values. He shut himself in his room, first with his textbooks, seeking reassurance, but latterly with his writing. He was engaged on an exposure of medicine under the National Health Service.

Always unpunctual, his writing made him more so. Locked on to the unwieldly sentences, which sounded so right when he delivered them to the air above his table, but which in some obscure way failed to emerge on to the paper with the same limpid clarity, he had no sense of time. They rang him from the wards and, impatient at the interruption, he said yes, yes, he would come. Twenty minutes or so. Then he lost himself again for an hour. When they rang again, he was infuriated. How dared they continually interrupt him like this?

Sister Addiscombe cursed him, Max Okiya was maddened by him, the nurses all imagined he was being deliberately difficult and playing hard to get. Dr Harrington thought him lazy and incompetent, as he had told Max, and was not at all adverse to taking this opportunity to make him responsible for the Masterson child. He knew how often David shuffled his work and responsibilities off on to Max, simply by reason of absence and lack of ability. Here would be a responsibility he should not evade.

David was furious. 'What does he think I am?' he demanded at meal times. 'This is supposed to be a training post, and he tells me I have complete responsibility for a child with schistosomiasis and her psychotic mother. He seems to think I'm a specialist in tropical medicine and a psychiatrist rolled into one. Not to mention a paediatrician.'

'You think he ought to understand you're none of these?' someone asked a little unkindly.

'My guess is he knows only too well,' another more obviously pointed out.

These remarks did not please David. 'One of the things that's wrong with medicine today...' he began.

The table groaned. 'Listen, chum,' the duty house surgeon interrupted, 'we don't need you to tell us what's wrong with medicine today. We're living it.'

'That's the trouble with all of you,' David urged excitedly. 'You *are* all living it. But you don't attempt to do anything about it. Why don't you fight?'

'Too busy,' someone muttered, wolfing dried apricots and prunes, optimistically designated fruit salad by the catering officer.

'Exactly, and that's why medicine is in the state it is. Because for years people like you have been either too busy to make an outcry, or too afraid of not keeping in with the consultants and missing the post you have your eye on. So medicine has been going from bad to worse, while you all do nothing about it. Well, I'm going to do something.'

'What?' the house surgeon asked, glancing at his watch as he did so.

'I'm going to take a stand.'

'What on?'

What on? That was the question, David knew. He hadn't a plan. A great many inefficiencies annoyed him, but quite how to come to grips with them he could not see. There were so many layers of diffused responsibility, consultants, nursing staff, secretariat, administrators – all topped by an increasing number of committees. He could see no hope of making an impression. Form another committee, and insist that its voice be heard? But he didn't want to make a committee's voice heard. It was his own voice that he imagined ringing through the land. He hesitated. 'Write to the press,' he suggested.

There was another groan.

'A letter to *The Times*, I suppose?' someone asked caustically. They dispersed to the afternoon's duties, leaving him glum, smoking a final cigarette and drinking the last of the coffee. He was still there half an hour later when Sister Addiscombe rang for him.

'Linda Masterson's injection,' she reminded him.

He had overlooked this in his desire to make a name for himself. He remembered it with the dull ache of fear he so often experienced when in contact with the busy routine of medical care, as opposed to the stimulus of medical politics. Linda had her injections every other day. David had given one supervised by Dr Harrington, and then a second on his own responsibility. On that occasion he had, to his amazement, managed without difficulty. He had given the injection slowly as he had been told, and everything had passed off all right, though the nursing staff had had a time with the child. Still, that was their worry. Now it all had to be gone through again. This time he might not do so well.

Unconsciously postponing the moment of test, he left the dining-room and went up to his bedroom to collect one or two oddments. Once there, he thought of a few points for an article on modern medicine – the place of the junior hospital doctor, his training and responsibilities – and made some notes while the points were fresh in his mind.

Sister Addiscombe, sounding tart, rang him again and informed him that an hour had gone by. 'After all, the poor child's had no lunch, no wonder she's getting fractious,' she had said to her staff nurse. 'And she knows she has the injection hanging over her, because we always starve her first. If that selfish young man doesn't hurry up, we'll have the mother here too, and then there'll be a fine old how-d'-ye-do.'

The imminent arrival of Mrs Masterson did in fact galvanise David into activity. He was a good deal more frightened of her than Max was. After one or two false starts he managed to get into Linda's vein, but he was harassed and worried by her screams and thrashing about, as well as by the prospect of her mother's arrival, and he failed to give the injection as slowly as he had done on the previous occasions. The result was that Linda had a worse reaction, and when her mother came she was vomiting and coughing in a way that terrified Mrs Masterson. Sister Addiscombe almost sent her away without seeing Linda, but knew the uproar such a demand would provoke, and decided the lesser of the two evils would be to let her sit with her daughter.

Unfortunately the vomiting and coughing were followed by an agonising tightness in Linda's chest and pain in her stomach, which made her cry out. She could not explain to her mother where the pain was, but gazed at her with terrified eyes, saying 'Here, here, hurts. Oh, Mummie, *hurts.*' Mrs Masterson began crying herself.

Nothing could have frightened Linda more. She began to scream again.

Sister appeared, sent for a nurse. Mrs Masterson was taken away, and restored with tea in the day-room. But in the meantime Linda had collapsed. Sister attended to her, and sent the staff nurse to telephone for David. She felt extremely irritable about the whole situation. If Dr Okiya had given the injection, she knew, none of this would have happened. She resolved to speak firmly to

Dr Harrington about the Masterson case. 'That woman can't be allowed to dictate to us all like this,' she said in the Sisters' sitting-room that evening. 'Dr Harrington will have to face facts. Either Mrs Masterson accepts the treatment we provide in the way we decide to give it, or she can take her daughter somewhere else where they're prepared to pander to ideas like hers.'

This was the attitude current among the nursing staff, who were not only one hundred per cent on Max's side (he had never been more popular around the hospital), but who exaggerated David's inefficiency and unpunctuality – from which they were, of course, the greatest sufferers.

While the hospital was still in a state of seething discontent, the local paper, the *Brookhampton Gazette*, gave the Mastersons a write-up. The *Gazette* reporter had been to interview Mrs Masterson, and proposed to print an account of her life in Zambia, her return home because of Linda's illness, and the bleak outlook for herself and her husband in Africa. 'There is no future for us now in Zambia,' Mrs Masterson had told the reporter bitterly. She had at last found the audience she craved, and she told the young man some lurid details of the children's ward at the hospital (it seemed reminiscent, he thought, of the workhouse in *Oliver Twist)* the African medical staff, and the old battleaxe of a Sister. Her daughter was not getting the right treatment, she was convinced. This was undoubtedly because they were not private patients any longer. As her husband was out of a job, they had to take what was offered under the Health Service. What was offered was a disgrace. Black doctors (the reporter shuddered, and left this out) and out-of-date attitudes. She was told, for instance, that she could only visit her daughter at certain hours. This, although Linda was seriously ill (thanks, of course, to the hospital's mismanagement) and although the Sister knew perfectly well she had flown home from Zambia especially to be with her.

Surely, the reporter queried, there had been an instruction from the Ministry of Health that in children's wards mothers were to be allowed to remain with the patients all day? Open visiting, it was called, and the *Gazette* had run an article on it. This new story would make good publicity. Children and the National Health Service, both good copy. He wrote the story up with enthusiasm.

CHAPTER NINE

Lavender Cottage, lost in the marshes, along a winding lane, its garden bordered with the low hedge of lavender from which it took its name, had been taken over furnished by Hermione, though sparsely, since Judith had removed her favourite pieces to the London flat. Hermione in turn had brought her own favourites from Fordham. Shortly after she had moved in she wrote to Judith asking if she might redecorate. Judith, then in America, had raised no objection. Hermione made new curtains, chair covers and bedspreads as she moved round from room to room painting and papering. She had a splendid time, and the cottage now reflected her own personality much more strongly than the flat at Fordham had ever done. This had never lost the atmosphere of an earlier generation, formal and servanted.

The cottage exuded feminine charm. In the Warrs' time it had been a comfortable country home, the big living-room filled with Colin's books, Judith's piano, the big chesterfield before the fire where Colin so often lay, his desk and the big reading lamp under the window. Piano and desk had gone with Judith, though Colin's medical books remained still in the low white-painted shelves.

Hermione recovered the chesterfield and the easy chairs in a pale lily-of-the-valley chintz, and painted the walls Georgian green. Judith had taken Colin's Persian rugs to London, leaving only the grey fitted carpet, and Hermione brought a green Indian rug. She had made white pleated lampshades and had been, too, up to London to the Japanese shop in Sloane Street for a white paper lantern. This hung, a huge oval, over the Regency table and chairs from Fordham that occupied the space formerly taken up by the grand piano. Now after three years all was complete. The dining chairs had seats covered in the lily-of-the-valley chintz, and the curtains and pelmets were made of a green Sekers silk that blended softly with walls and rugs. Hermione had brought the china cabinet from the drawing-room at Fordham, and it held her mother's Meissen orchestra and some charming green Worcester cups and saucers that she had picked up in Brookhampton 'of all places, darling.'

Upstairs in her bedroom the theme was grey. Grey and white striped wallpaper, silver-grey curtains and bedspread, a thick grey fitted carpet, more white lampshades, and lustres on the chimney piece. A cool room, perhaps even a little unfriendly, detached at the least. Here Hermione was comfortable and at peace.

Margaret Calderwood, though, decided that a more active participation in everyday affairs was required. All her life people had been deciding this on Hermione's behalf. The form Margaret's intervention took was to involve her in the activities of her Old People's Welfare Committee. Margaret herself was the secretary, but as she was also the Committee's physiotherapist, visiting the homes of old-age pensioners to give treatment, she was overworked. She hoped, by asking Hermione's assistance with the secretarial side, to induce her eventually to take over the job.

Sir Daniel Snelgrove, a wealthy Brookhampton businessman, was chairman of the committee, and Margaret was pleased to be able to introduce him to Hermione at dinner one evening. 'Sir Daniel Snelgrove, who is the chairman, as you know, Hermione, of our committee. My sister-in-law, Mrs Dunn, who is living down here now, and who has been helping me so much with the paper work.' She made a few more comments about the committee, and about one or two cases in particular, and then escaped to look at her casserole in the oven.

Hermione was encouraged to find that

this chairman was not at all forbidding, as she had secretly feared. She had heard a good deal about Sir Daniel Snelgrove. He had been knighted in the recent Birthday Honours – for services to industry, to the surprise of Jock and Margaret. They had expected him to reap a knighthood, but they had imagined it would be the result of his charitable work in the county. They both knew him as the power behind the scenes in local voluntary activities, and had hardly grasped how much energy he also put into running the family firm on the outskirts of the town. Daniel Snelgrove and Jock together had been responsible for turning the hospital's intensive care unit from an idea into a building project. Then, too, Snelgrove was chairman, not only of the Hospital Management Committee and the Old People's Welfare, but of the Rotarians, the Tuberculosis Care Committee, the local Bench, the Board of Governors of the Grammar School, the Friends of Brook-hampton Hospital, and innumerable other local groups, not to mention various sports associations and benevolent funds arising from the activities of his own works, Snelgrove & Watson. Hermione had imagined him to be a driving businessman, always in a hurry, keen, dark suited, with a tiny moustache. He turned out to be a burly, kindly figure, with a placid countryman's face, thinning sandy hair, and a quiet slow voice with a hint of the local burr. She warmed to him.

He warmed to her. She appealed at once to his protective instincts. Daniel Snelgrove had much to do with administrative women – busy, bustling middle-aged executives or wives, like Margaret Calderwood or the matron of the hospital. He respected them and enjoyed working with them. The salt of the earth, he was often heard to say. Secretly, though, he liked timid women who could be cosseted, gentle, fragile creatures, water-colour beauties. His wife had been one of these. She had seldom appeared beside him in public, and had led a secluded invalidish life until her death in a private ward at the hospital from inoperable cancer. It was from this event that Daniel's preoccupation with the hospital began. After his wife's death he had no personal life, and poured his abundant energies into the many good causes that he found ready to his hand. He was gregarious and appeared happy and en-grossed in his numerous schemes. He alone knew that there remained an aching void in his life. He never forgot his quiet, gentle Nellie. Hermione was another like her, he saw at once. He was startled to meet her as Margaret's sister-in-law, prepared to work for one of his committees. He set out to discover more about her, and under his expert probing Hermione soon found herself telling him half her life story.

Margaret came back to find them occupied, not in talk about old people's welfare at all, but apparently about a production of *Twelfth Night* that Hermione had enjoyed twenty years earlier. Stunned, she heard Daniel promising to take her to the Festival Theatre at Chichester. She signalled wildly to Jock, but he, returned late from the hospital after a meeting, was replenishing their glasses and pouring a first drink for himself. He gave her an uncomprehending stare.

At dinner the talk was general, though Margaret noticed that Hermione was more forthcoming than usual. After dinner, Jock and Daniel departed to the study, and the two women were left together in the drawing-room, though Daniel, before he went, remarked, 'I'll ring you up, if I may, and we'll arrange something?'

'I shall look forward to that,' Hermione said composedly. Margaret gaped.

In the study Daniel opened the conversation with a not unusual form of words. 'A rather disturbing matter has cropped up,' he said, settling down in one of Jock's deep leather chairs, and accepting a drink. 'Fortunately I've been able to scotch it this time, but it was a near thing.' He produced his battered old notebook that he carried

150

everywhere, and extracted from it a folded proof. 'From the *Gazette*,' he added, passing it across.

Jock studied it, frowning. 'Yes,' he said finally. 'Good thing you stopped it. Not good publicity at all. That bloody woman.'

'You know her already?' Daniel asked at once. 'Thought you would. Said so to Hopkins – he's the editor of the *Gazette*, you've met him, I think. Nice fellow. Sensible. One of his young cubs wrote this lot up, but he showed it to me before publication. Thank the Lord. I said I'd consult you. Thought you'd be sure to have the details.'

'The wretched woman has already set the entire hospital by the ears,' Jock said. 'Poor soul, one can only be sorry for her, fundamentally. But by and large she's a damn nuisance, no two ways about it.' He told Daniel the story of Linda Masterson, her treatment, and her mother's arrival from Zambia and disruption of the children's ward. 'Altogether,' he concluded, 'a tiresome situation. More whisky?'

'Thank you. Yes. I'll have a word with Hopkins, then I think this'll be the last we hear of that story. Now, tell me, the intensive care unit. I had a word with the architect the other evening, and I gather there's some difficulty about the power supply?'

'They seem to think at the Electricity Board that we use too much at the hospital

151

already. They don't like it.'

'So I heard. Now, what I was wondering was...' he went into technicalities.

'By the way,' he said some time later, as he pressed the starter of his Jaguar out in the drive, 'charming sister-in-law, Mrs Dunn. Most enjoyable meeting her. Seemed to like the theatre. I thought I might persuade her to come to Chichester one evening.'

'Splendid idea,' Jock agreed. 'Hermione doesn't go out enough, in my opinion. She came to live near us, you know, when Clare left school. We'd both like her to do more locally, only she's a bit shy, you know. But she's lonely, I think, now Clare's only home at week-ends. Take her to Chichester, by all means. She'd like that. Much more up her street, if you ask me, than social work.'

'That's what I thought,' Daniel agreed calmly, and drove off. Jock returned thoughtfully to the house. 'Something in the wind,' he announced to Margaret. 'Daniel's rather taken with Hermione.'

'Yes, I noticed. Amazing. I should have thought she was the last person—'

'Very attractive still.'

'Yes. Yes, I suppose she is. But she's out of this world.' Margaret found herself unexpectedly jealous. 'I should have thought Daniel would want someone practical and sensible, and interested in what's going on,' she remarked irritably.

'Probably just the opposite. He has enough of that.'

'Oh, do you think so?' Margaret, as always, was prepared to be open-minded. 'In that case perhaps we should encourage them to meet. He's such a nice man, I'm sure he'd be good for Hermione. But would she be good for him?'

'I think we can leave Daniel to look after himself. Very capable fellow.'

'Yes, of course. Of course he is. It's just that – well, men are such *fools*.'

Jock laughed himself sick. The next day, having a drink with Hugh, newly returned from Switzerland, at the Dog and Duck opposite the hospital, he related Margaret's remark, which was continuing to amuse him vastly, together with the possibility that Hermione would, as he put it, get off with Daniel. 'I'd like her to,' he added. 'She needs bringing out a bit. And then Clare can be free – she worries too much about her mother. Let Daniel do the worrying instead.'

'Good plan,' Hugh agreed absently.

'It's time Clare broke away from the stranglehold. She's gone a long way towards independence in the last few years, but I'd like to see Hermione have a life of her own.'

Hugh was hardly listening, Jock could see. 'What are you thinking about?' he demanded.

'I was wondering who that is with young

David Lyell,' Hugh admitted. 'I'm afraid I must be getting as gossiping as old Sister Addiscombe. "Who's that; I don't know him?" All the same, it isn't anyone from the hospital.'

'H'm?' Jock swivelled round and had a look himself. 'No, I don't know either,' he said, puzzled. 'Who can it be?'

In fact it was Ian Hardie, the young reporter from the *Gazette* who had written up the Mastersons. Frustrated and suffering from a deep sense of injustice because his editor had cut all the best bits out of his feature, leaving only a brief account of the Mastersons' Zambian experiences, he had turned up in the Dog and Duck to see what he could pick up from the hospital staff who were the main customers.

He found himself in conversation with David Lyell, who, as soon as he discovered he was talking to a reporter from the *Gazette,* had fastened on to him. The friendship was ripening fast. Each of them hoped to make use of the other, but they were still feeling their way.

At present David was explaining what was wrong with medicine. Everything, as far as Ian could tell. The buildings were old-fashioned, the administrators inefficient, the senior staff fossilised, the juniors inert, the pay appalling, overwork chronic, staff shortage acute and the food uneatable. He insisted on relating the menu that had been supplied at midday. Rissoles swimming in a fatty liquid, with swedes and potatoes, followed by stewed apples accompanied by lumpy custard and unutterable coffee. Ian Hardie was not unnaturally bored by the recital of these dishes. But he was hoping to be supplied with some inside information, so he concealed his fatigue and ordered more beer, hoping that he could put it on his expense account. A plan was growing in his mind. Why not a series of articles on different aspects of medicine today? They could all be built round the Brookhampton General Hospital. The Mastersons would come into it – the patient's point of view. His editor might stand for that article if it was accompanied by others giving a different side of the picture. This young doctor could write on the junior doctor's conditions (including even the food, if he felt so strongly about it). They could ask Dr Harrington, who had done an article for them a year ago, to do another. If he couldn't persuade his editor to run the series, he might sell the idea to one of the nationals. He might make his name.

David's thoughts followed a similar theme. If he could get in with this local reporter, he might do one or two articles for the *Gazette*, and then perhaps he could sell something to a London paper. He might make his name.

They arranged to meet the following evening, and separated, each to write the first draft of an exposure of the present-day Health Service.

Meanwhile Jock Calderwood and Hugh Ravelston had lost interest in them. To do so was a mistake, but of this they were ignorant. They were talking about Judith.

'It's so long since we've seen her,' Jock said. 'We haven't been able to tempt her down here. Of course, I can fully understand her feelings.'

'I think she's afraid to face it,' Hugh agreed. 'She thinks it will bring back the past too painfully.'

'She should have come sooner. No good putting these things off. I expect the prospect has built up now into a nightmare out of all proportion.'

They sat in silence, remembering Colin Warr and his death.

'In view of the way it's all turned out,' Jock admitted, 'it's possible that it would have been better for Judith to have stayed on in the cottage when Colin died. It would have been hell for her then, but she might have come through better.' She might, he thought, have been married to Hugh by now, both of them happy and raising a family. Instead, Judith was miserably alone in London, still missing Colin as though he had died recently, and Hugh equally alone in Brookhampton.

'Bring her down next week-end,' Jock added, taking a sudden decision.

Hugh opened his mouth to say that he doubted if he could persuade her, but Jock forestalled him. 'Tell her she's got to come,' he said firmly. 'Margaret and I want to see her. We'll put her up. She can't go on putting it off for ever.'

Hugh smiled lopsidedly. 'I think, you know, we'll find she can.'

He was correct. Judith could not possibly leave London that week-end, she asserted. Nor the next one. She had far too much to do. She maintained this even when Jock himself rang her and put considerable pressure on her to visit them, to name a day – maintained it almost to the point of rudeness, as he told Margaret. 'It's my belief the girl is still running away from life,' he said. 'I wish Hugh would give her an ultimatum. That might bring her to her senses.'

Hugh was coming to the same conclusion. They could not go on like this, he decided. It was fair to neither of them, left them both divided and unfulfilled. If they could not come together in a permanent relationship that had meaning for the two of them, then they must face a parting. He determined to go up to London at the week-end to tell her this.

Inevitably, since he had made plans, his

departure on Saturday was delayed.

Dr Harrington was going on holiday. He had been giving Linda Masterson her injections himself since David's failure. Now he asked Hugh to take on the responsibility.

Hugh found himself in the middle of a row. The hospital had already taken sides once over this issue, and now it divided again.

'Old Harrington ought to let Max do it, and stand no nonsense from that awful woman.'

'It's outrageous. We all know Harrington's simply pandering to that damned woman because the family are private patients. He wouldn't stand behaviour like that in one of his clinics.'

David fanned the flames. He was secretly offended that Dr Harrington had not asked him to continue with the injections himself, though at the same time he was extremely relieved to be able to escape the worrying duty. In his hurt pride he turned on Hugh. In his early days at Brookhampton he had particularly admired Hugh Ravelston, had hoped to know him better, to become a personal friend of his. This had come to nothing. Hugh had no time for him, and he had made scathing remarks as to David's competence on more than one occasion.

Hell may know no fury like a woman scorned, but the fury of an inefficient and lazy house physician scorned by the R.M.O. is far from negligible. In David Lyell's case it was regularly aired at meal times.

No one took much notice, to his increasing fury. He spent the next week-end writing another exposure of the Health Service, while Hugh, having given Linda her injection, went to see Judith.

CHAPTER TEN

Margaret Calderwood had received a letter from the U.S.A., which she showed to Jock as soon as he returned in the evening from the hospital.

'Look,' she said, passing him the letter. 'Tom's coming home. He's been appointed Director of the Virus Identification Laboratory.'

'Oh, splendid,' Jock said with enthusiasm. Tom was Margaret's only, and much-loved brother. 'I am glad. When does he take it up?'

'Not until next year. But he suggests they all come here for the Christmas holidays. To break the children in, he says—'

'Break us in, more likely.'

'I dare say. Also to have a look round to see how the housing situation is, and to meet some of the people he'll be working with.'

'Excellent idea. Expensive, I should have thought, but I suppose he's filthy with dollars.'

'I think he must be. He says that he's the brain drain in reverse.'

'Thinks well of himself, as usual.'

'The trouble is, he's right.'

'Oh, I know, I know. Sometimes I wish he wasn't so sure of it, but you can't really blame him. Only the truth, after all.'

'What worries me is Hermione.'

'She'll have to get used to it.'

'I know, but it *is* going to be difficult for her, and at Christmas of all times...'

'Don't see that Christmas is any different from any other time,' Jock said shortly. 'The two of them will have to make up their minds to meet and be agreeable. The sooner the better. Hermione can't expect Tom to stay out of the country for ever, simply so that she isn't inconvenienced.'

'Yes, but–'

'Dammit, it's well over ten years since they separated.'

'More like fifteen. Clare was quite small.'

'There you are then. Nothing to it.'

'Don't be obtuse, please, Jock. You know Hermione as well as I do, and there'll be trouble.'

'Dare say you're right. We'll have to live through it, and so will she.'

'I'm afraid she will be very upset, though, and I think she'll feel we've let her down.' This was what was worrying Margaret. 'After all, when we urged her to come and live in Lavender Cottage, we never thought Tom was going to be around, with his new family. Hermione will think we ought to support her now.'

'We can't forbid your only brother and his family to come to our house simply because he and Hermione had a divorce fifteen years ago.'

'She'll want us to.'

'Then she's going to be unlucky.'

'I think she's going to feel – well, betrayed.'

'Nonsense. If she does feel that – and I admit it's exactly the sort of damn-fool attitude Hermione might well take up – the sooner she gets over it the better. Any beliefs of that kind are melodramatic poppycock. Emotional blackmail, and neither of us is going to be blackmailed by Hermione. If we don't react, don't play her game, she'll have to pull herself together and behave sensibly.'

Margaret looked at him with amused affection. 'I do so hope you're right, darling,' she said. 'It does sound most admirably simple.'

'Is simple,' he retorted. 'You women will complicate issues so.'

Margaret sighed. 'No sense in putting it off,' she said. 'She and Clare are coming to dinner on Sunday. We'd better break it to them then.'

'Good idea. Not to worry, you'll find she'll survive,' Jock said confidently. He was far from oblivious of the difficulties ahead, but he could not see why Margaret should spend the week-end worrying about Hermione. When Sunday came, Margaret decided to postpone the breaking of the news until after dinner. She saw no reason why the meal, which she had cooked with care, should be spoilt. She realised, too, that Clare would leave to catch the nine-thirty train back to London, and she thought her departure might be used to terminate what could only be useless discussion.

Accordingly, when they were drinking their coffee, she threw her bombshell. 'Hermione,' she began, 'I wanted to tell you, I've had a letter from Tom. He's coming back.' As soon as the words were out of her mouth she knew she had begun in the worst possible way. Hermione turned towards her a face of such glowing hope that her belief was plainly apparent. Tom had tired of Barbara, had left her and was returning to his first love. Stumbling over her words, Margaret ploughed on, hating the blow she had to deliver. 'They're all – he's got a post – not until next year, of course – he takes it up next autumn – but he said they would all come over for Christmas. He and Barbara and the two children,' she ended, spelling it out, 'and they want to come to us for Christmas.'

'Be nice to have them,' Jock said firmly. 'Margaret was a bit worried in case you didn't feel up to meeting them all, but I told her that was all old history, and you'd be glad to. Of course, I know it may be a bit difficult for you to get used to the idea,' he added, as it was clear from the look Hermione had turned on him that she thought his jovial attitude callous in the extreme. 'But well worth an effort, don't you agree? I'm looking forward to having him back.'

'All one big happy family, I suppose?' Hermione asked sarcastically. She was shocked out of her dreams, and found herself suddenly with a biting tongue she had not known she possessed.

'You haven't any real objection to meeting him, have you?' Jock asked bluntly.

Hermione regarded him speechlessly. She was so much taken aback by the realisation that both Jock and Margaret assumed that the past was over, that a meeting between Hermione and Tom would be a minor and routine encounter, that she could find no words. Were they so completely lacking in imagination that they were blind to the agony this meeting must be? Even if they lacked true understanding – and of course Hermione had always known that she possessed far more sensitivity than the rather mundane Jock and Margaret – surely they would at least sympathise with her distress? But apparently they simply didn't care at all. They had no intention of putting her first. They were looking forward to seeing Tom again, apparently even intending to welcome that female pathologist he'd married, and she, Hermione, was expected to fit in with their plans. Her heart might be breaking, but it was nothing to them. Selfish and callous, one could call it nothing else. And at Christmas of all times.

'And at Christmas of all times,' she said bitterly.

'It will be a good opportunity for us all to get to know each other,' Jock maintained with a false heartiness. Margaret had been right. Hermione was going to play up like merry hell.

'I shall see if Mary can take me in,' she said poignantly. 'Otherwise poor darling Clare and I will have to be company for one another.' She smiled bravely through a mist of tears. At least, that was what she thought she was doing. Margaret saw her as infuriatingly smug and ostentatiously martyred.

'Don't be silly,' she said brusquely. 'Of course you mustn't go away. I'm sure Clare doesn't want to spend Christmas in her old school, anyway.'

Clare's expression told her how right she was.

'It doesn't matter what Clare and I want,' Hermione responded throbbingly. 'No one is going to think of us or our feelings. But don't worry, I shan't spoil your festivities with my unhappiness. Clare and I will be far away. You need not worry about us.' She paused, too wrapped up in herself to notice the expressions of extreme irritation worn by all her hearers. 'I know that it will be dull for poor Clare to spend Christmas at St Ursula's, but where else can we go?'

'No need to go anywhere,' Jock responded. 'Stay here, and join us as usual. It's time Clare got to know her father.'

Hermione shook her head theatrically. 'You don't understand,' she murmured. 'You simply don't understand, I'm afraid.'

'No, I don't,' Jock declared. 'And a good thing too. Of course I know it'll be difficult just at first, a bit awkward perhaps for both of you, but you must make up your mind to face it. You can't go round for the rest of your life avoiding Tom, pretending he doesn't exist. He's Margaret's only brother, and we're both delighted he's coming back to the country so that we can see something of him. After all, he is Clare's father, and in fairness to her, if for no other reason, you should meet him. It isn't as if you parted on bad terms, either. Let's all behave like civilised human beings,' he ended on a note of exasperation. Usually expert in managing people, he had no patience with drama.

'It's easy for you to talk, Jock,' Hermione said. 'No doubt you're quite right. But I'm afraid I haven't the strength for it.' She sank back into her chair, looking frail.

'Think it over, think it over,' Jock said

bracingly. 'Know you can manage it if you try. Sure you will. Clare, it's time I ran you to the station. Got your things?'

Clare, looking stunned, rose obediently to her feet and began moving towards the door, like a sleepwalker.

'So I am to be left all alone to remember the sad past and the empty future,' Hermione enunciated with clarity, sounding as if she were participating in an elocution lesson.

Clare looked baffled. 'Mother–'

'No, no, you must go back to all your London friends, and your busy life at work that you enjoy so much,' Hermione said accusingly. 'I shall manage somehow. After all, I still have dear old Woodie,' she added bravely.

'I'll be down next week-end,' Clare promised.

'Next week-end?' Hermione paused, the atmosphere heavy with doom, and Jock wondered irritably if she was about to assert that she was unlikely to live to see it. He attempted to remove Clare as speedily as possible, and began shepherding her towards the door, asking where was her case, and had she a coat? Clare, however, would not co-operate. She returned to Hermione, and began 'Do you want–?'

'It doesn't matter what I want,' Hermione broke in. 'I'm the last person to be thought of. Go up to London, darling. Catch your train and be happy.' Her lip quivered and drooped.

'Well, she's got to, Hermione,' Margaret interrupted briskly. 'If she misses the nine-thirty she'll have to catch the five-thirty tomorrow morning. That would be ridiculous. Say good-bye and let her get off, or she'll miss the train.'

'Good-bye, darling,' Hermione enfolded her daughter in a passionate embrace. 'I shall be quite all right by myself. I'm sure I shall.'

Clare was almost in tears now, and Jock could cheerfully have throttled Hermione.

'Come along, my girl, I'm not driving along the lanes at eighty,' he said loudly, putting his arm round her shoulders and urging her forward. This time they succeeded in leaving. Jock threw Clare's case into the back of the car, settled himself into the driving seat, and started the engine.

'No good worrying about your mother,' he asserted, and patted her knee. 'She'll get used to the idea. She's just a bit cross that she'll have to meet your father with his second wife, that's all it is.' He was determined to reduce the situation to manageable proportions for Clare.

'Do you think so?' she asked dubiously.

'She and your father separated perfectly amicably. They simply drifted apart, and after she had refused to go to the States with

168

him, it came to a natural end, the marriage. If she had been fond of him, she'd have gone with him. It's nonsense to pretend she was heartbroken, she wasn't. I can't for the life of me see why they shouldn't meet again without all this hullabaloo. I think it must be simply that she feels supplanted, out of it. Tom's coming with Barbara and the children, so Hermione feels she has no one but you, and she can't help playing up a bit. Don't let it worry you. Margaret'll be able to talk her round, I'm sure. No need to look forward to Christmas at St Ursula's.'

'You know–' Clare began, and stopped dead.

'What?'

'I always thought – I suppose it was silly of me, because no one actually said – at least, I don't think they can have done, because it wouldn't have been true, would it?'

'What wouldn't?' Jock asked patiently, his eyes on the road.

'I always thought my father was dead, you see.'

'Oh,' Jock said, startled. 'You never knew? You mean, all these years – you didn't know he was in America?'

'I knew he went to America. I thought he'd died there. Years ago. In a car accident or something. I don't quite know what I thought, expect that he didn't exist.' Her voice wavered.

They were at the station. Jock parked the car, and hauled her case out. 'They had a divorce,' he said, 'in 1954, and he married Barbara soon afterwards. They have two children, and he's a virologist. You'll like him. Run for the train, darling, here it comes, and *don't worry*. It'll all work out.'

She ran, and he returned to the car, furious with Hermione. The bloody woman must have told Clare her father was dead. He drove back home, frowning.

'Hermione's gone back to the cottage. She wouldn't wait for you to drive her – she's still in a mood, I'm afraid,' Margaret said when she greeted him.

'Just as well,' Jock said heartlessly. 'She'll be better when she's slept on it. Hope so, anyway. All this has been rather a shock to Clare. She thought her father was dead, she says.'

'Oh *no*. Oh Hermione really is the end, sometimes,' Margaret said. 'How could she have let her think that? Her own *father*. I do think that's very naughty of her.'

Hermione, sitting alone before the heart-shaped mirror in her charming grey and white bedroom, would have been consumed with anger to know that Margaret dubbed her behaviour naughty. She was not unaware that she had behaved badly, selfishly even, but out of a searing agony, she would have considered, and with some justification.

CHAPTER ELEVEN

Hermione had been brought up in Fordham in very much the way she herself had brought up Clare – sheltered, protected, cut off from her contemporaries and any struggle for existence. The only child of Charles and Vanessa Seabrook, she had been shy and retiring from birth. Charles Seabrook adored her, and hated any suggestion that she should be pushed into mixing with other children, when she so obviously found it painful. Had she been a son, he would have dealt with the situation differently. But a charming daughter was there to be spoilt, cosseted and made much of.

Vanessa Seabrook was a warm and out-going girl, who had courted her beloved Charles and persuaded the conventional and secretly shy young doctor into marriage. He needed her warmth and reassurance as much as her daughter did. But unfortunately Vanessa had always suffered from high blood pressure. Having Hermione had been difficult and dangerous for her, and there could be no question of another child. She died in her early fifties. Charles and Hermione were left alone, but with Tom Dunn in attendance.

Vanessa had encouraged him. Hermione at that time was seventeen, and Vanessa knew that she was immature and not ready for love. But she knew too that her life was likely to be short, and she could not prevent herself from longing to see her daughter safely married, and scheming to bring this about. Tom Dunn was a brisk and kindly – if unimaginative – house physician at the local hospital, who had been invited as a matter of routine to one of the Seabrooks' sherry parties. He had gone as a matter of duty, but had stayed on for supper, apparently riveted to Hermione's side.

When Vanessa died, Tom had taken it on himself to escort Hermione, and to comfort her in the desolation that had engulfed her on her mother's death. Charles Seabrook encouraged him, almost against his better judgement. He did not think the pair suited to one another, but, despairing and lonely himself, he was relieved and thankful to have Hermione looked after. Though he adored her, he did not at that sad time feel equal to making any great effort on her behalf, and when Tom shortly afterwards wanted to marry her, her father found an additional reason for not opposing the match. Scrupulous and introverted, he suspected that his own motives for disliking the proposed marriage were entirely selfish.

Without Vanessa to laugh him out of his complicated ponderings, he accused himself of potential jealousy and possessiveness. He spent considerable time admonishing himself, but little in assessing the realities of the situation.

So Hermione at eighteen was able to play the lead in a love story written and directed by herself. Unworldly, immature, without her mother to bring her to earth, she revelled in a dream. She had a white wedding, and looked ethereal, fragile. Tom was carried away by her beauty, and was so gentle and thoughtful on their honeymoon that his friends would hardly have recognised him. But he had fallen helplessly in love with this enchanted princess whom he had had the amazing good fortune to marry. He paid court to her. This was only what Hermione expected. In all her life, she had never occupied any position other than the centre of the stage. She was radiant. She made love obediently, since Tom found it so moving and essential, though she failed to understand what this mundane activity had to do with the poetry of their love.

They returned to Fordham, where Charles Seabrook had allocated them their own rooms in the big old-fashioned house. Tom left the Fordham hospital for a second house job, which meant that he had very little free time. Hermione happily spent the days, weeks, months, in a dreaming trance, arranging her rooms, wheedling out of her father the furniture she liked best, ordering curtains and covers, buying beautiful lamps and china to decorate their lovely home. She was a happily married woman, looking after the house, with a handsome young doctor husband, who devoted himself to medicine. With Tom away, there was no reason why she should not share her father's meals – indeed, it would be unkind to do otherwise – and she faced him across the big dining table as she had done all her life.

Tom used to try to persuade her to join him at the hospital for week-ends when he was on call, but she was afraid of the place. The other doctors frightened her, with their boisterous talk that she never understood, the entire alien routine upset her. Tom would go off to the wards, leaving her to fend for herself, and the experience was misery. She began to make excuses, saying it was not fair to leave her father alone, and couldn't Tom come to see her at home, that would be so much nicer? He did his best, but often they didn't meet for a month at a time. Hermione was secure in her happy dream, and had no inkling that their separation could be physically and emotionally demoralising for Tom. Theoretically she knew the facts of life. In practice their implications eluded her completely.

Tom's next post added to her bewilderment. He had taken up pathology, and found a post in the public health laboratory service. This meant that he could live at Fordham with Hermione again, and he began to bring his colleagues home for meals or drinks. Their conversation was totally unintelligible to Hermione. This astonished her. She had never envisaged herself as anything but the centre of attention, the charming and admired hostess, in her own home. When Tom had courted her, he had not talked pathology all the time. Now he seemed only interested in his friends. She might as well not exist.

'I might as well not exist,' she wailed, when he came cheerfully back from seeing his friends off.

Slightly drunk, and very much bewildered (the evening, surely, had passed off quite normally?) Tom tried to persuade her to forget her misery in making love. For the first time – but not the last – she repulsed him. 'Leave me alone, you're disgusting and you stink of that awful beer.' Now he too sulked.

They made it up, but the pattern was repeated, not once but a hundred times. Tom began to feel that Hermione was deliberately trying to freeze his friends out. He took to avoiding the difficulty by meeting them in pubs. That he was not home so much, and did not bring his strange rowdy friends with him, was nothing but a relief to Hermione. Tom knew a perpetual undercurrent of resentment, but he tried constantly to push this away, because he could not at this period accept any flaw in his lovely Hermione. Other flaws, though, appeared. Their love-making was a failure. Hermione often evaded it; she never pretended, when they did make love, to receive any pleasure herself, she was often asleep when he returned from his convivial evening in the pub. He began to suffer from a sense of sexual inadequacy. He was puzzled, resentful, defeated, at a loss. But Hermione was very beautiful, and she could be charming to him still when the mood took her – though more often she seemed to regard his presence as an interruption. An interruption of what no one but herself could say, since she seldom appeared to be doing anything. Tom refused still to accept the possibility that the responsibility of their failure could be hers. He blamed himself, and continued to put her first – if he thought about her at all. But he began, too, to have affairs. They were unimportant, hardly more than sporadic attempts to reassure himself of his own virility. They left him guilty and afraid.

After two years in the local laboratory, Tom had a year at the London School of

Hygiene and Tropical Medicine, where he took the Diploma in Bacteriology. He travelled up and down daily by train from Fordham, but his return was often delayed. On the course he met a girl, a pathologist like himself, who not only attracted him physically but who, unlike Hermione, understood what he said. This was Barbara Fielding, whom he eventually married. They became companions, and Tom found his life full and rounded in a way that built him up and renewed his enthusiasm for his job. After the course, though, he tried to break away from Barbara. He returned to the Fordham laboratory and made a determined effort to settle down to work and domesticity. He missed Barbara more than he would have believed possible.

It was during this period that Clare was conceived, by two people still conscientiously trying to bolster a failing marriage, neither of whom really wanted a child. Tom soon saw that his attempt to make a normal family life with Hermione was doomed to failure. It was the last thing she wanted. She was not going to be like other wives, and any attempt to force her into that mould would be useless. He began to feel that his own efforts to establish the marriage were futile.

Hermione for her part had submitted to Tom's desire for a child in one of the moods when she wanted to be a normal wife and mother. She soon regretted this, but by then it was too late, and she had to watch herself steadily increasing in size, unmistakably pregnant. She loathed the sight of herself in this condition, and became even more remote as she turned her back on the whole affair – which, however, not surprisingly, proceeded inexorably towards Clare's birth.

Tom was not in the country when this took place. He had been awaiting his call-up for National Service ever since he had taken his diploma, and was now in Malaya in the army.

Clare was two when he returned home. He was determined once again to make his marriage work. Hermione was a better letter-writer than conversationalist, and he had vowed to himself that he would turn his back on any thoughts and desires other than those compatible with family life. But Hermione did not make it easy for him. She had had no sexual life during his absence, of course, and she felt no need for it now. To allow the messy business to begin again was to risk another pregnancy, which she intended to avoid. In any case, she had become used to having her bedroom to herself, and she saw no reason why Tom should be allowed to clutter its feminine charm with his clothes, textbooks, notes, and the remains of his recurrent snacks. (Tom was always missing meals, and demanding

178

instead cheese and biscuits and apples and glasses of milk or beer, which he consumed roaming about the house, a habit which particularly infuriated Hermione.) So she firmly put him into the spare room, gave him a bookcase and a desk there, and informed him this was his study-bedroom.

He did not protest. He felt her rejection deeply – and with bitter irony – but he could not see how to deal with it. At times he was angry, and asked himself why he had steeled himself to break with Barbara. Hermione, for whom he had thought he was making the sacrifice, obviously did not want him. Chiefly, though, her rejection renewed those feelings of inadequacy and anxiety from which he had been free during his army service. Hermione was not interested in him, and who could blame her? He was a boring, excruciatingly ordinary chap, no match for her. He could not even make her happy in bed, he had no conversation but pathology, no friends but his colleagues. Limited and incapable even of fidelity, though he loved Hermione. A small-time lecher. Barbara too would soon have tired of him, as Hermione had done. He was capable merely of executing a few laboratory techniques and playing with his two-year-old daughter. Anything above these levels was beyond his scope.

Not that Hermione let him play with

Clare if she could help it. Here she displayed a strange jealousy. She had not wanted Clare, and as a red and screaming infant she had disliked her. She had refused to breast-feed the baby, and until she was crawling, Clare had been brought up by Woodie. But when she became a person in her own right, Hermione became devoted to her. The only occasions on which she became involved in life were when she competed with Tom for Clare's attention, or quarrelled with him because of his interference (as she described it) with Clare's schedule.

After his discharge from the army, Tom managed to land a post which pleased him very much, at the Virus Identification Laboratory. At least his success in his career was proving genuine. The laboratory was not near enough to Fordham for him to travel home daily, and for the first month he stayed at a hotel and came home at weekends. During this time he found a flat near the laboratory, but when he told Hermione this she was unwilling to move into it. Apparently it had not crossed her mind that she might be expected to leave her home. She did not go so far as to refuse. She made constant excuses. 'Not this week, Tom, it's Clare's whooping cough inoculation.' 'Oh dear, I don't think I can manage it this week, I promised Woodie I'd help her spring clean.' Once or twice she left Clare in Woodie's care, and occupied the flat with him, but so much in the ephemeral manner of someone sitting on her suitcases at Victoria Station that he was more ill at ease in the flat than he had ever been.

Hermione loathed the flat. Tom had taken it furnished, and while reasonably comfortable it looked – and was – distinctly secondhand, and could not compare with her lovely home. It was ugly, and not at all what she was used to. Then she found housekeeping an intolerable burden. To plan her day round shopping for food, Hoovering, cooking and washing-up was a tremendous strain for her, accustomed as she was to leaving anything of this sort to Woodie. Unfortunately, too, her efforts were not rewarded by praise and admiration. Tom had never been punctual, nor much interested in organised meals. He was quite happy with his snacks. He was engrossed in his work, and he wandered home at all hours and scrounged around for something to fill the aching void of which he only then became conscious. The meal Hermione had prepared earlier was ruined and dried up in the oven. As it had caused her a great deal of thought, worry and care, she was angry and disappointed, and told him he was selfish and thoughtless. He was surprised and apologetic, but Hermione continued to sulk. Not that she knew she was sulking. She was simply terribly, terribly hurt.

Soon Tom began to experience the same sensations as Hermione. He was relieved when she wasn't around, and he began to make excuses not to go to Fordham at week-ends. Charles Seabrook thought he had found another woman, but he was wrong. Tom at this time was immersed in his work, and lived for that alone.

After a year he had the opportunity of going to the U.S.A. to study tissue culture. He did not invite Hermione to accompany him – not that she would have gone if he had. She wondered if he would expect her to go with him, and was thankful that he did not. The prospect appalled her. Everyone said that there was no domestic help in the States, she would have to see to everything herself, and in a strange country, too. There would be a whole group of new and alarming colleagues of Tom's to meet, and all their wives. No doubt there would also be parties. She thanked heaven for the dollar shortage (the ostensible reason for her remaining at home) and settled down to another period free from Tom when she need make no effort to be what she was not. She was able to tell people how much she missed him, what an important fellowship he had won, how outstandingly well he was doing in his career, and how hard he had always worked.

'He has always been absolutely *dedicated,* you know,' she asserted. And this was how she began to see him herself. The dedicated scientist, aloof, unpractical (Tom, who was the most practical of men, able to turn his hand to cooking, washing-up, installing a boiler, mending Clare's toys or a fuse, dismantling the car or seeing to the plumbing), with no sense of time, anti-social (he was the most gregarious of men), cut off, indeed, from anything but his own speciality, which of course was totally incomprehensible to any normal person. She began to build her dreams round this figure. A man who might one day make a great medical discovery, a world scientist, with no home life and none of the usual needs – but a great man. When the great man wrote suggesting a divorce she was stunned. Here was life, inescapable, real, and she had no notion how to deal with it. She kept his letter to herself, told no one, not even her father.

What had happened to Tom was that he had met Barbara again. The meeting was unplanned. They had run into one another at a conference in New York. The five years of their separation dropped away as nothing. Their love burst into a consuming passion. Not, though, a passion that burnt itself out in a few brief months. Based on strong mutual attraction, and intensified by their parting, which both of them had found agonising, it was nourished now by companionship and their mutual interests. Their relationship grew and deepened. This time, Tom decided, he was not going to allow Barbara to pass out of his life because of some imaginary duty he told himself he owed to Hermione, who had made it very clear she had no interest in him. Their marriage had been a mistake from the beginning. Hermione was bored with him, disliked his company and his habits. She would be thankful to see the back of him. 'I don't think,' he wrote confidently, 'that this letter will come as any surprise to you.'

It came, of course, as a total surprise. Safely ensconced in her dream world, Hermione had never supposed that her husband, however errant, would cease to be her husband. The shock was intense. For months she pretended not to have had the letter. If she ignored the situation it might no longer exist. But the facts proved inescapable. Tom wrote again, then again. Finally he wrote to Charles Seabrook. He told him what he believed and what he had originally written to Hermione, explained that he had had no reply at all from her, and wanted to know how she was taking it. Charles Seabrook read the letter at the end of morning surgery. He had recognised Tom's handwriting on the envelope, knew at once that the letter meant trouble or some sort, since he and Tom did not correspond, and took it away from the breakfast table, where he was under Hermione's eye, and into his consulting-room. Now, drinking his coffee before he went out on his rounds, he pondered. He had seen this coming for years. The marriage, he had seen for himself, had been virtually non-existent since Tom went to Malaya, and in a bad way long before that.

At tea-time he tackled Hermione. She looked distinctly caught out. 'I didn't answer because I didn't know what to say,' she said sulkily.

'You could have discussed it with me,' her father pointed out. 'You don't have to struggle with this alone, you know, my dear.' He was sorry for her, but he was sorry for Tom, too.

'He is my husband,' Hermione burst out.

Her father sighed. 'Well, is he?' he asked.

Hermione stared. 'You know very well he is.'

'And you are his wife?'

'Of course.'

'Then why aren't you in California with him?'

'You're on his side,' Hermione wailed, and burst into tears.

'There, there, Hermione,' her father said, troubled, patting her on the shoulder. 'You can always rely on me. But we must work out what is best for both of you. The marriage can't go on like this.'

Hermione, among sobs and gulps, could just be heard to mutter, 'Why not?'

'We'll talk about it again when you're calmer,' her father said evasively. 'Now I must pop along to the hospital before surgery.' He drank the last of his tea, and made his escape.

The subject was not raised for several days. Then Dr Seabrook re-opened it.

'You must decide, Hermione,' he said firmly. 'If you want your marriage to continue, you must go out to California and join Tom. If not, I'm afraid you must face the fact that it's ended, and do as he asks. That's only reasonable.'

Hermione paid no attention to the end of the sentence. 'Go out to California?' she repeated. 'To California?' The prospect appalled her. 'I couldn't do that,' she said decisively.

'Are you sure? You could take Clare with you, and—'

'I'm not going to California,' Hermione shouted. 'You can't make me. I won't go.' She sounded about twelve years old, and her father watched her with affection and irritation.

'I don't see any other way of saving your marriage,' he said firmly.

'I'm not going. I don't see why I should.'

'Think it over,' her father suggested. He knew she would never go, and he doubted if he could have found it in his heart to urge her. How could Hermione succeed in mending a relationship when she had never succeeded in making it in the first place? The possibility of her pulling this off, standing alone and without guidance in a strange country, facing a husband she had never understood, was so remote as to be without reality. He wondered if he himself ought to fly out there with her? Sheer melodrama, he decided. Best to let the moribund marriage die peacefully.

'If you don't feel you can go to California,' he said a few days later, 'I think you should write to Tom and tell him you will fall in with his suggestion.'

Hermione was relieved. He wasn't going to try and bully her into joining Tom in California. There was a way out, after all. All the same, it was a bit much of Tom to expect to have everything his own way.

'It's a bit much of Tom,' she said grumpily.

Dr Seabrook felt like shaking her. 'How long is it,' he asked instead, 'since you were a true wife to him?'

Hermione did not even understand what he meant. 'What?' she asked. 'I've always been here. I never suggested a divorce. I've always been here with Clare, he's the one who went junketing off, and now asks for a

187

divorce, as if I mean nothing to him.'

Dr Seabrook looked helplessly at his daughter. 'Write to Tom,' was all he said.

Hermione did write. A careful, cautious letter, compounded half from an idealised fantasy of their marriage, and half from reality. It made an odd mixture, and Tom read it with alternating gusts of irritation and sympathy for his dotty unworldly wife.

He was determined, though, to marry Barbara. To have a real marriage, not this crazy hotchpotch of fiction and meaningless reality that was all he had known with Hermione. He wrote telling Hermione this, the first she had known of the other girl's existence. Now it was clear to her that he had known 'this female pathologist', as Hermione was always to refer to her, for years.

This was a further shock. Hermione had never thought of Tom as unfaithful. For one thing, she had always assumed that he adored her, the tiresome creature. For another, it had never crossed her mind that men were unfaithful to their wives outside books and the Sunday papers. Now she found she had been 'betrayed with that female pathologist' for, as far as she could tell, years.

Oddly enough, this knowledge made the final break easier for her. She could now place them all in a drama. She, the betrayed wife, lacking worldly sophistication, ethereal, spiritual, longing to give her more earthy husband the devotion he spurned. He, the remote scientist, unaware of his wife's great personal qualities, demanding merely the easy physical companionship so lightly offered at his work. Barbara, hard, white-coated, lacquered from head to toe, competent in the laboratory and no doubt equally so in bed, a typical professional woman with no softer side, but with the determination and ability to grab what she wanted that the gentler Hermione lacked. One day Tom would understand what he had done, what he had thrown away. In the meantime, though, she, broken-hearted, but too idealistic to chain him to her side unwillingly, would give him the release he asked.

Some at least of this drama was based on fact. If Hermione had loved Tom in the flesh as much as she did in her dreams, he would never have left her. He was always aware that his love for Barbara was a more manageable affair than his devotion to Hermione had promised to be at the outset of their marriage. But now with Barbara he was sharing a living relationship that grew constantly, while with Hermione there was nothing except his own inadequacy. He assumed that his earlier hopes had been no more than the mystical dreams of a boy. When Hermione wrote, though, agreeing to the divorce and asking him (typically) how to set about it, he was consumed with guilt, and almost brought the whole business to a halt. He had never liked her so much. If she had taken a plane to California with Clare, he would have left Barbara and made another attempt at building his marriage. If Hermione had not been too selfish to travel to California, and too proud to let Tom know how lonely and bereft she was feeling at the end of all her hopes, she could have had him back. Instead she gave him his divorce with an apparent lack of feeling which deceived him absolutely, and endorsed his own belief that she did not care for him at all.

Dr Seabrook was relieved when the matter was settled. He looked forward to a comfortable old age with his daughter and his granddaughter. He knew Hermione and himself, and he suspected that the small Clare would be as much as either of them needed to love.

Hermione's drama as the forsaken wife changed by imperceptible stages into a drama of grieving widowhood. She began to play a new role, the relict of a distinguished man, a brilliant scientist, now, alas, no longer with them. By implication, dead. Soon she invented a car accident. At first this had been part of an imaginary death-bed scene she had concocted to comfort herself. Although Tom was no longer in her life, he had died loving her and her only. Died in her arms, both of them secure in their love. After a few years she no longer knew fact from fiction. Questioned, she would have admitted Tom's existence, in his laboratory in California. But unless challenged, she believed in herself as a widow, in Clare as fatherless. Dr Seabrook was angry with Hermione when she implied, more than once, to Clare that her father was dead. He remonstrated with her, but received only dramatic replies. 'He has chosen to be dead to both of us.' 'Clare has no father, as you know.' 'It's not by my wish, as you know very well, but she is in fact fatherless.' He could not deal with Hermione in this mood, and eventually he allowed the question to go by default, though he remained uneasy.

'One day,' he warned her, 'Clare may blame you for this.'

This day had come.

CHAPTER TWELVE

For years Clare had had a somewhat contemptuous affection for her mother, shot across with pangs of intense love. Tonight as she sat in the Waterloo train she experienced both these reactions, but accompanied too by a raging fury. One moment she knew she would never be able to forgive Hermione for concealing the fact that her father was alive and accessible. Then suddenly she saw that only fear could have made Hermione do this – fear that Clare might prefer her father's company to her own. She would show Hermione, Clare decided loyally, that nothing could disturb their mutual devotion. A second later something did – a gust of cold anger against her mother. She remembered all those long years of boredom and emptiness at St Ursula's and at home in the quiet flat, with only Hermione and old Woodie, the sterile years of her lonely girlhood. She relived the struggle she had faced to break free, to fight her way into a worthwhile life of her own, and saw clearly how fatally easy it would have been for her to have succumbed to the pressure of home and Fordham. There had been so many points at which she had all but given in. Afterwards, too, leading the coveted new life had not been altogether easy. She had been too sheltered as a child to be able to swim unthinkingly in the waters of freedom. There was so much that she knew nothing about. She had never had a host of friends before, she had never gone out and about in London, she had never looked after her own clothes even, done her own washing and ironing. Leaning to stand on her own feet had been hard, though exhilarating.

Now it turned out that throughout her childhood her father had been available, cut off from her, Clare was sure, only by Hermione's decision. Her father, surely, might have opened all these doors to her in childhood? She need never have endured the long days of Fordham, sinking steadily into apathy. Another blow struck her. Perhaps she was mistaken. She might be blaming Hermione unjustly. This might have been none of Hermione's doing after all. Perhaps her father had simply not been interested in her. She was his eldest child, certainly, but obviously not his only child. Jock had made that clear. Tom and Barbara were coming with the children. Her half-brothers and sisters. Had her father been disappointed that she had been a girl? Men were said always to want sons. Had he abandoned her with Hermione, two failures, and gone on to other successes?

The train drew in to the platform at Waterloo, and Clare stumbled out, clutching her canvas bag, muddled and on edge. She pushed her way along the platform, where travellers out of London surged, catching the last train down to the coast. Head down, frowning, lips set, her week-end grip banging against her legs and those of any incautious passer-by, she slammed along, to find herself all at once held firmly.

'Wait a minute, stop and say hello, you unsociable brat.'

Vaguely she looked up, bewildered, half-aware that she had heard her name called more than once. Hugh, returning from his London week-end. She stared at him.

'Good God, what's the matter with you?' he demanded, astonished at the pale tense face she had turned up to him.

'Nothing,' she said childishly and grumpily, scuffling her shoe.

'Oh no, not much,' he agreed sarcastically. He scanned her face. 'Had a row with Mum?' he suggested.

'Not exactly. Sort of. It's too complicated to explain here.'

'No, it isn't. Come along and have a drink, and you can tell me what's up.' He took her case off her, said 'come on,' and began walking rapidly back towards the barrier. She followed him.

'Now then,' he said, when they were seated at a small round table in an unknown pub full of late drinkers making the most of their remaining time, 'what are you going to drink?'

'Gin and tonic, please.'

'Oh no, you aren't.'

She giggled in spite of herself.

'What's funny?'

'You've hardly said a word to me since we met except no. Why shouldn't I have some gin and tonic? And why are you so negative all at once?'

'Perhaps because I feel negative,' he said bitterly, thinking of his wasted week-end. 'However, be that as it may, I don't advise you to have gin. Useless if you're miserable. Which I can see you are. Only makes you worse. Keep off the stuff. What about brandy?'

'Brandy,' she repeated. Brandy was for emergencies at home, being put to bed with brandy and hot milk, or else for old men after dinner, in an aroma of cigars and heavy talk.

'Brandy,' he said. 'You can have it with dry ginger if you must have fizz.' He went to the bar. Clare sat on at the little table, vacant but comfortable now. Hugh was in charge.

He came back, dumped down two glasses and a bottle of dry ginger.

Clare looked at the glasses. 'That seems an awful lot of brandy,' she suggested faintly.

'What you need,' he said briefly. 'Stop carping, and get outside that.' He pushed the glass across the table. 'Now shoot.'

'My father isn't dead at all,' she announced indignantly. 'And he's coming home for Christmas. With his wife Barbara and their children.' She surveyed him wide-eyed over the top of her glass.

'No, well,' he tipped the brandy in his own glass absently, turning it about in his long fingers, frowning. 'No. You can't expect the poor chap to be dead simply to suit you and your mother.'

'Not to suit me,' she exploded. 'To suit *her*. That's just what I mean. What right had she to let me think he was dead, all these years? I'm twenty now. Nearly twenty years she's made me believe I hadn't a father, and there he's been all the time, only I never knew. All her doing. How *could* she?'

'It wasn't exactly the right thing to do,' he agreed cautiously.

'Now there's nothing to be done about it,' she went on furiously. 'It's too late now. I'm grown up now, and we've never even met. Or at least not since I was about four, and I honestly can't remember. It's – it's irretrievable. My childhood gone. All finished. Without him.' She stared accusingly, and drank more brandy. 'I could have grown up having a father. But she didn't let me, and now it's too late. It could all have been entirely different. All those years at school, when I thought there was only me and Mother. Horrible, dreary years. You don't know how I hated them, and yet what an effort it was to break out of them. To refuse to go on living that awful life. I couldn't tell if I was doing the right thing at all. I know now. I know now that I should have done it years earlier. Now I can see how strange and abnormal that tiny little eventless existence was, and how obvious this must have been to everyone else. Leaving it has even been good for Mother. But nobody told me so at the time. Only Mother said how hard and ungrateful I was being. Unnatural and unfeeling. And I believed her. I thought I was being selfish and horrible. I simply knew I couldn't bear it all any longer. But I nearly didn't make it. She nearly won. If I had only known about my father I should have asked him what to do.' She threw the final sentence down dramatically, as a challenge, and glared.

'Don't kill me with a look,' Hugh said. He found her very lovable and endearing, and he was touched by the story she had told. 'I shouldn't have stopped you,' he added. 'But,' he pointed out, 'you didn't do it. You made out on your own, h'm? Right, so you had a hard time. Harder than you need have done. But you came through. It was worth doing, wasn't it?'

'Oh yes, but–'

'You managed without this mythical father – who easily might not have turned out to be the *deus ex machina* you are so determined to make him. You feel your mother let you down–'

'She has. It isn't just what I feel, she has. It's no good saying she hasn't, because she has.'

'I know she has, but so what? She's not infallible, she can make mistakes, like anyone else. She loves you, and because she needs you she made a mistake. Just because she's your mother doesn't mean she's automatically fitted to be your guide to living, you know. She's simply another human being, who had a broken marriage and got into a mess. It was bad for both of you, and you have every right to feel you've had a raw deal.'

'My father–'

'Don't try to persuade yourself that your father would have put everything right for you. He had a broken marriage too, and got into his own mess. When he and your mother separated they can't have been all that much older than you are now. Thought of that? Just two young people in trouble, churning up their lives – and yours, too, of course, but inadvertently, entirely by accident. You can't blame them because they weren't a couple of wise old grandparents.'

Clare giggled again. She began to feel better.

'There's no reason I can see to assume that your father would have taken charge of your life and given it a neat little twist in another direction, and all of you could have lived happily ever after.'

'I suppose not,' Clare admitted. She had drunk most of the brandy now, and was beginning to experience a comfortable glow and a conviction that she could cope with it all. 'He's coming for Christmas,' she added.

'Rather fun to encounter your father for the first time when you're adult,' Hugh suggested. 'You'll be able to meet him on equal terms, and see him as a human being, not simply as a father figure.'

'I suppose it might be quite fun,' Clare agreed. 'For me, at least. Perhaps it will be rather hell for Mother. So she seems to think. She's talking of spending Christmas at St Ursula's.'

'You don't have to go if you don't want to,' Hugh pointed out.

'I suppose I don't.' Clare was surprised and comforted.

'You can decide for yourself – according to the circumstances at the time. And as the time is six months away, I suggest you postpone worrying about your decision.'

The pub was emptying, and they went out

into the dark night. 'We'll find a taxi,' Hugh said, 'and I'll take you home.'

In the taxi he put his arm casually round her, and she sank back against the support of his hard body. She had almost forgotten now about her father and Hermione and the unfairness of her childhood struggle. Only the present counted. The rough tweed of Hugh's jacket against her cheeks, the strength of his arm and the warmth of his body. She would remember this all her life, she knew. The taxi ride, with Hugh holding her in his arms. She saw no farther. Simply to be held by him like this was enough. She stared up at him. He looked beyond her, his face was taut and expressionless. She longed above all to see love flood it – love for herself.

They reached the house in Earls Court where Clare had her flat.

'Out you go,' he said abruptly.

'Oh,' she exclaimed, realisation striking her for the first time. 'Oh, you've missed the last train. All because of me. Oh, Hugh, I *am* sorry. What–'

'It's quite all right,' he said curtly. 'Ben will put me up. I'll go down on the first train tomorrow.'

'I am sorry,' she said again. No wonder he suddenly seemed irritated. There she had been, selfishly happy in his company, and he had to find a bed for the night, rise early in the cold dawn to catch a train for Brook-hampton, and face a day's work.

'Go on in,' he said briefly. 'See you.' The taxi made a complete turn and disappeared down the Earls Court Road.

Ben was unruffled as ever when Hugh rang him from the callbox round the corner. 'Of course,' he said. 'There's no one here. Though I approve of your caution. All my mistresses are out of town, though. In-considerate lot. You'd think they could work out some sort of rota.' But when Hugh appeared, Ben discontinued his mockery of his own sex life, and began enquiring about Judith. The transition was natural. Hugh had spent the week-end in Judith's com-pany, but he had passed the night's blamelessly in Ben's flat. Ben thought this a mistake. If Hugh and Judith were incapable of carrying on an illicit *affaire,* the time had come for them either to get out or get married. He said as much.

'No dice,' Hugh retorted. 'Judy depends on me – or so she says – but she doesn't find me physically attractive. She–'

Ben was staring. 'She doesn't...'

Hugh shrugged. 'I don't suppose it's permanent. Or do I? If it is, the sooner I get out the better. But I think, and so does she, that it's simply that she hasn't yet forgotten Colin. She's not ready to be excited by anyone.'

This was what Judith had been telling him. 'I can't turn my back on our life together,' she had said sadly. 'I know Colin said life was for the living, but I can't forget him.'

'No one wants you to forget him.'

'No. But I can't seem to have any very strong feelings about anyone else.' She looked unhappily at him. 'It's so unfair on you. I'm taking such advantage of you.' She took his hand. 'I'm simply a drag on you. Someone to whom you have a duty, but who gives you nothing.'

'You give me your companionship,' he reassured her. But in fact he agreed with her. What was he supposed to gain from their friendship?

'I did the wrong thing at the beginning,' she told him. 'I should have stayed on at the cottage, gone on living there. Then I would have had to grasp that Colin was dead and I'd got to go on living. It would have been painful, but it would have been better. Instead I went rushing off to the States. Anything to get away from the place where Colin died, and where we had both lived. All my happy memories. Everyone urged me to go. You did yourself. But it was the wrong thing to do. I stayed on there, simply because I couldn't face coming back. Back to no Colin. I kept putting it off and putting it off. Well, you remember.'

He did.

'Then when I did come back, I found I was back at square one. All my feelings about Colin must have been in cold storage. Back in London I had to grow used to his death as if it had happened only last week. In a way I still can't grow used to it, and the fact that I can't is something to do with my stay in the States. Something to do with the fact that I didn't stay and face reality, live through it all the hard way. Because now there's no reality at all. Colin hasn't just died, he died over three years ago. My life with him finished then. But I'm still in some sort of limbo. Existence began after he died, but not living as it used to be.'

Hugh was desperately sorry for her, and longed to take her into his arms. At one time he would have done so, would have tried to bring her to life, tried to instil confidence into her that together they would make a new and meaningful life. Now he lacked the confidence to impart to her. She had succeeded, by her constant evasions of his approaches, her gentle but firm detachment, in destroying his belief in himself.

When Colin died, Hugh had been in love with Judith. He had doubted his own ability to succeed Colin. Nothing had changed this original opinion. Colin had been an outstanding man. It was natural that Judith should not find Hugh adequate to succeed him. He couldn't help feeling, though, that he had failed her – and Colin too. For Colin had asked him to look after her, had urged him, almost in so many words, to grab her and marry her, and settle down to raise a family. That he was unable to sell this future to Judith was another symptom of his own inadequacy. He had failed in medicine, failed with Nicola. Now he was failing with Judith. All of a piece.

Yet something in him rebelled at this interpretation. He only half-believed it. He could have made Judith marry him, he knew this. If he had been willing to settle for second-best, he could have married her soon after she returned from the States. She was fond of him, she needed him in her life, there was no one else. She would have acquiesced if he had insisted on marriage. She would acquiesce now if he put his foot down.

But he did not want to marry her in that spirit. He wanted a real marriage, not a kindly, tolerant companionship. He wanted, too, a wife who would put him first. Judith made no pretence about this. Music came first with her. After that Colin's memory. Then her affection for Hugh. It wasn't good enough. But he couldn't leave her.

'I don't think I've ever had a girl-friend who thought so little of me,' he said dryly to Ben, his mouth lifting in a smile of bitter self-mockery.

Ben was angry. 'Then why in God's name – after all, you've always had your pick of girls. All right, I know you think you have an obligation to look after the girl, that you promised Colin Warr and so on. But for Pete's sake, why can't you accept the inevitable and look after her like an uncle? And get yourself a girl for home comforts? It's time you settled down.'

'Speak for yourself. I don't notice the little woman and the nappies around in this flat. All I hear about from you is a multitude of girl-friends. Isn't it about time *you* settled down?'

'Safety in numbers,' Ben said with a benevolent smile. 'It isn't that I wouldn't like to settle down, you know. I would.' His black eyes flashed with amusement under his heavy brows. 'It's just that I can't make up my mind which of them to settle down with. And you'll agree it's liable to lead to a certain amount of awkwardness if one marries in this frame of mind. You wouldn't like to take one of them off my hands, I suppose? I'd probably be rather annoyed if you did, as a matter of fact, but there's no doubt it would simplify matters for both of us.'

Hugh laughed without amusement. 'And for Judith too, I dare say.'

Ben looked at him. He wanted to tell Judith Warr a few home truths. Perhaps she was unhappy, desolate without Colin. But she should learn to consume her own misery. Instead she allowed it to consume Hugh. This might have been forgivable if she had loved him, but Ben doubted this. She was simply making use of him. If she had loved him she would have valued him. This was exactly what, by Hugh's own account, she did not do. 'I don't think I have ever had a girl-friend who thought so little of me,' was what he had just said. And not for the first time. Ben had heard similar comments before. He found them intolerable. Who did Judith Warr think she was? He remembered Hugh in their student days, and later when they had been housemen and then registrars together at the Central. He had been sought after by all the girls. A glance from Hugh Ravelston had brightened their day. Staff nurses, physiotherapists, almoners, secretaries – he could have had his pick. Now Judith Warr dangled him contemptuously on a string, it seemed.

'Cut loose, Hugh. Pack it in.'

Hugh looked at him, frowned. 'It's not as simple as that, you know,' he said. 'Part of the difficulty, of course, is that I'm down at Brookhampton and she's up here.'

'Then let her damn well get down to Brookhampton,' Ben wanted to say. But he kept his mouth shut.

'It doesn't really give us a chance, you

know. We meet so seldom that we never seem to get our relationship going before we have to break it off again for another month or two. Judy thinks I ought to move to London.'

Ben swallowed, but said nothing.

'She seems to think I ought to have gone into the research labs, not stuck out for clinical medicine.'

Ben swallowed again, and began to count to twenty very slowly.

'Of course she's not the only one to think that.'

Ben had reached three only, and said nothing.

'Everyone said I would have more chance of some sort of successful career, in spite – of – of everything, if I had stuck to bio-chemistry. Judith knows that, you see, and I think she feels I ought to be up in London making my mark, instead of down in Brookhampton stodging away as a second-rate physician in a second-rate hospital. Sometimes I think she's half-ashamed of me and my dull little job.' Only to Ben could he have admitted this, yet it was a relief to share his suspicion. 'There she is herself in this sort of lively artistic circle, you know, full of interesting people doing fascinating things, and then I turn up from the wards, only able to talk about patients with messy diseases. I'd be more acceptable if I was doing research in some lab – more up to her musical friends.'

'What you do,' Ben said very carefully, having regained control of his temper, 'depends on what you feel, and not on what Judith Warr's friends imagine.'

'Oh, quite. I'm not going to give up my sort of medicine simply to make an impression on a lot of pianists and fiddlers. I haven't quite taken leave of my senses. But I am rather wondering if I ought to move to London.'

'To be near Judith?'

'Yes. One of us has to make the effort, and I think it will have to be me. She has to be in London for her career – mine has gone phut anyway, but hers hasn't. And she has other absolutely valid reasons for not wanting to be down in Brookhampton. I shall have to be the one to do the moving.'

Ben sighed. 'It won't be all that easy to find a good post. The pressure is still on in London, as far as jobs are concerned. London hospitals aren't all that short-staffed.'

'I know. It won't be easy. And one side of me doesn't want to leave Brookhampton. A lost has happened to me since I first went there – in a state of acute demoralisation – and I've roots there now. I'm fond of the place. I don't honestly want to become just another peripatetic registrar with no future, doing the rounds of the dead-end jobs.

Frankly, if I can't have a career at the Central I'd rather stay at Brookhampton. However–'

'You'd still like to get back to the Central,' Ben said accusingly.

Hugh smiled sarcastically. 'Well, I shan't. We both know that. I can't make up my mind what to do, though. There's a side of me that wants to stay where I am, and build myself the sort of life you can have down there. Satisfying in its way, genuine, and right outside the establishment.'

'The sort of life Dad has,' Ben contributed.

'Exactly.'

'And the other side of you?'

'Says I'd be throwing away my chance of happiness with Judy simply out of inertia, satisfaction with the second-best.' He frowned. 'If I don't make a move, I'll lose her merely by not trying. That seems extraordinarily feeble.'

'I see your point,' Ben agreed. 'Er – I don't want to seem inappropriately crude, but first things first, after all. You don't want to turn your life upside down for a girl who never intends to get into bed with you.'

Hugh winced, and reddened.

'It sounds brutal, I know, but I think you ought to cut loose.' Ben had decided to come out with it. Obviously Hugh hated the idea of leaving Brookhampton. He was prepared to do it entirely to please this damned

Judith Warr. 'You say the relationship doesn't have a chance because you're separated by distance. Isn't it more because all these years it's remained spiritual and not sensual? We both know perfectly well that, however unpoetic it may seem, you can't have a successful marriage without sex.'

'Of course I know that,' Hugh retorted irritably. 'Don't think I'd be such a fool as to embark on marriage if Judith remained physically aloof.'

'You think she might wake up to you if you were available in London? It seems to me – I'm sorry, Hugh, but it sticks out a mile – that you shouldn't even consider moving from Brookhampton *unless* she desires you physically. Not needs you, or depends on you, but actively desires you.'

'I nearly seduced Clare in a taxi tonight,' Hugh confessed. 'Only iron self-control enabled me to pack her off intact.'

'I'm glad to hear it,' Ben said severely. 'Hands off my young cousin.'

'I think it must have been the result of my abstemious week-end.'

'Perfectly natural,' Ben agreed. 'But not, I repeat, *not*, with Clare.'

'No, that's what I thought. Pity. Ten years ago I wouldn't have been so careful. She's a very attractive armful.'

'What was she doing in your arms at all? Here am I imagining you depressed and lonely because of Judith, and quite worried about the situation, and now you suddenly let slip that you've managed to pack in a quiet armful of Clare in a taxi as well. I must say, this sounds thoroughly healthy, and more like your old form. But she is my cousin, and I shall constantly be asking you your intentions if you continue in this way.'

'I can't afford to get involved with Clare as well as Judith. That would be a fine old muddle.'

'It sounds a far more enjoyable muddle than the one you're in at present,' Ben pointed out, and then recollected his role as Clare's protector. 'Lay off the girl, though.'

'I did lay off the girl. Though it was a struggle. I was taken by surprise, you see. There was I, all avuncular in this taxi, seeing the girl home because I thought she was in a state of emotional shock, when – wham.' He laughed. 'I pushed her out of the taxi fast.' He paused. 'Trouble is,' he added reminiscently, 'it keeps on happening.'

'What do you mean, it keeps on happening? Do you make a habit of driving round London in taxis with Clare?'

'No. It's when we're sailing. I can't seem to take her for granted any longer. I used to – you said so yourself.' He sat and brooded. It would be so easy and pleasant to have an affair with Clare. Why did he have to have two girls in his life, both of them for different reasons untouchable? When he sailed with Clare now, he found he couldn't take his eyes off her. His body sprang to life, made urgent calls for her body, her lithe young beauty. He fought the demands down, but their relationship was no longer easy and straightforward, as it had been in the past. Sometimes he hated her for her power over him, her recurrent ability to disturb him. He could control the urge to make love to her, but not always the urge to hurt her, to strike back at her for daring to exercise this physical domination over him. He was becoming obsessed by her body, which she seemed now to flaunt as she trod the decks. Yet he knew that she was the same as she had always been, it was his desire that had changed. He must get away from Brookhampton to London, he knew, or he would find himself making love to one girl and promised to another. He frowned. 'I must get away to London,' he said.

Ben grinned unsympathetically. 'You'll find Clare here too, you know, if you're running away from her fatal fascination. I suppose she *is* a virgin?' he demanded suddenly.

'Oh, of course,' Hugh replied with certainty.

'How do we know? She gets around, she's very attractive. Let's not be olde worlde, these days–'

'I feel sure she is,' Hugh said curtly.

'Pity. It'd be so nice for both of you if she wasn't. You need a nice devoted girl for a change. However, it's out. I won't allow it.'

'Doesn't matter whether you will or not,' Hugh said. 'I won't.' He changed the subject, and talked again about prospective posts in London. Rather against his better judgement, Ben found himself promising to see how the land lay, to make some enquiries for him.

'Nothing grand,' Hugh remarked. 'Don't let them think that. Just any old thing that happens to be going in any old hospital.'

Ben mentioned the matter to Professor Barham, who had succeeded Sir Alexander Ramsay in the Chair of Medicine at the Central. Ben, who had been Resident Medical Officer at the Central for five years, was now the most junior consultant on the professorial unit. His career had followed exactly the lines forecast for Hugh Ravelston, whose grandfather had been Professor of Medicine before Ramsay. This had been in the days before what was dramatically but accurately known as Hugh Ravelston's disgrace. Ben was having the career they had all, in the early brilliant days of success, mapped out for Hugh, the youngest and most brilliant, it had been said then, of a brilliant family. Now, though, he would be lucky to find any post.

'London? Not here, I hope?' This was Barham's immediate reaction when Ben mentioned Hugh's name. And Barham was a kindly man, less conventional than many of his colleagues.

'Oh no, not here,' Ben agreed hastily.

'Because there'd be no hope of that.'

'I'm sure he knows that. He said–' Ben was inspired to quote '–"nothing grand. Just any old thing that happens to be going in any old hospital."'

'Poor fellow,' Barham said, mollified. 'We must all do what we can. I was away in Nyganda when the Ravelston affair blew up, of course, so I've only heard the story at second hand. He was Vanstone's registrar, I remember. I didn't, frankly, have much use for him, then. A typical Vanstone type, smooth and rather superficial, but with considerable ability, of course. Vanstone's no fool, after all.'

'Hugh can give that impression,' Ben admitted. 'He isn't like that at all.'

Barham looked at him. 'Friend of yours, of course. I remember now. You want me to do something, do you?'

'If you could,' Ben said.

'Of course I can,' Barham retorted. 'It's a question of whether I will.' He grinned suddenly. 'Listen to me,' he added. 'Growing well into the part of the pompous old professor. All right, I'll do what I can.'

CHAPTER THIRTEEN

What Professor Barham came up with was not, after all, a post in London, but in Nyganda. He explained the possibility to Ben.

'Taussig needs help at the hospital in Ikerobe. He's not the easiest man to get on with, and not everyone wants to go permanently to Ikerobe. But it might be a chance for Ravelston.'

'It might indeed,' Ben said, speaking slowly and thinking fast. He knew at once, of course, what Barham was doing – opening the back door unobtrusively for Hugh. Barham had always had a reputation for kindness. This was it in action. He had spoken nothing but the truth when he had said earlier that there wasn't a chance of finding Hugh a post at the Central. But at the sister-hospital in Ikerobe? That would be another matter. Young men doing well at the Central were not anxious to go to Ikerobe for longer than the usual six months. Out of sight was out of mind, they often rightly considered. Their colleagues would steal a march while their backs were turned, grabbing the best posts. Moreover, it was uncomfortable there, though the experience, as Barham always pointed out, was magnificent. But there would be little competition for a permanent post there, rather a sudden unobtrusive melting away towards urgent commitments elsewhere.

The Medical Superintendent at Ikerobe was Andy Taussig, a dedicated and extremely difficult man. He needed, Barham stated, a permanent assistant. He was tired of rotating registrars, and his Nygandan assistant, a very sound physician trained at the Central, had gone into politics and was now officiating as Minister of Health. If Hugh went to Ikerobe for five years – any post might be available after that. He would be in the swim again. There was no doubt, the offer was well worth his consideration.

But what, then, about Judith? She was his real reason for thinking of leaving Brookhampton. Ben doubted whether she would contemplate going to Nyganda with Hugh. On the other hand, it would be tactless in the extreme to let Barham suspect that Hugh's reason for seeking a London post was a girl. That would never do.

Hugh would have to decide for himself. If this offer led to a break with Judith, so much the better, Ben reflected.

'I feel sure Ravelston could manage to get along all right with Taussig,' he said to

216

Barham, as if this were the only difficulty he saw in the scheme.

'Not at all Taussig's type, as I remember him,' Barham commented. 'However, Taussig's mellowing – and all Ravelstons are loaded with ability. We'll throw them together and see what happens, eh?'

Ben agreed.

'Tell Ravelston to come and see me. He'd better ring up and make an appointment one afternoon.'

So Hugh found himself, after an absence of five years, back in the room belonging to the Professor of Medicine at the Central. A room that had once belonged to his grandfather, and which he had last visited when Sir Alexander Ramsay had sent for him at the time when he had had to leave the Central, his career shattered. Ramsay had been kind to him then. Hugh had not been expecting this, and it had thrown him off balance, destroyed the iron self-control he had been exhibiting. He had never thanked Ramsay for what he had done. He had been too raw and embittered at the time. Now Ramsay was dead, and the opportunity gone for ever.

'Last time you were here, I expect you saw Alec Ramsay,' Barham said, almost as though he had read Hugh's thoughts.

'Yes. He was very good to me,' Hugh answered, this being uppermost in his mind.

Barham was surprised. He had been making enquiries about Hugh Ravelston, and the general consensus of opinion was that he was as proud and be-damned-to-you as old Sir Donald Ravelston himself.

'In what way?' he asked. Bill Barham liked to have everything elucidated, and he had few inhibitions about demanding the information he needed.

'He found me a job.'

'I thought that was Jock Calderwood?' Barham, Hugh could see, had made it his business to acquaint himself with the history of the whole affair in detail.

'You mean through Ben?'

'That's what I had assumed.'

'Ben asked him. But he wouldn't. Well, who would? Ramsay talked him into it. And a bad bargain he got.' Hugh looked back into the past, and saw himself as he had been when he began to work in the laboratory at Brookhampton, with his failure gnawing at him.

Barham watched him, and said nothing.

'And I never thanked him,' Hugh added. 'Such a little thing to do, but I was too wrapped up in myself to do it. I probably owe him my entire career, but I didn't spare a word. It may not be much of a career,' he commented hastily, recollecting that he was in the professorial medical unit at the Central now, where his attainments were

218

more compatible with failure than success, 'but at least it's medicine, and it easily might not have been.'

'Ramsay helped a lot of people,' Barham said. 'I rather doubt if many of them thanked him. He cared a lot about the hospital in Ikerobe, you know. He would have liked to get you for it. D'you want to go?'

'If I can,' Hugh said, his mind made up at that instant. Until then, he had been uncertain. But Barham's mention of Ramsay's feeling for the place solved his dilemma. It was true that the hospital at Ikerobe had been very near to Ramsay's heart. He had founded it, seen it through its early days, fostered it and left it, on his death, well established. He had said more than once that he would be satisfied to be remembered for that alone, and he had always been anxious for young men from the Central to put in a period there. 'It shows up a man's true quality,' he had said.

'There's work there crying out to be done. All you need is a pair of hands,' Barham said.

Hugh knew this to be true. Out of loyalty to Ramsay, he could not have turned the offer down, even if he could have afforded to do so. And he could not afford to. There was no doubt about that. A helping hand from Barham was a stroke of luck for someone in his position. The future would not be at all what he had planned, but he accepted his fate with what he hoped was a convincing display of gratitude. Then he went away to think out what he was going to tell Judith – so lost in thought, in fact, that he wandered down the familiar corridors towards the hall and the courtyard without remembering that this was his first visit to the hospital since the day he had left with his name a by-word.

Others were not too lost in thought to remember. The Ravelston nose was unmistakable, and familiar. Even those who were too newly qualified to have known Hugh personally, recognised a Ravelston when they saw one, and guessed the rest. In its day, the Ravelston affair had rocked the hospital. There were sidelong looks and sudden halts in conversation.

'Isn't that Hugh Ravelston? What's he doing here?'

'What, the one who was struck off?'

'Yep. Had an affair with a patient, or something. Must say, he looks the type birds fall for.'

'I always thought it was a car crash – manslaughter and drunk in charge.'

'Versatile fellow. Maybe it was both.' They stared after his retreating form with fascination, and condemnation tinged with admiration.

'Surely he's not getting back here? Even if

he is a Ravelston? Not after that lot?'

'Nepotism is still rampant in the teaching hospitals. I've always said so. Now you can see for yourself.'

'I can't believe it.'

'Wait and see.'

The news percolated through the various levels, and Barham, at a sherry party that evening, found himself under interrogation.

'By the way, Bill, hear you had young Ravelston up to see you? Hugh Ravelston, I mean.' Jimmy Marlowe, the heart surgeon accosted him.

'Splendidly efficient spy system the Central runs,' Barham said affably. 'No need to write little notes, here. Just think of something, and bingo – it's round the hospital.'

'I gather you did more than think of Hugh Ravelston,' Marlowe pointed out dryly.

'Hugh Ravelston?' Someone else had overheard them. 'I'm told he was seen in the medical school today.'

'Yes, Bill saw him.'

'Oh, did you, Bill? How's he wearing? Poor devil, he had a very raw deal, if you ask me.'

'But no one did ask you, Verney, as I remember it.'

'Not bloody likely. I was very newly appointed then. No one cared what I thought. Or what Ravelston thought, for that matter. You have disgraced the fair name of this, our illustrious hospital – out.'

'Old Sir Donald Ravelston could have saved him, but he was harder on him than any of them. That shocked me at the time. I thought Ravelston deserved all he got, except that.'

'Ramsay stood up for him.'

'Ramsay was a soft-hearted old idiot.'

'I dare say. What I'm trying to find out is whether Bill here is a soft-hearted young idiot.'

'Thank you, Jimmy. Those few words touch me deeply. Soft-hearted in this iron-hearted society? Good. And young? Of course, in the prime of life. Bless you, my dear fellow.' He patted Jimmy Marlowe on the back affectionately, looked at his watch, muttered 'got to be off,' and was gone.

'Bill gets more wily every day,' Marlowe complained. 'Can't get a straight answer to a straight question out of him any longer.'

The subject of their speculation was sitting in the train to Brookhampton, staring out of the window, pondering his next step.

He had not been to see Judith. He was afraid to do so. He faced this fact bleakly. It gave him the jitters.

Judith, he knew inescapably, would try to stop him going to Nyganda. He must not allow her to succeed. He would despise himself if he could be talked out of what he had decided to do, what he had told Barham he would be glad to do. What disturbed him most was the knowledge that Judith would neither sympathise with his decision nor be prepared to share his life in Ikerobe.

It was because he knew this that he had not been to see her. He had enough turmoil in his mind, without adding to it by an ultimatum from Judith. He would, quietly and alone, face the implications of his decision, and then carry them out.

He wished he had never started Ben on the plan. He would have liked to have turned the clock back, and be able to stay comfortably – if ignominiously – at Brookhampton for ever. He could tell Barham he had thought again, did not, after all want the job. And then what? The end of Hugh Ravelston. Barham had stretched a point in seeing him at all. In any case, Hugh asked himself disgustedly, what had he meant when he had talked about what he owed Ramsay? Had it been a meaningless form of words, or had it reflected a genuine state of mind? He knew at once, as he had known all along, that if he was to continue to live with himself he must accept the offer.

This brought him back to Judith, and desolation. He would have to go without her. They would never marry. This was the end of their road.

He could not face this, and his thoughts revolved in a circle again. Was he wrong to put the job first? Ought he to put Judith first, to refuse the job if it meant leaving her? His pride revolted. There was nothing to stop her from accompanying him, except her refusal to allow him to interrupt her career. If they had been married, fair enough, one of them would have had to compromise. But they were not married, not even lovers. She was a girl he saw once or twice a month. A girl, he suspected, who was bored by him. She would have gone to the ends of the earth with Colin.

Again he shied off, and began the circle of uncertainty. When he arrived at Brookhampton he remained undecided. He could not quite accept the possibility that he and Judith might separate. What about his promise to Colin? He shook himself irritably. Colin had not intended him never to move from Judith's side. On the contrary, he had assumed that Judith would accompany Hugh, rather than the opposite.

He experienced a double sense of failure. He had been unable to make Judith love him. He was a superficial young man, who had made a mess of his life through girls and fast driving, just as his grandfather had said, and who had not enough character to hold someone worth while, like Judith. Now he would be on his own again.

He set his shoulders. In that case, he had better make the best of it and get on with the job he had been offered. He went to his room and wrote two letters. One to Barham confirming his acceptance of the job in Nyganda if Taussig wanted him for it, and another to Judith, telling her what he proposed to do.

I am afraid that this involves you too in a decision. I have to take this job. It's a great opportunity for me, much better than anything I had a right to expect would come my way again. It's also the only means by which I can repay something of what I owe to Ramsay. What I should like is for us to be married so that we can go out there together. I know this is asking a lot. Asking, in fact, that you should give up your career, to help me with mine. You know what my feelings are. If you decide not to come to Nyganda, I shan't blame you in any way. But I think we must both face reality and make our decision now. Either marry me and come to Nyganda, or we must face the fact that marriage is not for us.

It could hardly be plainer, he thought, as he read it through. But the time had come. They could not go on as they were. And the necessity for a decision now might just push Judith over the edge. Otherwise she would procrastinate for ever.

He had a wave of depression. The end, he knew, had crept up on them long ago. If Judith would procrastinate for ever, and he knew it, then they had passed the point of no return. His love for Judith, which had begun in sorrow, had ended in unfulfilment and separation. How long had he known this? For ever? Always? Now he accepted it. They were finished. He knew an odd sense of peace. The conflict was ended. Life was before him, open and unencumbered.

A moment later he was horrified. Judith was not an encumbrance. He had to smile at the notion. But latterly she had been a burden. He had loved her for a long time. It had brought pain and responsibility, and a weight of guilt, since he felt he was failing all along the line. When she refused to go to Nyganda, as he knew she inevitably would, he would be free of his obligation. They could be friends, without forcing themselves into a relationship that strained them both.

In the morning, though, he was optimistic. Everything would be all right. He was cheerful at breakfast, and teased the new houseman who had replaced the un-lamented David Lyell, now in a geriatric hospital in East Anglia, writing a novel to rival the entire output of A. J. Cronin and Richard Gordon. The new arrival appeared to be interested only in rugger. 'Which comes as a relief, I must say,' Hugh remarked to Max at lunch time.

'I know it seems very Philistine,' Max agreed, 'but thank the lord for a straightforward rugger-playing houseman, instead of a cross between an agitator, a cub reporter and Dylan Thomas in person.'

'I don't think he either wrote poetry or drank,' Hugh said accurately.

'Not actually drank, no. But he was always in the Dog and Duck.'

'Talking to that reporter from the *Gazette*.'

'Well, roll on the day we'll see one of his so-called exposures in the *Daily Blaze*.' They both laughed with considerable amusement at the bizarre prospect. 'By the way,' Max added. 'Linda Masterson goes home today. Cured at last. Until next time, of course. They're going to South Africa, I gather. Another cross we don't have to bear. Life is looking up, in fact.'

'No more Mrs Masterson. That must be a considerable relief to you.'

'More of a relief to Sister than anyone.'

'What an objectionable woman she was,' Hugh said reflectively. 'And how she managed to set us all by the ears.'

'She was even supposed to have driven a wedge between you and me,' Max added. 'Did you know that?'

'I know I was damned unpopular with

young David when I was giving Linda her injections,' Hugh said. 'Lazy, incompetent young hound. Far from being grateful to me for getting him out of a spot, he was constantly implying that I was committing some sort of ethical offence in giving them.'

'Racist,' Max said, and began to laugh.

'Who, me?'

'Yep. You, according to the boy David. You should have struck a blow for integration at the Brookhampton General, and refused to have any dealings with a patient whose mother had been – er – "blacked" I think is the word current in industrial disputes, but it hardly seems appropriate for Mrs Masterson.' His white teeth flashed.

'Certainly it would hardly be appreciated by her.'

They both laughed, and Max remarked, 'David regarded you as a smooth and privileged member of the gilded rich, siding always with the boss class, a typical blue-eyed boy from the teaching hospitals.' He put his arm round Hugh's shoulders and shook him gently. 'So now you know,' he said, his dark eyes dancing.

'But – but surely somebody told him – he must have known–'

'No,' Max said softly. 'No, nobody told him. We all rather went out of our way not to, I think.'

Hugh flushed. He had not expected this.

He had never imagined the junior medical staff ranged four-square behind him, as one man loyally concealing his disreputable past from the loose-mouthed David Lyell. He owed them a great deal. And now he was leaving them. He was leaving as he'd grown fond of the place, as he'd found out what it meant to him.

Meanwhile Judith was reading his letter. 'This is it,' she said to herself. 'Now you've got to face it, my girl. This is where you choose. Your whole life will be entirely different. This time you have your eyes wide open.'

She could not imagine life without Hugh. She knew she had often treated him badly, but her intentions towards him had always been good. She did not expect to feel about him as she had about Colin. Colin had swept her off her feet. She knew Hugh would never do this, and it was the last thing she wanted. Once in a lifetime was enough. She expected a steady, rewarding companionship with Hugh. She liked the idea of having him in her life, of not being alone. When he was with her, though, she knew she was unfair to him. She found herself constantly resenting the fact that he was not Colin, could never be Colin. This made her irritable and touchy. During her marriage, she had imagined herself to be placid and good-humoured. She had enjoyed her relationship with Colin, her domesticity, her music. One coherent and satisfying whole. Everything fitted together nicely. She admired Colin, had always done so, and hoped one day to be worthy of him, to grow to maturity alongside him. One day she would mean as much to him as he already did to her. Instead he had died and left her to face life without him. She had somehow become a temperamental and demanding neurotic, who gave Hugh Ravelston hell, and who refused even to sleep with him. She brought him no comfort, either of body or spirit, and she knew it.

Snap out of it, she had told herself more than once. She was unable to. But now she dared not go to Nyganda with Hugh. If she abandoned her musical career she would go to pieces. Her career was her only solace, the only meaning that life still held.

She took her decision. They must separate. She felt a sensation that could be nothing but relief, a lightening of the spirit. It was followed almost instantaneously by insecurity. She could not let him go, she could not face life alone.

'Oh, grow up,' she told herself irritably. Then paused, amazed. What had she said? Grow up? This was the crux of it.

She had never grown up. She had married Colin, whom she adored, when she was only twenty, and he was forty. He had been a most confident and fatherly husband. She had remained his child-wife. She had complained about this from time to time, had reiterated that she wanted to be treated as an adult. But when Colin died she had fled from the prospect. She had fled to the U.S.A. and her music, had put her emotions into cold storage. She had recognised this herself when she returned to London, she had seen that during her three-year absence she had been marking time. She had found it unsettling and depressing to be back in London, to face the fact that Colin was indeed dead, dead and gone, that he was not to be found in their old haunts, that he was nowhere, he had gone away from her and she had to do her growing-up alone. She had refused to go down to Brookhampton, because as long as she stayed away, there was still one place where Colin lived on. She could not bear to go there and find him absent, finally dead at last, in his grave.

The grave's a fine and private place,
But none, I think, do there embrace.

Now she understood that she had never faced his death, had embarked instead on another period of marking time. She had made use of Hugh, so accessible, such a convenient shelter behind which to hide from life. She had never been in love with

231

him, but she had told herself that this was only to be expected. She was fond of him, and she was able – because he allowed her to do so – to use him as an understudy for Colin. She made no new relationship with him, she remained encased in an invisible glass shell, speaking and moving, pretending, always pretending. She had been afraid to mourn Colin, afraid to admit that life went on without him, and that she had to remake hers alone before she was ready to join it to another. The only occasions on which the truth impinged at all were those moments when Hugh tried to make love to her. These occasions had always been an agony. Now she saw why. Only in them had she experienced her loss.

She had made use of Hugh. It had been done in ignorance, but it had been done. He had lived through it, had experienced this false attempt at loving through the years. Colin would have been angry with her. He was the most genuine of men, he would have hated to see her self-deception. Most of all, her deception of Hugh.

Now she must end it. She must send Hugh to Nyganda alone, and stay here in London herself. She must learn at last to stand on her own feet. Until she achieved this, any relationship she tried to make would be false. This was what had been wrong between her and Hugh.

She sat down, while she still had the courage, to write to him and explain this.

He thought he had prepared himself for the inevitable. He had expected to go to Nyganda alone, he knew that he and Judith did not share enough to take them through a lifetime together. He thought the ending of the relationship which she rightly described as false could only bring relief to both of them.

But it brought pain and loss and despair. He had failed again. He was thirty, and he had nothing. No one who loved him, no one who valued him, no professional achievements to his credit, simply emptiness and failure.

He set his lips. There was always a remedy for these troughs of depression. He went to the wards and immersed himself in work.

Here at least he was needed. There was, for instance, Grayson, the man fighting for breath in Cartwright. When the intensive care unit was completed, was equipped and fully functioning, a patient like this would be looked after there. His heart would be monitored and the latest resuscitation equipment would be ready. As it was, his care depended on a busy Sister and staff nurse, already overworked, on a rushed and exhausted houseman, and on Hugh himself. Now the Sister was on holiday, and the experienced staff nurse who knew the ward and the patients had at last been persuaded to go off sick with the influenza she had been fighting for four days. The Nigerian girl who had replaced her was doing her best, but she was nervous and worried, and it was as much as she could do to cope with the daily routine. She was assisted only by two first-year students and two Spanish orderlies who still spoke very little English. Hugh longed for the resources of the Central, both in machinery and in experienced, highly trained staff.

Longing, though, was useless. He had to depend on himself. The houseman could give him little help, since he was busy in Jenner, looking after a girl with a spontaneous pneumothorax.

There was no particular reason, in any case, to expect Grayson's condition to change for the worse. But Hugh had a nasty feeling it would, and he kept popping in to look at him. Grayson was a little wiry man of nearly sixty. He had lived in Brookhampton all his life, and was a foreman at Snelgrove & Watson's. He had been admitted with bronchitis, which crippled him each winter, though somehow until now he had managed to struggle to work daily. He had a rasping cough and smoked like a chimney, despite all advice to abandon the habit before his lungs gave up the struggle and life abandoned him.

Hugh went to the ward now. He was only just in time. As he reached the swing doors, one of the Spanish orderlies came flying out and nearly cannoned into him.

'Ogh, Doctor,' he ejaculated with obvious relief. He hated telephoning – with some reason, since no one ever understood what he was trying to say. 'Nurse want. She say–' he took a breath and enunciated clearly, this was something he had practised '–she say car-diac emer-gence-y.'

Hugh waited to hear no more. He pushed through the swing doors and pounded up the ward. It would, he knew, be Grayson.

It was. They had got him on to the floor beside his bed and the Nigerian staff nurse was bent over him.

'Airway clear?' Hugh demanded.

'Yes, sir.'

'Legs up,' Hugh said briskly, beginning to raise Grayson's legs as he spoke. Actions were better than words when dealing with the Spanish orderlies. The man took over, and Hugh knelt down on the floor beside Grayson and felt vainly for the carotid pulse. His pupils were enlarged and there was no sign of life. Grayson's heart had stopped. He thumped him savagely in the middle of the sternum.

It worked. Bob Grayson's heart began to beat again. Regularly, too. They were probably not going to need the defibrillator or

235

the pacemaker this time, though he sent for both. But the pupils were small now and the pulse steady. Grayson looked at him. He seemed not to know that he had lost consciousness, though he was puzzled, as well he might be, to find himself on the floor. 'You'll be all right,' Hugh said encouragingly. He hoped it was true.

'Course I will,' Grayson said stoutly. 'Always have bin, haven't I? What am I doing down here, though? Must've dropped off, and fallen out of bed, I suppose. Never done that before.' He looked at his wrist, which Hugh was holding. 'Worried about me pulse, are you, doc? Needn't be. I'll live to draw me pension.' He grinned.

'I haven't a doubt of it, you old devil,' Hugh agreed cheerfully. In fact he had many. But the pulse was strong, and the danger seemed to be over. Until next time.

Grayson was feeling about him. 'Pass me down me fags, Nurse, there's a good girl,' he suggested.

Hugh put his foot down. 'No,' he said firmly. 'You can't have one. You've got to be sensible about this smoking. Otherwise you'll kill yourself.'

Grayson sniffed sceptically.

'I mean it. In any case you're off cigarettes absolutely for the next twenty-four hours, and that's flat.'

Grayson was furious. He began to swear

vigorously. It was hard to believe that a quarter of an hour earlier he had been dead for a full three minutes, that at one time there would have been small chance of his recovery.

CHAPTER FOURTEEN

'Did you know mother's got a boy-friend?' Clare asked. Wearing faded jeans, an old gingham shirt with the sleeves rolled up, her feet bare, she was standing by the mast on the foredeck, looking down on Hugh in the cockpit. She spoke idly, sleepy from sun and wind.

Hugh grinned. 'Rumours had reached me. Daniel Snelgrove, I believe.'

'He takes her to Chichester, to the theatre, and out to dinner occasionally too, and she comes back all pink and girlish.'

'Perhaps she'll remarry,' Hugh suggested, giving Clare an acute look intended to find out if the prospect daunted her. He saw more than he had bargained for. Clare seemed unmoved by his suggestion, merely agreed, 'Perhaps; rather fun if she did,' and leant lazily against the mast, a ripple of movement passing from head to toe as her muscles stretched and relaxed. Hugh stiffened as he watched her. 'Stop looking at her, you fool,' an inner voice warned him automatically, the voice that seemed to have been warning him for years. But he continued to stare, and his body reiterated its demands.

'...jealous,' Clare was saying.

'What?' he asked, startled.

'You weren't listening,' she said calmly. 'Never mind. What were you thinking about?' She regarded him tranquilly. She had grown used to loving him. She knew it was hopeless, but she could feel herself expanding in his company, growing, maturing, opening herself to all that life offered. His presence was a steadily burning flame. Not for her, she knew, but she might warm her hands at it while she had the opportunity. In return she tried to offer him peace and easiness of spirit. She was under the impression that she made no demands whatever.

'No, tell me,' he persisted. He thought she had made some comment on their relationship, and he half-longed, half-feared, to be precipitated into a new situation with her. But she had not been talking about herself, or about him, he was disappointed to find. Disappointed? Relieved, surely? He had had enough of women and their ways. He was going to do without them and rebuild his career.

'I was saying that Mary Farquharson is jealous,' she said.

'Of Daniel?' he asked, foolishly cocking an eye at her, and regretting it immediately. Her face was alive with mischief, her eyes met his with no barrier, and her soft lips were tender with a gentle amusement.

'Of Daniel,' she agreed. 'Mother doesn't quite know how to cope, I don't think,' she added, her lips quirking. She jumped down into the cockpit beside him, steadying herself with a hand on his shoulder, and suddenly it happened. He was grasping her as though he would never let her go, and his mouth found hers with no tenderness, only a bruising insistence. Her head bent back, she looked astonished.

He was astonished himself. He wrenched himself free.

'That means nothing,' he said harshly. 'A momentary triumph of body over mind.'

She had never known such pain.

'Get into the dinghy,' he said, in the same hard voice. 'I'm sorry about that. Stupid of me. I didn't mean to do anything of the sort. I apologise.'

'It doesn't matter,' she said in a dead voice.

'You shouldn't be so bloody attractive,' he said. 'You make me forget myself.' He looked at her with hatred.

She clambered into the dinghy, speechless. What had happened? Why did he all at once speak to her in that killing voice? Clare was too inexperienced to be able to translate Hugh's behaviour into any pattern of meaning. They had been comfortably chatting together, as far as she was concerned. Then he had suddenly seized her and kissed her in the most magnificently exciting way. Then, as suddenly as he had begun, he had stopped. He asserted that what he had done meant nothing, which, though disappointing, was not altogether unexpected. A kiss from Hugh was wonderful, but she knew it could lead nowhere. Did he imagine, though, that she would make difficulties, take advantage of it to try to pretend he owed her more, was that why he seemed now to hate her? Surely he knew her better than that? She had never made demands on him. She never would. Somehow, though, she had failed him utterly. She could not tell how, or what she had done that was so inescapably wrong. She sat hunched in the dinghy, trying to hide her hurt bewilderment.

Not succeeding, though. Hugh read her as clearly at this moment as he understood himself. His fury was followed by a wave of compassion. She looked so vulnerable, she was so young still. Her bones that a few seconds earlier he had longed to crush in passion he now wanted only to protect and cherish for ever. Her narrow drooping shoulders, and her dark head bending forward on her thin child's neck – they were his to cherish and love.

He grounded the dinghy, jumped out to hold it steady for her. Together, in silence, they pulled it up the shore above the high water line. Then he took her by her thin shoulders and said, 'I'm sorry. Try not to mind me. I'm just bloody-minded.' He kissed her again, briefly and affectionately this time, on her cheek that smelled of sun and wind and salt. 'I love you,' he heard himself add.

She took not the slightest notice, so he said it again, rather more firmly. She gave him a puzzled, scared look. He repeated it. 'I love you.' He kissed her neck, and it was soft and lovable and warm. He knew he was not going to resist any longer, and he turned her head and kissed her again, on the mouth, not affectionately at all, but long and with deep satisfaction.

'There,' he said, pleased. Then realisation hit him. 'Oh, my God,' he added. 'What have I done?'

This time she followed him. 'It doesn't matter,' she said. She looked at him sideways. 'It was very nice, and I'm glad you did it. But I know it doesn't mean anything. Ben would say very educational for me.' She shot him another sideways gleam and went ahead of him up the path. 'No need to worry,' she said airily.

She had saved him. She had made it easy and without awkwardness, and he must be grateful to her.

Only he wasn't. He didn't want it to be easy, and he didn't want to be saved. Educational, indeed? What the hell had Ben been saying to the girl? He was serious about her. He had never been more serious about anyone. Ben could mind his own business. She was lovely and fragile and courageous, and he wanted to drown in her beauty and her love for ever. It was useless for her to plod methodically along the path ahead as if what had happened had no meaning, simply because Ben had been filling her with a load of nonsense. He pulled her back on to him so that her head lay against his shoulder, and spoke into her ear. 'I said I loved you,' he reminded her.

She twisted round to look at him. 'I know you did. But you didn't mean it.'

'What the hell are you talking about?' he shouted.

She looked at him, her eyes huge and startled.

'Did you?' she asked.

'Yes, I damn well did.' He glared at her.

She dropped her eyes. 'What about Judith?' she asked in a small voice. She turned her head away and looked over the marshes to the great clouds rosy with the first of the sunset. She could hardly bear to hear his answer, the answer she knew was coming.

'That's all over,' he said flatly.

Her head shot round. 'What?'

'I said it's all over,' he repeated. He knew it was nothing but the truth, and he felt an immense surge of relief and happiness. It was all in the past. He was free. Free to love Clare. The way ahead was for the two of them together. 'It's you I love,' he said, spelling it out for her, as she looked at him warily. 'My frightened love,' he said, and touched her cheek.

'I am frightened. I don't believe you. You – you've *always* been in love with Judith.' She spoke accusingly.

'Not for quite a while.'

'But you were once.'

'Yes. I loved her very much.'

'More than you do me now.' It was a statement, not a question.

'No. As much as I love you.'

She stared disbelievingly at him.

He grinned. 'Once upon a time, when I was young and handsome, and a registrar at the Central, birds used to fall into my arms with loud chirps of gladness if I so much as batted an eyelid at them. They didn't stand about arguing and contradicting. I suppose I'm too old and decrepit and provincial and unsuccessful these days to have the same effect.'

'You're not unsuccessful,' she said, roused. 'Don't be so silly. Anyway, you know I love you. I always have.' She smiled at him brilliantly.

'Come on,' he said. 'Back on *Sea Goose*. We can't spend this evening chatting up your mother and Mary Farquharson. I expect it means baked beans instead of – of?'

'Lobster. Daniel's coming to dinner. But we can do better than baked beans on board, you know. I could make–'

'Come on then. I want to talk to you about a lot of things. One of them is, how would you like to live in Nyganda?'

'Nyganda? Why?' It was only later that night, when she lay alone in her room at the cottage reliving all that had happened, that she realised that at that point Hugh Ravelston had proposed to her, and she had taken it for granted.

'Mother,' she said the next morning at breakfast, before Mary Farquharson had appeared. 'I am going to marry Hugh Ravelston. I hope you don't mind.'

'Mind?' Hermione dropped the marmalade spoon into her coffee. 'Are you sure?' she asked quickly, fishing it out. Could the silly child have imagined it? There had been no sign of what Mary would have called 'anything in the wind', and Clare had always been so dreadfully offhand with the young man. Hermione had frequently deplored it. 'I always thought you–' she began.

'You don't mind, then?' Clare said comfortably. 'We shall be married before Hugh goes to Nyganda.' She poured herself coffee and munched cornflakes.

She was distinctly smug, Hermione realised. So it was true. 'Darling,' she breathed. 'Of *course* I don't mind. I am absolutely delighted. Such a *charming* young man, however did you – I mean I am so pleased. We must have a little engagement party, don't you think, darling? One of my little dinner parties would be nice...' she mused. 'Daniel, perhaps, and of course Jock and Margaret, and is there anyone you would like? *Not* Rachel, darling, I don't think she'd quite fit in. We could have a brace of pheasant, d'you think, and ... did you say Nyganda?' she demanded alertly. 'Nyganda?'

'Hugh may have a job there.' Clare put her cornflake bowl aside and reached for toast and marmalade.

'Oh,' Hermione said doubtfully.

'There's a hospital at Ikerobe attached to the Central London Hospital, where Hugh trained, and they are probably going to offer him a post there.'

'Oh, Africa. I must see what Daniel thinks.'

Clare looked amused.

'Anyway, we can certainly have a little celebration dinner. Now, if we...'

'We must have a little celebration dinner,' Clare reported to Hugh. 'And she is asking Daniel whether it's all right to go to Nyganda. She rather thinks a brace of pheasants will meet the case.' She grinned, then put her arms round him. 'Oh God, I do love you,' she said. 'Are you sure you still love me? It hasn't worn off since last night? You didn't make a mistake, or something?'

He kissed her.

She heaved an enormous sigh. 'You are absolute heaven,' she said. 'You know that? You feel wonderful, and you look wonderful, and I am mad about you.'

Hugh's eyes danced. 'That's my girl,' he said. 'Though I'm afraid all this will wear off,' he added cautiously.

'Why should it? I've felt like this for years.'

'What a clown I've been,' he said, meaning it. 'All these years that I could have had you, and held on to you.' He held her as tightly as she held him, and lost himself in her warm comfort.

They were in his sitting-room at the hospital, familiar and homely to him, if dreary, and strange and exciting to her. She had gone there to see him on Sunday morning, as he could not get away until lunch time.

'At last,' he remarked, 'we can have a real celebration in that ghastly Rose and Crown. Come on, we'll order champagne and generally stir the place up.'

'I'm not exactly dressed for the Rose and Crown,' she said dubiously.

'Good God, lunch at the Rose and Crown isn't dinner at the Savoy.'

'They may not let me in, showing all this leg.' The day was hot and sunny, and Clare was wearing an extremely scanty slip of a cotton dress, patterned in that season's hot orange and pink, sizzling together, that ended halfway up her thighs. With her limbs tanned by the sea wind, her dark tousled head and her huge brown eyes, she was riveting. Heads turned when they entered the dining-room, but no one attempted to throw them out.

After lunch they drove out along the lanes to the Calderwoods. The land lay bare under the steady afternoon sun, the shadows short on the stubble, and the larks high in a clear sky. The estuary stretched ahead, and a salt wind came flicking towards them, as they walked round the side of the old house to the lawn and the rose garden, where Jock and Margaret were drinking coffee.

'Hullo, you two,' Jock said. 'Just in time for some coffee. I'll get more cups.'

'No, I will,' Clare said, and sped indoors. Hugh watched her. Jock and Margaret watched Hugh, and then looked at one another. When they compared notes afterwards, they agreed that they had known at once. Neither of them had seen Hugh ever before with naked love blazoned across his face, nothing hidden, no ironic overtones.

Clare came back carrying two coffee cups, her expression serene and glowing.

'Do you two,' Jock asked, 'by any chance have any news for us?'

Two heads swivelled towards him in startled enquiry.

'It's written all over you,' he explained.

'That's the champagne,' Hugh replied. He appeared to think he had made everything clear.

'I see. Champagne?'

'Celebration lunch. At the Rose and Crown.'

'Might one tentatively enquire what you were celebrating? Or would that be out of order?'

'I thought you'd already decided?' Clare said pertly.

'I like my information to be official.'

'We're getting married,' she said.

'Quite soon,' Hugh added.

'Probably this afternoon, I should think,' Clare said, and lay back in her deck-chair shaking with mirth. Then she sat up abruptly. 'Hiccups,' she announced indignantly.

'Hold your breath.'

'What does Hermione say?' Margaret asked.

Clare laughed again and then hiccupped wildly.

'I don't know that you ought to have let her have all that champagne,' Jock remarked mildly.

'Hold your breath,' Hugh said to Clare. 'Apparently,' he went on, to Margaret, 'Hermione says she'll give a little dinner party.'

'So she's taken it all right,' Margaret said, relieved.

'And she's consulting Daniel about whether it's a good idea to go to Nyganda,' Hugh added with a grin.

'Ben will be pleased,' Margaret said to Jock, after Hugh and Clare had gone off for a sail. 'He'll like to have Hugh in the family.'

'So am I pleased,' Jock said firmly. 'I shall like to have Hugh in the family too. I'm very fond of the boy, though at one time I never thought I should be.' He looked back along the years. 'What I'm not so keen on is having Archie Ravelston in the family. All those rather grand Ravelstons, in fact. Thank the Lord the old man is no longer with us. I couldn't have had him here looking down his nose. Rodney's all right, though he's unmistakably marked out for eminence too, I'm afraid.' He chuckled.

'As Hugh was once,' Margaret pointed out.

'He's a much more worthwhile individual since he crashed, you'll admit. It did him a great deal of good.'

'Yes, you're right. All the same – oh well, it can't be helped.'

'Looks as if he's working his way back into the Central, you know. In five or ten years' time he may be back in the main stream of medicine.'

'I hope so. He deserves it.'

'Unfortunately, deserts have very little to do with it.'

'No need to be cynical. The next problem is, how's Hermione going to take it, losing her one ewe lamb?'

'That, my dear, we are inevitably going to find out,' Jock said.

CHAPTER FIFTEEN

Hermione did her best to relive her own marriage through Clare. Clare did her best to frustrate her. Margaret and John adjudicated. Sometimes Hermione's antics were amusing, sometimes infuriating, occasionally heartrending.

There was enormous and protracted argument about clothes. Hermione would have been shocked if she had been told that fashion and interior decoration were the real content of her inner life, the chief matters of importance to her. But this was the case. She prided herself on her own impeccable taste, and judged others by whether she approved their choice of dress or furnishings. As Hugh remarked, a woman could lack every good quality and be selfish and disagreeable, but if she had taste Hermione would admire her, and would be prepared to rate her more highly than Margaret Calderwood or Jean Ravelston, whom she dubbed 'ordinary'. 'Just like my own mother,' he went on. 'She despises Jean but she's prepared to wallow in admiration for anyone who happens to have the knack of draping a piece of silk or who can advise her unerringly on what colour will look best on the west wall in the dining-room. I'm afraid they're both quite mad.'

Clare agreed. 'We needn't take much notice of them,' she pointed out.

'No,' he said. 'Because we have each other.' He held her to him and touched his cheek gently to her cropped head, ruffling her dark hair. 'Extraordinary how everything falls into proportion as a result.'

'Just as well it does,' Clare said. 'Or we'd go mad too.' She was remembering her latest conversation with Hermione.

'Your trousseau, darling, now we must really begin to put our heads together. You must have some truly pretty things.'

'Oh, honestly, Mother–'

'Some dainty nightdresses and négligées. Ruffled perhaps? So pretty. And you could let your hair grow.'

Clare said a rude word.

'Clare! I don't know where you picked up that word, but I absolutely forbid you to repeat it. How Hugh will *imagine* I brought you up–'

'He won't think I got it from you, if that's what's worrying you,' Clare said with a chuckle.

But Hermione was not mollified. 'I'm afraid it's that awful Rachel Bloomfield. I suppose we'll have to invite her to the wedding, though what Hugh's family will think

I don't know. Very distinguished, darling, the Ravelstons, you know. Daniel has met them, and he was telling me about them.'

'I wish to goodness she'd decide to marry Daniel, and turn her energies into organising her own wedding, instead of mine,' Clare complained. 'If only she'd be sensible about my clothes she'd be so useful. She could make me a lot of dresses. But I daren't let her. "I've just made the skirt a *weeny* bit longer, darling, and put a tiny little gore here, and here, because it was so dreadfully straight and not really very becoming, don't you think? I felt it would suit you so much *better.*" I've had enough of that, and never again. What shall I wear for the party?'

The Calderwoods were giving a party at Marsh Farm to celebrate the engagement.

'Buy something to confound everyone. Lash out.'

'All right. But where shall I lash? What do you want me to look like?'

'Sexy.'

'Oh. Not pure and ethereal?' She opened her large eyes at him and glowed.

'No. It doesn't matter about that. I shall be around to see that no one gets any wrong ideas.'

'Do you want me to wear a mini-skirt, then?'

'You always do,' he said in surprise.

'Mother said not now I'm getting married.

254

I'd be letting you down, she says, and I must stop wearing teenage clothes.'

'If you lengthen your skirts I'll beat you. You look magnificently long-legged and sultry, and that's how I want you to go on looking.'

'Sultry? Me?'

'Sultry. You. Scorching.' He reached for her, and clamped his mouth on to hers.

She thought about this conversation on and off during the entire week that followed, and was constantly pausing to stare at herself in mirrors, practically taking a tape measure to her legs and a thermometer to her body. This, too, was leading an intense life of its own. Sensations she had never known before swept through her, burst out all over her, Rachel told her. 'You're vibrating with excitement and sex,' she asserted. 'Not that I'm at all surprised. He is the most fab hunk of man.'

'Come with me and buy a frock for the party. Hugh says it must be sexy. I want it to be sophisticated – all these people from the hospital, and probably some of Hugh's family. I don't want to look juvenile.'

'You won't,' Rachel said with her fat chuckle. 'You haven't looked the slightest bit juvenile since you had your hair cut and stopped wearing those awful clothes your mother bought. And now you–'

'I don't want to look virginal, even if I am,'

Clare remarked with a burst of confidence.

'You don't, particularly. I thought perhaps you weren't any more.'

'By the skin of my teeth,' Clare said with a cheerful grin. 'Not that I see the point, myself. But Hugh seems to think it's important. That's what he says, but of course he keeps forgetting. So far he's remembered before it's too late. Though I find his remembering rather disconcerting. And it's all because I *am* inexperienced. Apparently. I honestly don't understand it at all. Aren't men weird?'

Rachel agreed.

'After all, what difference does it make? When we're going to be married anyway in six weeks.'

'Is it as soon as that?'

'I've just given them a month's notice at the office. They've all announced that they expect to be invited to the wedding, although I warned them it would be down in Brookhampton, so it's going to be a bit of a crush. However, marvellous Uncle Jock will cope, as always.'

Marvellous Uncle Jock was a little startled, though, to hear from Hugh that the engagement party, scheduled for the next week-end, was to be followed by what threatened to be a mammoth wedding in a month's time.

'I thought you'd wait until the New Year,'

he commented. He was talking to Hugh in the deserted laboratory at the end of the day. 'Tom and Barbara will be here then. I know Margaret's told Tom he will have to give Clare away. She thought it would make a very nice introduction for the two families, this wedding.'

'Then she can't have mentioned it to darling Hermione,' Hugh said with a sarcastic smile.

'Hermione playing up again?' Jock asked, cocking an alert eyebrow.

'You can't really blame her. She's terrified, you know, of meeting Tom. Then I think she's equally terrified of losing her friendship with you and Margaret, of being supplanted, so to speak, by Tom and Barbara. Clare says your friendship means much more to her than she lets you see. Hence Daniel, you know. He's being encouraged, I'm afraid, as an insurance policy – and, of course, to be brandished at Tom.'

'Poor Daniel, he deserves better than that.'

'He seems to me quite capable of taking care of himself.'

'Exactly what I said to Margaret. But I'm beginning to wonder.'

'Anyway, darling Hermione is damned if her ex is going to steal any of her thunder at her daughter's wedding. So she's all in favour of us getting married before Christmas. I'm all in favour of it too. And for more than the obvious reason. I want the pressure taken off Clare.'

'I see what you mean. It's hard on Tom, though.'

'He's done nothing for Clare. Why should she put herself out for him?'

'He is her father.'

'If he were here, I can tell you one thing for sure, Clare would still want you to give her away.'

Jock was suffused with pleasure, which he tried to conceal behind a dutiful defence of Tom Dunn. Hugh interrupted him. 'Darling Hermione and Clare are as one on this,' he said. 'You're wasting your breath. Tom must put up with it. After all, he took his decision to leave them years ago. Now he has to take the consequences.'

'Poor fellow, I don't think–'

'I'm not for one moment saying his decision wasn't justified,' Hugh said irritably. 'I'm sure it was the only possible action in the circumstances. Darling Hermione must have been sheer hell as a wife – how Daniel can be so blind escapes me. But he has a price to pay, and this is it. Presumably he's quite able to stand it, even if he doesn't care for it. He's not a frail plant, is he?'

'About as frail as a bulldozer. But it will still hurt him.'

'He'll have to wear it.'

Jock sighed. 'No need to rub it in, though.'

'No wish to rub it in, but I'm damned if I'm going to see Clare sacrificed for him. She was sacrificed for darling Hermione, blast her, for the first eighteen years of her life. Now this is her wedding, I intend to see it's the only wedding in her life, and she's set her heart on being taken comfortably up the aisle by you. You mean a lot to her, and so does getting married to me, thank God. She wants us both there, one on each side of her, and I'm going to see she gets us. I'm not having it all mucked up in order to spare Tom Dunn a momentary twinge or two.'

'Fair enough,' Jock agreed. What else could he say? He'd have to explain to Margaret, of course, but he was deeply moved – as much by Hugh's warmth as by Clare's devotion. In the last few years Hugh had become part of his family, and he felt an affection for him that was all the stronger because it had at first been unwelcome and half-strangled at birth.

'After all, we all have twinges,' Hugh said casually.

This was it, Jock thought. He knew Hugh's off-hand manner of throwing out his secrets. They had to be grabbed with both hands and dragged out of him – which was what he wanted, though he remained unable to help at all. 'Tell me about yours,' Jock said firmly. He expected to hear about Hugh's break with Judith.

He was wrong. Hugh was thinking of his career. 'Oh, I have them,' he said. 'Just as Rodney told me I would.'

Jock remembered clearly how Rodney had warned them all that Hugh would not long be satisfied with a mediocre post in the provinces. Biochemistry and a brilliant future in research was what Rodney had seen for him.

'Frustration and being passed over is as hard to take as Rodney said it would be,' Hugh explained. 'But it's the price I knew I'd have to pay. It doesn't make me waver. That's what Rodney didn't understand. To have gone into the research laboratories and done biochemistry would have been to pay a much bigger price altogether, and an intolerable one. Intolerable for me, that is. I'm not a natural investigator, like you and Rodney, and of course Uncle Archie. I'm more like the old man. Intuitive. Interfering. I need people, not bacteria or viruses, or D.N.A. or amino-acids.' He paused, then added quietly, 'I chose with my eyes open. The practice of medicine does in actual fact mean more to me than success. I've proved it the hard way, and it's the truth. I'm only half-alive in the laboratory – where does worldly achievement come alongside that? But I don't waver when I pay the price of my idiocy as the playboy of the Central. I accepted it years ago.'

Jock knew this was a realistic appraisal. 'It's a waste,' he said. 'But you're right. And it's done you no harm, you know. You might have remained the playboy of the Central for ever.'

'Too true. The youngest Ravelston, cocky, spoilt and superficial.'

'Teaching hospitals are places to get away from, once you've qualified. It's not the accepted view, I know. But I've never regretted leaving. Do the job for its own sake. That's maturity. Not for the applause and the admiration of the tight little phoney world where you were once a student and are now, you hope, part of the hierarchy.'

'I accept that. But only just.'

'Oh, it's a glittering world in its own way, and it's easy to feel a success there, simply because it is so tiny and circumscribed. Everyone sees your triumph – or your disaster, of course. But if you do well – clap, clap, clap – it's like being head boy or games captain all over again. Except that the players are adults. Or supposed to be. Most – not all, but most – of the best people in medicine can be found working away un-obtrusively far from the teaching hospitals and the tiny little rat race they engender. I'm not altogether happy about Ben, you know. He's always been very level-headed, but his own success is going to mark him inescapably.'

'I don't think you need worry. He'll be all right. His values are sound as a bell.'

Jock was delighted. 'I'm extraordinarily glad to hear you say that,' he said. He turned the talk to the arrangements for the party, which were becoming complicated. There was a sort of V.I.P.s' dinner party being given by Hermione, and London guests to be put up overnight at the Calderwoods. Jean and Archie, Ben, of course, and Rachel Bloomfield, though this news had not been broken to Hermione.

Ben drove Rachel and Clare down on Saturday afternoon. Clare had bought herself a brief tunic in a silver-like chain mail. The dress, sleeveless, came to mid-thigh, and she wore silver tights and shoes. Mary Farquharson was impressed, and told her she looked like a lissom young page from a medieval court.

'She looks entirely feminine to me, thank God,' Hugh retorted unsympathetically. Clare snorted companionably, and they both moved on.

Jean Ravelston had arrived without Archie, who had refused to disturb himself for any party at the back of beyond. She was apologising profusely and somewhat tactlessly to the Calderwoods '...so I simply couldn't persuade him to leave just now, you see. But he'll come to the wedding, of course, if I have to drag him here in chains.'

'Let's hope it won't come to that,' Jock said gravely, the twinkle in his eye unnoticed by Jean, who was worried by her first sight of Clare. Had this glittering silver girl any heart?

'Will she be kind to him?' she asked Margaret, her battered face crumpled, as so often, with anxiety for her unmanageable family.

'Will he be kind to her, is what we're all asking,' Margaret responded tartly. 'He loves her now, but will it last? If it doesn't, she'll be totally lost.'

'Oh,' Jean said. She looked at Clare, and began to warm to her.

'She's a good girl,' Daniel Snelgrove said. 'Kind to her mother, too. Hermione is not always the easiest creature.'

Jock and Margaret caught one another's eyes, and looked hastily away. The understatement of the century, they felt.

'She'll make him a good wife,' Daniel continued firmly. 'Pity we're going to lose them both, though,' he added to Jock. 'You did warn me, of course, that we wouldn't be able to keep him long. But it's a pity. He was shaping very nicely, I thought. We'll have to think again, now, about that appointment. That reminds me...' they drifted off, engrossed in talk about the next management committee.

Ben winked at Hugh. 'Just hatchin' a few plots,' he murmured, jerking his head towards the corner where Daniel and Jock now had their heads together. It was the first opportunity he had had to talk to Hugh. Clare had temporarily disappeared, and Hugh took time off from doing the rounds with her for a quiet chat. 'Glad you managed to come down,' he said. 'How do you think Clare's looking?'

'Dishy. She's in great form too, tremendous, tearing spirits. Have I found time to let you know how pleased I am about this?'

'No. I'm listening.'

'On second thoughts, you can take it as read. You didn't find time to invite me this evening, so why should I put myself out?'

'*Invite* you. I took it for granted–'

'Clare invited me,' Ben said with a deliberately vapid grin, 'otherwise I don't suppose I'd be here.'

'Rubbish. Your parents are giving the party, of course you don't need an invitation. Anyway, you're the best man, you have to officiate at the engagement party. Don't be daft. Goes without saying.'

'I'm the best man? Is that something else that goes without saying? I don't recollect being asked.'

'Stop being so stuffy. I take it for granted and well you know it. None of your teaching hospital pomposity here,' he added, remembering his recent conversation with Jock. His eyes gleamed with amusement, and Ben laughed hugely. He was delighted out of all proportion. 'He's got it out of his system at last,' he said to his father later. 'He's over it. He's started pulling my leg about teaching hospital pomposity.'

Clare returned. 'Mother's leaving – with Daniel, needless to say – to see to things at home,' she announced. 'She says she expects us all in an hour flat. She's in a ghastly tizz about her old dinner party,' she added, her gaze wandering reflectively round the Calderwoods' drawing-room, where about a hundred people, mainly from the hospital, conversed in crescendo. There were nearly another hundred shrieking in the hall and dining-room, but Margaret Calderwood was unruffled. Clare longed for Hermione to take her own dinner party for twelve as calmly.

'She'll be one short,' Hugh reminded her. 'Archie isn't here – did you tell her?'

'No, I forgot.'

'Never mind, we'll take someone along,' Hugh said comfortably. In the end, he asked Max, which was to be a considerable shock to Hermione, who had never before entertained an African at her dinner table.

Max had arrived late, with Peter Barlow, the new rugger-playing houseman who had superseded David Lyell. 'Sorry to be so unpunctual,' he apologised. 'But we had an emergency.'

'Anything interesting?' Hugh asked at once.

'Sandra Clifford, I'm afraid. In heart failure, as you foretold. I was telling Peter on the way out here, she was the case you and I met over. Must be five years ago now.'

'Oh dear.' Hugh frowned. 'It had to come, but I'm sorry to hear it.'

'Her father came in with her,' Peter volunteered.

'Mrs Clifford's here, helping in the kitchen,' Hugh explained.

Peter raised his eyebrows. 'That sort of mother, is she?'

Hugh shrugged. 'She'd think this party more important than Sandra, any day. Mind you, there are two hundred people here; it would have been awkward for Margaret if Mrs Clifford had let her down. I suppose if Ted was at home anyway?' He sighed. 'I don't know – what can you do?'

'Nothing,' Max said flatly.

'In all fairness,' Hugh added, softening a little, 'we must admit that it's pretty well impossible to look after these children with cystic fibrosis so that they can live a normal life. And Sandra was one of the earlier ones. Much less was known when she was small than we know now.'

'Better mothers than Mrs Clifford have failed,' Max agreed. 'It demands super-human qualities in parent and child, in my opinion, and a lot of luck as well. We shouldn't blame Mrs Clifford. It would probably have ended like this whatever she had done or not done.'

'I suppose so,' Hugh agreed. He looked worried. He was wishing that he had been able to superintend Sandra's exercises every morning, as he had done when he had been the Cliffords' lodger. Her life might have been prolonged by a year or two.

Max saw this. 'I know,' he said sympathetically. 'But you mustn't be unreasonable. Neither of us can give any patient all the time we'd like. We have to accept this. It's a fact of life – medical life. We can't even blame it on to the National Health Service.'

'I don't see why not. I for one am perfectly prepared to blame the N.H.S.'

'No. This would always be the case. There are never going to be enough potential doctors and nurses, let alone ancillary staff, to care for everyone under ideal conditions. Not with the demands modern medicine makes (not to mention, of course, the demands modern patients make). What we give to one we take from another.'

'At the Central–'

'All right, at the Central they'd do better than we can do here. Absolutely true. But where do they find their staff? They're taking them from us, from the provincial hospitals. All these highly trained so-called top people from the teaching hospitals might be working in provincial general hospitals. But they keep them at places like the Central in order to maintain their high standards.'

'Perhaps.'

'So we staff ourselves with Indian and African doctors and nurses. In our turn we're taking staff, who might be working in under-developed countries, in order to maintain the standards of European medicine. Do you think, if I was at home, I'd be worrying about a child with cystic fibrosis? Sandra would have died in infancy, and I'd be trying to cope with kwashiorkor, schistosomiasis, malaria, poliomyelitis and leprosy. For an area the size this hospital serves, there wouldn't even be me. There'd be the equivalent of one staff nurse and one orderly, doing their best, and sending cases to me by Land-Rover *in extremis*.'

'But–'

'I ought to be out there myself, doing just that. I know it, don't worry. But politically it doesn't happen to be practicable for me to go home – I'd find myself unable to practise medicine, to say the least, so I do what I can under the conditions I find here. I try to look after Sandra Clifford, to the best of my ability and in accordance with what is customary in this environment. If I were working at St Mary's, Paddington, I would have been able to do far more – except that Sandra doesn't happen to have been born in Paddington, any more than she was born in Nigeria. If she had been born in Paddington, though, she might have had a team of doctor, nurse and physiotherapist following her into her home. I've been out with them. It's a magnificent service, and it actually saves beds and staff in the long run. But we don't have it here. We can't even staff the wards properly. You know very well you can't run a one-man-home-treatment service all on your own. Eh?'

'No. But I can't help feeling that I could have done more.'

'Of course you could have done more. You know you can always squeeze out that extra fraction of time or energy with an immense effort.'

'Well, then–'

'Right through your life you'll be making that extra effort, hour after hour, day after day. That's medicine. Sometimes, though, it isn't quite enough. Then you'll blame yourself because a fraction more might have been. Wait until you get to Nyganda. Then you'll understand at first hand that you personally can't save everyone who comes to you. Do what you can and leave it at that. Don't be such an old worry-guts, Hugh.'

'Sandra–'

'We would both like to have succeeded

with Sandra. We didn't. We've failed. It won't be the last time we fail, either.'

'She's not dead yet,' Peter Barlow pointed out quietly. His seniors appeared to be over-looking this fact.

They both looked at him. 'No,' Max agreed. 'You're quite right.'

'I thought this was supposed to be a party, not a case-conference,' Clare said, joining them.

'So it is,' Max said. 'And you're looking very lovely, if I am allowed to say so. I would like to wish you so much happiness,' he added with some formality but complete sincerity.

'That is nice of you, Max,' Clare said. 'I'm glad you're here. I didn't see you, and I thought perhaps you weren't going to be able to come.'

'We were late, I'm afraid. This child, Sandra Clifford...'

'Back to the case-conference,' Hugh said warningly.

'No, I want to hear,' Clare assured them. 'Tell me about Sandra Clifford.'

Peter Barlow saw a staff nurse he was interested in, and moved purposefully off. Max grinned at Hugh, and remarked, 'He's more interested in her than in Sandra, I'm afraid.' Hugh grinned, and said, 'It's natural, at his age.'

'Oh, listen to Grandpa,' Max said to Clare.

She laughed. 'He has a faint interest still, in the female sex, you know. Or so I am hoping.'

Hugh made a face at her. 'This party is not unconnected with my interest,' he said. 'To revert to Peter, though. He's all right.'

'I agree,' Max said. 'I wasn't suggesting anything else. I'm quite happy for him to chase staff nurses in his spare time.'

'He's a great improvement on the boy David, at any rate.'

'Thank the lord we've seen the last of him,' Max said. 'I hope never to hear of him again.'

This hope was doomed to disappointment. David Lyell, writing busily away in East Anglia, at last struck oil.

CHAPTER SIXTEEN

David Lyell had sent his articles on the Health Service and its failings round the national press. Until now, they had returned like homing pigeons, bearing their rejection slips. What could be wrong with them? David cogitated. He remembered what Ian Hardie had told him. He had despised the advice at the time, but now at last he began to wonder.

Actualities, Ian had said more than once on looking through David's manuscripts. 'This won't do. No editor wants all this generalising and theorising. Useless to write "young doctors today are frustrated, their pay is low, their accommodation dreary, hours of duty interminable and the food bad". You won't make the grade that way, boy. You should say, "Dr Tom Brown, twenty-five years old and a house physician at the Brookhampton General Hospital, is fed up. Chocker. Not only is his take-home pay only eight pounds per week. But it was mutton stew and boiled potatoes again for lunch and the heating in his bedroom hasn't worked since he arrived five weeks ago".'

David had sneered at the time. Not that he

had let Ian see this. This style, though, might do for the local rag, but not for David Lyell. Not for the sort of writer he was going to be. But now, forced by the rejection slips to reassess his writing technique, he wondered. Cheap? Sensational? Perhaps. But somehow he had to put a foot in the door of the world of journalism. Once he was in things would be different. He was certain he had a future as a medical journalist.

Always extraordinarily lacking in elementary discretion, once he had decided to take the plunge, he overdid it. He began writing up the Brookhampton Hospital by name. After all, his contract had expired, he told himself. He would never go back there. What did it matter? He wrote about the appalling food. Ian Hardie had never seemed much impressed by his tales of hardship, but David was determined to make the misery of bad cooking come alive for thousands. Millions, perhaps.

He failed. The article, like all the others, came back to him. He pondered. There must be some story he could get across. The situation was ridiculous. Here he was, his head stocked with medical gems which he knew the public were eager to hear, yet because he had no influence no one published them. It was the same old story. No influence in medicine, and now no influence in journalism. Without influence, how good he was counted for nothing. He could be another Conrad, but they'd take no notice. The injustice of it. People like Ravelston – who despised him – had it all their own way.

Ravelston. He'd like to expose him, he thought bitterly. And the whole establishment racket. Personalities, Ian had said. Personalities are news. Right. Through Ravelston he would demonstrate the unfair influence of privilege.

At once the whole beautiful story sprang complete into his head. He would write up the Linda Masterson case. It had everything. It was all there. Money-making consultants – already past it – infiltrating their private patients into the wards and giving them preferential treatment. Racial discrimination, with an able young registrar forbidden to treat the child because of the colour of his skin. The entire resident medical staff ready to strike, solidly behind him, anxious to demonstrate that he was not to be dealt with in this way. If he was not to treat the child, then no one should.

David was genuinely convinced by now that he had led the junior hospital doctors in what would have been a walk-out. A battle for freedom and their rights. He forgot that all that had happened was that at lunch and supper for two or three days he had held forth to an inattentive, pre-occupied and constantly changing audience, used to his Welsh volubility and accustomed to discounting his latest excitement. They went on thinking about their impending clinics or ward rounds, or alternatively about their wives or girl-friends, and their hopes of a better job where they could live out.

By now, though, David was certain that Max would have been, so to speak, avenged by an embittered corps of housemen advancing under the dragon of Wales, had it not been for the interference of the Resident Medical Officer, that snake in the grass, scion of the Establishment, lackey of the consultants – Hugh Ravelston. He had selected at the moment of crisis to treat the child himself. He had cut the ground from under their feet in order to curry favour with the paediatrician. Ravelston had no principles. He was interested only in his career, and he saw a fine future for himself in private consultant practice.

At the *Daily Blare* they had a long memory for names and a nose for news.

'Ravelston?' someone said. 'That rings a bell. Wasn't there a case a few years ago?'

The library came up with the full story.

David's article did not return to him with a rejection slip. On the contrary, he had his first cheque. He had a shock, too, when he read the *Blare's* version of his article. A double shock. He had known nothing of

Hugh Ravelston's past. Now that he had discovered it, though, he was not sorry to see it raked up again. Serve him right.

His article, though, even allowing for the additional material added by the *Blare,* seemed a little over-sensational. Surely he hadn't gone as far as this?

He checked with his typescript. He found that he had. They had cut a good deal, which had given his story increased emphasis, and added considerably to the quality of innuendo which was already part of it. They had sub-titled it in a way that horrified him. But they were printing it. That was what mattered. Next time he submitted an article they would know who he was, they would give real consideration to it. He had embarked at last on a writing career. Hugh Ravelston could look after himself.

That was not what his friends felt. They read the article with horrified fascination.

'Of all time for this to happen,' Jock and Margaret faced one another across the breakfast table. 'As if it wasn't bad enough at the time,' Margaret said. 'Without having it all dragged out again now, just when things were beginning to go right for him at last.'

'If I could lay my hands on that little swine Lyell, I'd half-kill him,' Jock said between his teeth. 'He was useless as a house physician,

276

by all accounts, and now he's done this. Irresponsible young bastard. If anyone deserved to be struck off, he does. All these names and allegations, and what amount to extracts from confidential case histories.' He scowled, and scanned the article from beginning to end with some care. 'No,' he admitted regretfully. 'The lawyers have done their job. Trust the *Blare*. I don't suppose there's a detail actually printed here that isn't either factual or else generally available to any member of the public who cares to go looking for it. The real dirt is written neatly between the lines.'

Ben had his attention drawn to the article by a friend at morning coffee. 'I hear Ravelston's in the news again. Friend of yours, isn't he?'

'Eh?'

'Haven't you heard? The *Daily Blare* has ferreted out the whole story, including the fact that he was struck off, and tied it in with some weird account of a patient down at Brookhampton and the colour-bar.'

'Good God.'

'There are copies being passed round here. I thought you'd be bound to have come across one and read it.'

'No. Not yet.'

'Bad luck, really. He must have thought he'd just about lived it down by now.'

Ben gulped his coffee and sent for a paper.

He hated what he read.

Max saw the article before Hugh himself. It was brought to him by a worried Peter Barlow. Max read it and swore. Then he went in search of Hugh.

'I want to talk to you.'

'Oh yes?' Hugh paused on the stone stairs, easy in his mind, smiling cheerfully.

'Not here. In your room.'

'What's the hurry?' Hugh asked, surprised.

'If there wasn't any hurry I wouldn't suggest it,' Max said irritably.

Hugh looked at him. 'All right,' he agreed. They walked downstairs and along the corridor in silence. Hugh led the way into his room. 'Well, what is it?' he demanded. He was expecting to hear some difficulty about a patient, some awkward mistake made by one of the housemen.

'You're not going to like this,' Max warned him, and showed him the article.

'*Struck-off doctor in hospital colour-bar storm,*' the headline screamed. Hugh went white. There was a photograph, too, one that had been taken five years earlier, in the car park outside the Central, showing him young and shadowed and weary. He had hated it at the time and he hated it again now.

Max watched him. Hugh had been white, but now he was flushing. Max remembered his early days at Brookhampton, how raw he had been from the pain of rejection by his own profession, how difficult he had found it to come to terms with life. This publicity was going to flay him.

Hugh said nothing. He was reading the article, his colour ebbing and flowing, his fingernails showing white against the back of the chair he had grasped. Max decided it was essential to make him talk. No suffering in silence. Fury would be infinitely preferable. He began to curse David Lyell with all the epithets he had acquired during his varied existence in Africa and Europe. They made a motley but satisfying collection.

Hugh smiled wearily. 'Oh yes, he's all that,' he said. 'But I don't suppose he'll ever know it. He'll probably do very well now, wouldn't you say?'

Max swore again, at some length.

'Oh well,' Hugh said. 'Better get on.' He paused, absently tipped the chair he had been holding back and forth, rocking it on two legs. 'Here we go again. I know it all by heart. I lived through it once, I shall have to live through it again, that's all.' He banged the chair back on to four legs, with a resounding crash. 'Thanks for warning me,' he said, handing back the *Daily Blare*.

Max took the paper and dumped it down on Hugh's desk. He left the room. Hugh would have to face this alone before he returned to the wards. In fact, though, he did not remain for long in his room. No use skulking about here, he thought. However long he left it, the result was going to be the same. He glanced at the telephone. He had a sudden impulse to ring Clare.

He mastered the impulse. He remembered Nicola all too clearly. She had not liked it when his career had crashed and burst into the headlines. What was Clare going to feel in the same circumstances? She knew the story of what had happened to him, of course. But in outline only. That was very different from reading it sprawled across a newspaper page, with innuendo and biting phrases. He dared not drag her into the middle of this mess. He was afraid to – afraid that Clare, like Nicola, would somehow slip away, vanish into another life, leaving him alone.

He remembered Nicola's first visit to Brookhampton, when he was lodging with the Cliffords in Malden Road. She had been horrified. 'How can you live in this frightful place?' she had exclaimed. 'Somebody ought to do something. Someone could find you a better job than this. This place is a ghastly *hole*.' Comfort had been what he had longed to receive then, not outrage. But there had been no comfort from Nicola. He had counted on her to be his one surety, his remaining happiness in a sea of trouble. But she had drifted delicately away. This had been a shock to him, and a gnawing pain. For the first time in his life – until then privileged and carefree – he had had to grasp that a beautiful girl might not find him good value. No Alfa-Romeo now, no gay life in London, no future career as a consultant at the Central. He had been forced to watch her love steadily evaporating as his prospects dwindled. She was out when he telephoned, her conversation was evasive, she put him off when he tried to meet her in London. Finally she announced her engagement to his cousin Don.

He braced his shoulders. Useless to live in the past. A great deal had happened since those days. There could be no comparison.

In any case, the present was enough to deal with. One thing at a time. He had a job to do, he would go and do it. Later there might be a time for other needs, for hopes and fears.

He walked back up the stone stairs to Cartwright. As he was doing so he had his first glimpse of the possibility that this was not, after all, going to be quite so bad as last time. Bad enough, no doubt. But different, at any rate. For last time his work had been taken away from him. Now, whatever his private hell might be, he could at least lose himself in his work. In the wards he was needed still, whatever his public reputation, and to many of the patients lying there and meeting death with what courage they could muster, the information that he was suffering because of a photograph and a few captions in a newspaper would seem odd. Out of proportion.

There was to be another difference that he did not foresee. At lunch-time he went into the dining-room, stony-faced, calling on his fortitude to live through the mingled contempt and gossiping amusement that he had encountered at the Central five years ago. The kindest of them, as before, would say nothing, pretend that life was normal and undisturbed. But there would be others not so kind.

He walked into the dining-room to find himself in the midst of an indignation meeting.

'Here he is,' Gibson, the surgical registrar, said. 'Give him his drink first.' He found a glass of whisky pushed into his hand.

'What's this?' he asked, bewildered.

'We thought you might need it,' they said in chorus.

'Correct us if we were wrong.'

'You weren't wrong,' he said. 'What an excellent idea.'

'Our ability to prescribe can occasionally extend to our colleagues,' Dr Jayant Rao remarked in his usual pedantic style.

'All we could think of, more likely,'

Gibson said.

'What he really felt like doing,' Peter Barlow remarked, 'was descending on this Lyell character and battering him to a pulp. That being impracticable at the moment—'

'We considered you might not be entirely appreciative if the hospital was totally denuded of the medical staff while we all stormed off to this place in Suffolk—'

'Instead we had a whip round and Peter went over to the Dog and Duck and purchased a bottle of Johnny Walker. I won't say we haven't most of us had a small nip—'

'Speak for yourself.'

'—but the remainder is for you to consume in the next twelve hours.'

'I shall expect to collect the empty at breakfast tomorrow, and it had better be empty,' Peter said. 'And incidentally, I'm sorry to say there are two press photographers parked outside the main entrance.'

'Blast. I suppose it was inevitable. I'm surprised, in a way, that they've stopped there.'

Peter laughed. 'You wouldn't be if you'd seen the porters. Four of the largest of them ranged across the entrance looking like American gangsters somehow got up in the uniform of the dear old N.H.S., and all with their mouths turned down in that obstinate way reminiscent of a Giles cartoon, that we're all so familiar with. Another whisky?

You might as well, the lunch is down to its usual standard.'

'Thanks. I really think I'd like to pay for it, though. It's magnificent of you to have been out and fetched it, at least let me foot the bill.'

'Certainly not. It's a present from all of us. A small token of esteem and respect. We shall be hurt and offended unless you accept it. You don't want to hurt our tender feelings, do you?' Gibson spoke lightly, but Hugh was conscious, as he had been since he came into the room, of the warm friendliness behind the trivial chat. Suddenly the whole affair seemed less overwhelming. This reaction might not last, he knew, and might have been at least partly born of the whisky. But undoubtedly there were gleams of light among the shadows. He began eating the rissoles, mashed potatoes and processed peas that constituted the catering officer's contribution to their well-being for the day, while the rest of them suggested a number of obscene and disastrous fates for David Lyell.

'I must say, I feel quite apologetic and ashamed that I even took his place,' Peter Barlow said. 'Rather a despicable place, it must be.'

'At least you have one pleasure denied to the rest of us,' Gibson pointed out. 'The fact that you've never had to meet him – or sit opposite him at meals (as if the meals aren't bad enough without the addition of our home-grown poison pen) – should be a source of satisfaction to you.'

'I expect it should,' Peter agreed.

'And as for taking his place, at least you can be one hundred per cent certain that we couldn't have been more delighted to see you instead of him.'

'The bastard. If I'd had any notion of what he'd get up to once he left–'

'As if he wasn't quite enough of a trial when he was here...' They resumed their detailed and uncomfortable plans for David Lyell's future, while Hugh finished his rissoles and began on something that at his prep school had always been known as frog spawn, though here they had found a more revolting label. Then he downed his coffee, while a resolve formed.

'I think, you know,' he interrupted them all, 'I'd better go and have my photograph taken. Then they can go away and the porters can get back to their normal duties. I shall have to face it sometime, so I might as well get it over before out-patients, and not have to creep furtively round all afternoon.'

'Give a press conference,' Peter Barlow said, his eyes shining. Angry he might be, but Hugh could read his young excitement too, written all over his eager puppy-like features. For him this was a glimpse of life as he had always hoped to see it. Hugh grinned at him. 'You'd better come as bodyguard,' he suggested.

'We'll all come as bodyguards,' someone yelled, and there was a growl of acquiescence. The room suddenly had more resemblance to the last night of term in the dormitory at Garside than to a respectable medical mess. Hugh saw that in a few moments they would be out of hand.

'No,' he said firmly. 'I must do this properly. As you say, Peter, it will be a press conference.' Peter looked gratified. He had successfully demonstrated his worldly wisdom. 'It won't simply be a quick photograph and away, I'm afraid. I wonder if I ought to ask the Secretary of the Management Committee to support me?' He drank his coffee and pondered. 'I'd better take advice,' he decided. 'I'll see what Dr Calderwood thinks.' They watched him while he went across to the telephone and rang the laboratory.

'Ah, Hugh,' Jock said. 'I was just going to get on to you. I take it you've seen the *Daily Blare?*'

'Yes, I have. That's what I was ringing you about. Apparently there are press photographers storming the entrance, and–'

'There should be extra porters on duty there,' Jock said quickly.

'There are indeed,' Hugh said, under-

286

standing now who had placed them there with impeccable timing. 'You old manager,' he added affectionately. 'The thing is, I thought I'd better face the inevitable, and have my beastly picture taken and be done with it. I suppose I'll have to give some sort of interview.'

'Yes, that's what we think,' Jock agreed. 'Daniel and I were just discussing it. Hold on.' He could be heard muttering. Hugh looked across to Gibson and said, 'Sir Daniel Snelgrove seems to be with him.'

Gibson raised his eyebrows. 'He doesn't waste much time, does he? But then he never has. Fantastically efficient bloke, I always feel.'

'Hugh?' Jock's voice came on the line again.

'Yes?'

'Daniel says he'll come with you, and so will I. Say as little as possible, but you'd better make a statement, and answer a few questions. Come up here and we'll rough something out. Oh, and get hold of Okiya. We'll want him.'

Hugh put the telephone down and told the expectant faces turned towards him, 'He says he and Snelgrove will come with me, and I'm to go up there first to draft a statement.'

'Excellent,' Gibson said.

'Indeed yes,' Rao agreed. 'The Chairman

of the Medical Committee and the Chairman of the Hospital Management Committee. What you would call the top brass, eh? Couldn't be better.'

'Oh yes, and they want to see Max. Could you find him, Peter?'

'I'll do that,' Barlow said, and shot eagerly out of the room. Hugh followed more slowly, and climbed the stone stairs to the laboratory.

When Clare, who had been shown the *Daily Blare* at morning coffee in the office, left there that evening, she found Hugh's photograph staring at her from the front page of the *Evening Standard*. Her heart turned over.

Hospital denies colour-bar allegation, this headline asserted. The photograph was captioned *Dr Hugh Ravelston, alleged to be the centre of a storm over whether black doctors should treat white patients at the Brookhampton Hospital, seen today with Dr Maxwell Okiya from Nigeria.*

The article began on the same lines, and continued, *Dr Maxwell Okiya (see picture) denied that there had been any question of ceasing treatment of the child mentioned. 'Our main object,' he told our reporter, 'was to maintain continuity of treatment. We were all agreed about that. The child's mother was upset. She was newly returned from Zambia, where she rather considered she had been unfairly dealt with. She appeared to associate me with her unfortunate experiences there (in fact I come from Nigeria) and this made her a little excitable. This was reacting unfavourably on the child, and for this reason I asked Dr Ravelston to continue treatment for me. No, it was my decision, not Dr Ravelston's, quite definitely. Yes, I asked him to treat her.'*

A few paragraphs farther down *Dr J. M. E. Calderwood, Chairman of the Medical Committee, said that there had been no representations at all from the junior medical staff about this case. 'Nor would I expect there to be,' he added. 'No medical man would contemplate interrupting a patient's treatment in this way, whether her mother wanted her to be treated by pink elephants, white doctors or spotted giraffes. Our aim was to lower the emotional tension, which, as Dr Okiya has pointed out, was having an undesirable effect on the child.'*

Then there was a statement from Sir Daniel Snelgrove to the effect that there had never been any difficulties at the hospital over race, colour or creed, and warmly phrased paragraphs about the indebtedness of the hospital to its overseas doctors and nurses.

Of course, Hugh had not escaped personal interrogation. 'Is it true, Dr Ravelston, that you were struck off by the B.M.A. five years ago for unprofessional conduct?'

He had been expecting this question, yet it

289

still cut deep and he flushed painfully. He replied, with typical Ravelston accuracy, 'The G.M.C. Yes.'

'This was as the result of a road accident?'

'Yes.'

'You killed a man?'

Sir Daniel Snelgrove interrupted. 'It would be fairer to say that the driver of the other car died as a result of his injuries,' he pointed out.

Hugh was grateful to him for his intervention, but he did not feel it improved matters. The questions continued.

'The court considered that it was your responsibility?'

'Yes. I was exceeding the speed limit.'

This answer did improve matters, though Hugh was unaware of it. In fact, it caused a small sensation. The reporters were genuinely shaken by his reply. He was exceeding the speed limit, so he was guilty? They shuddered, but pressed on. 'Was that all you did that contributed to the crash? There was a verdict of manslaughter, wasn't there?'

'Yes, there was,' Hugh agreed. 'No, the other car had the right of way, you see. And I had had a drink before I left East Callant – all this was on the way back to Central London, at one in the morning,' he added, the occasion once more vivid in his mind.

'Were you drunk?'

'No, certainly not. I'd had a couple of whiskies when I arrived at this dance, about eight in the evening, and then some beer. Just before I left, I had a whisky. I've often wondered, of course, since it happened, if my reactions were slowed at all. If I hadn't had that drink before I left, would I have missed the Zephyr? I jammed my brakes on, you see. If I'd accelerated, I think he'd probably be alive today. But there you are, you shouldn't drink at all if you're going to drive, and I did. It was my responsibility, all right.' He suddenly noticed that he was thinking aloud in front of these reporters. In reliving the crash, he had forgotten that every word was being taken down. He tried to remember what he had said, and looked guiltily across the table at Daniel, who had told him to say no more than a word or two in answer to any question.

But in fact he had done himself some good. They were sympathetic. The climate of opinion was more favourable than it had been five years earlier. The medical profession – and particularly the younger members of it – was not now regarded as quite so privileged as it had been, there was more understanding of the demands made on it. This story, the reporters felt, illustrated one of these demands. The accident was unfortunate, deplorable. That a man had died was horrible. But a similar

291

accident could have occurred to any of them. They had often exceeded the speed limit. They had often driven after drinking, after more than one whisky, too. If they had met with a similar accident, they would have incurred the same verdict, presumably. They would have carried a load of guilt – or not, according to their temperaments. What they would not have incurred was the additional penalty. No one would have tried them again and decided, as a result of the verdict of manslaughter, that they were no longer fit to represent the *Daily Blare* or the *Evening Standard*.

'For this you were struck off?' they asked, in disbelief.

'Yes.'

They thought it hard. They prepared to write up the story sympathetically. People had been very nice to them at the hospital, too, giving them the committee room for their interviews, and even cups of coffee. They departed in good humour for the telephones and the London trains. Tomorrow's press was better.

That was not the end of the story, though. Television, for instance. Hugh was asked for an interview. At first he refused, but they were persistent, and finally he agreed to appear with Max. This was tough. The interviewer was much less friendly than the reporters had been. He behaved as though they were a couple of quacks, Max said, to be exposed for the benefit of suffering humanity. 'Personally,' Hugh said, 'I felt as though he suspected me of having robbed a bank.' 'Or of running a lucrative practice in illegal abortions,' Max contributed. They both laughed. 'Whereas in fact, you know,' Hugh remarked, 'he was hardly conscious of either of us. He couldn't have cared less about us. He was just engaged in showing his producer, or whoever it is he needs to impress, what a vigorous interviewer he is, worthy of more programme time.' 'Each to his own little rat race,' Max agreed.

Clare missed the television appearance, as she was in the train to Brookhampton. She arrived, supperless, tired and weary, after a long and agonising day. She had been under pressure at her office, where they were experiencing a rush of work. All day at the back of her mind, as she raced about, up and down passages and stairs – no time to wait for the dilatory lift – as she banged her typewriter, answered the telephone, fought with the switchboards of other organisations (and often, of course, her own) fetched and carried for her seniors, ran this current of anxiety for Hugh. How was he taking it? How was he standing up to this new and unjust onslaught into his privacy? What was he feeling? She was torn with pain for what he must be going through now, and for what he had endured in the past. She knew little more than the bare outline of what had happened to his career. Ben, always ready to confide details of Hugh's love affairs, was reticent about his damaged career, while it had always been apparent that Hugh himself hated talking about it. She had never pressed him.

She took a taxi to the hospital, and asked at the porter's lodge for Hugh. The porter had been turning people away all day. He gave her an appraising look, remembered that the London train would be in, and said firmly, 'Dr Ravelston's not in the hospital.' He was not a porter who knew Clare by sight.

'Oh,' Clare said. She had been quite unprepared for his absence, and she could have cried on the spot. Something got through to the porter, who looked at her again, and said, 'Well, I don't think he is. What name is it?' She gave her name. 'I'll try the medical quarters,' he said. 'But I don't suppose – Miss Dunn to see Dr Ravelston,' he announced. 'Yes, Miss Dunn. Yes, here, in the hall. Very good.' He took the plug out and turned to her. 'He's coming along now, miss, if you'd just wait.'

He came round the corner into the hall, looking deathly tired. But his face lighted up when he saw her. 'They said it was you,' he said, kissing her, 'but I didn't really believe them. What are you doing here? Why didn't you ring me?'

'No time. Busy. I came down because of the papers, you see.'

'You came because of the papers?' he repeated.

'Yes.'

They had been walking along the corridor towards his room, but he stopped dead. 'You came down, all this way, this evening, because of the papers?' he repeated blankly.

'Yes. I told you.' She was searching his face with her great brown eyes, trying to discover what he was feeling. Was he angry, miserable, upset – what? He looked exhausted. This was all she could tell.

'You weren't coming down here anyway?' he asked, as though he couldn't believe her.

'No. Why should I be?'

'I don't know. God, I don't know. You just came to see me?'

'Yes.' What was the matter with him?

'My God, you don't know how I wanted you,' he said. 'Oh, my God.' He put his arms round her and held on to her tightly.

'There,' she said, making little patting movements without knowing it. 'There. It'll be all right, darling. It'll be all right.'

'It'll be all right,' he repeated automatically. Then he came to life. 'By God, it will be all right,' he said in strong tones quite unlike his earlier remarks. He hurried her along the corridor. 'We'll live through it, won't we? And it isn't very important, simply unpleasant.' He shut the door and took her into his arms again. 'You didn't mind?' he asked.

'Mind? Why should I mind? It's you I want to know about.'

'I don't care,' he said. At that moment it was the truth. 'Not now you're here. How did you know I wanted you so much?'

'I should have thought it was obvious,' she said.

He smiled at her. 'It might not have been,' he said. 'But I'm glad it was. You wonderful girl.' He continued to hold her to him.

She tilted her head back to look at him. 'What's been happening all day?' she asked.

He began to laugh. 'Quite a lot, my darling, quite a lot. We've had a press conference in the committee room, and–'

'Yes, that's in the *Standard*.'

'What? Have you got it? Let me see.'

She gave him the evening paper. 'Strewth,' he said, as immediately his own face and Max's stared out, slightly pop-eyed, both of them.

'Uncle Dan Snelgrove and all,' Clare commented. Jock and Daniel could be discerned in the background, plus, Hugh saw at once, two of the porters with their mouths turned down, obviously ready to make a fight of it given half a chance. He began reading the article, together with its subsidiary columns about his own career, and what the *Standard's* medical correspondent had to contribute about continuity of treatment and also the number of overseas staff of all categories employed in the hospital service.

'Well, it might have been worse,' he commented finally.

'I should think it might have been much worse,' Clare said. 'It's a pity it had to get into the press at all, but as it has, it's not nearly as bad as it might have been. I could *slaughter* that miserable David Lyell,' she added.

Hugh laughed. 'You're not the only one. The entire resident medical staff have thought up a number of most unsavoury situations for him.'

'I should think so too.'

'Max and I have been on television,' he remarked. 'That was not exactly enjoyable.' He described the interview to her. 'Still, it might have been worse. And now you're here, and everything's all right.' He dropped his head forward and kissed her hard on the lips. Then he let his breath out in a long sigh. 'I feel a lot better,' he announced. 'Have you had supper?'

'No. Have you?'

'No. We must have some. I suppose I'll be recognised pretty well anywhere we go, this evening. We'd better brave the Dog and Duck. At least the clientele there is almost entirely hospital.'

'We can go home,' Clare suggested. 'Woodie will make us a meal. Omelette – no, scrambled eggs and bacon, she does those better. Soup first. Cheese afterwards. How's that?'

'Sounds good. But what will darling Hermione say?'

'Mother can shut up for once,' Clare said through her teeth. Then she giggled. 'What price Uncle Daniel Snelgrove?' she demanded, her eyes sparkling. 'Isn't he supposed to be the arch-fixer. Let *him* fix Mother. Can I use your telephone?'

He pointed at it.

'Do you remember his number?'

'No, but the switchboard know it. Just ask for him. They'll find him all right. They're always scouring the countryside for him.'

She did this, and was soon talking to Daniel. 'This is Clare,' she said.

'Oh, hullo, my dear – nothing wrong with your mother, I hope?'

Clare made a face at Hugh. 'No, she's fine,' she assured him in dulcet tones. 'It's just – look, I wondered if you'd do me a favour?'

'Of course, my dear. Glad to.'

'You see, I'm at the hospital. I want to take Hugh home for a meal, because we've neither of us had any supper, and we're very hungry. We don't want to go to a restaurant or a pub or anything, not this evening. And – and I don't want Hugh to have to tell Mother the whole story. We just want to be quiet and relax. So I wondered if you could–'

'Rely on me. I'll see to it. Don't worry. You get along to the cottage and have your supper. Everything will be quite all right.' He rang off.

'He is good, you know,' Clare said. 'I'm sorry I made that rude face. Come on, we're going. Supper.'

When they reached Lavender Cottage Daniel's Jaguar was already parked outside, and as they walked up the brick path the front door opened and Daniel and Hermione came out.

'Darling,' Hermione said. She enfolded Clare, and kissed her. 'And Hugh,' she added, brushing his cheek with hers, as she had taken to doing since the engagement.

'Come along, Hermione,' Daniel said a voice redolent with *now remember what I told you*. To everyone's amazement, including that of the two principals, Hermione obeyed the unspoken injunction. 'I'll see you later, darling,' she said. 'Daniel and I are going out for a drink.' She went on down the path and sank gracefully into the front seat of the Jaguar.

'That man can fix anything,' Clare said, as they stood in the hall taking off their coats.

'There's one thing he can't,' Hugh said.

'What's that?'

'The Nygandan post.'

'The Nygandan post? What do you mean?' She stared at him. 'Will this publicity affect that?'

'It's off, as from today.'

'When did you hear? You didn't tell me.'

'I don't need to hear. I know.'

'Oh,' she said, relieved. 'Don't be depressed, darling. I don't see any reason why this should interfere with Nyganda in three months' time. People have fantastically short memories. All this will be completely forgotten in a week or two. Come into the sitting-room and have a drink. What you need is to be warm and comfortable, and have a proper meal, and it won't look so bleak.' She led the way confidently into the room, where a log fire blazed cheerfully, a lamp shed a pool of light reflecting the mellow wood of beautiful old furniture. Firelight flickered, too, on decanter and glasses on the low table before the sofa, and on the spines of the books in the white-painted shelves. 'Come along,' Clare urged. She sat down and patted the sofa invitingly. 'What are you going to drink? Some of Daniel's dry sherry, or whisky?'

'Whisky, please. My God, you look lovely,'

he exclaimed, as she leant forward to pour the whisky. 'Thank you, darling, here's to you.' He raised his glass. 'All the same, you know,' he added, 'I'm right. The Nygandan job is undoubtedly off. Shall you mind?'

'Me? Of course not. I want you to have the job you'd like. I don't care whether we go to Nyganda or not. Of course I don't. But are you sure—'

'They have very long memories at the Central, that's what you don't understand. Barham was stretching a point in offering me the job at all. Now he can't do it.'

Here, of course, he was correct. Barham said as much to Ben. 'I'm afraid, you know, we shall have to drop our little plan for Hugh Ravelston to go to Nyganda.'

'Yes,' Ben agreed heavily. He had been thinking about this most of the day. 'Of all the bloody luck.'

'Ravelston is unlucky,' Barham pointed out. 'And it isn't only politicians who need luck on their side in order to reach the top.'

'Certainly Hugh seems ill-starred. Of all things to happen, just now.'

'You've read the story, I suppose?'

'Every stinking word of it.'

'Then you can see that, quite apart from the fact that any publicity at all is anathema in this place, this particular publicity is deadly in the circumstances. It means I can't put Ravelston forward for the Ikerobe post, with all this spread over the press about colour-bar.'

'I'm sure he is the last person—'

'My dear fellow, I don't doubt it for a moment. But now is hardly the time to choose to send him to Nyganda, you'll agree?'

'I'm afraid it isn't.'

'Even if I could get it past the Medical Committee – which frankly I doubt – I can't any longer honestly feel myself that it would be a desirable appointment. Not in the circumstances.'

This was final, Ben knew. Barham had withdrawn his support. He could not blame him. Had the responsibility been his own, he would have found it difficult to advocate the plan.

'The question is,' Barham went on, 'which of us is to break the news to him.'

'Eh?'

'Oh, I'm quite willing to do it myself. Don't misunderstand me. But it's never pleasant to be turned down, and I wondered if it might not be less traumatic if it came from you.'

'I expect you're right,' Ben had to agree.

'Nothing is going to soften the actual blow of losing the post, because he wanted it badly, I could see that. But we need not rub salt into the wound by an official brush-off, I don't think, do you?'

'No, I'll tell him. I'll ring him up this evening.'

'I expect he already guesses.'

'I'll confirm it for him,' Ben promised. Gloomily he rang Hugh, only to be told he had left the hospital. He gave a message, and Hugh telephoned when he returned, at about midnight.

'Hullo, there you are,' Ben said. 'Where've you been?'

'Out at Lavender Cottage with Clare.'

'Oh, she's down, is she?' Ben awarded his young cousin top marks at once, and almost felt easier about the news he had to deliver.

'Yep. She's catching the five-thirty up in the morning, poor sweet. What are you ringing up about, just to condole with me, or have you a specific reason?'

'I'm afraid I have a specific reason.'

'Thought so. Nyganda is off. You don't need to tell me.'

'I didn't suppose you had failed to realise. But I promised Barham I'd–'

'Oh, this is an official intimation, is it?'

'Afraid so.'

'Does he want me to withdraw?'

'He didn't say so. I think he simply proposes to drop the idea, I don't think you have to take any action.'

'Oh well, if he does want a letter you can tell me, and I'll write one. Otherwise, as you say, we regard the project as closed. There's nothing else he can do, I see that. I told Clare it was off, but she refused to believe me.'

'She doesn't yet know the teaching hospital mentality – lucky girl.'

'As she's going to marry me, I don't suppose she ever will.'

'It's not necessarily a disadvantage.'

'Perhaps not. I must say, everyone here is being extraordinarily nice about it all. D'you know, when I came into lunch, I found they'd laid on a bottle of whisky for me? Meanwhile, upstairs your father was closeted with Uncle Dan Snelgrove, drafting out a plan of campaign. And the porters practically formed themselves up into a riot squad. All rallying round, you see. Almost cosy, if you know what I mean.'

'So they should rally round. It was a very poor show at the Central when it first happened, I thought. I didn't say so at the time, because you had other things to think about. But it was simply a rat race. All anyone cared about was leaping on to the rung of the ladder you were about – they hoped – to vacate, before anyone else got there. You're much better off where you are. If you can only accept it.'

'I'd better, hadn't I?' Hugh asked, a little bitterly. 'It seems to me I haven't much option.'

'No good kicking against the pricks,' Ben

said firmly. 'I thought you liked it at Brook-hampton, anyway.'

'I don't like anything very much at present. But I'll get over that.'

'I haven't a doubt of it,' Ben agreed comfortably.

Hugh laughed. 'You're right, blast you. But you could go so far as to express a little sympathy, just for the look of the thing.'

'You seem to have had bucketfuls of that.'

'As a matter of fact, I have.'

'Quite. That's what you said. You don't need my sympathy,' Ben retorted briskly, and rang off. The telephone at once rang again, and the switchboard told Hugh Dr Okiya wanted him in the children's ward.

He went up there. The door to the side ward was open, and sounds of activity came from within. Hugh's heart sank. This was Sandra Clifford. He went in, and Max looked up. 'I don't think her heart is going to stand much more,' he said. 'I thought you'd want to know.'

'Yes.'

The Night Sister came in. 'Her parents have arrived,' she said.

Max looked at Hugh. 'You know them both,' he said pointedly.

Hugh sighed. This was a duty he could hardly evade. 'All right, I'll see them,' he said. He went out into the passage.

'In the office,' Sister said.

He went in. The Cliffords were sitting there, looking small and forlorn. Irene was carefully made up and well dressed as usual, and seemed composed. Ted was in his working overalls, white and miserable. They both looked pleased to see Hugh, and smiled hopefully.

'I'm afraid it's no good,' he told them. 'You know we warned you we were worried about Sandra's heart?'

'I know,' Ted said.

'It looks as if it may not last out much longer. We've done what we can, but I'm afraid her lung condition is throwing this very heavy strain on her heart, and–'

'But surely you can do *something*,' Irene interrupted. 'I mean, that's what hospitals are for. She's been coming here all her life. Why have you let this happen to her?'

'Now, Irene, you mustn't–' Ted began.

'I thought modern treatment and modern drugs were supposed to be so good. Why can't you stop this sort of thing happening?'

'Sandra's lungs have always been her weakness. We can't yet give her new ones. I wish we could.'

'I thought you could have new lungs and a new heart. It said in the papers–'

'Not yet, I'm afraid. One day. But not in time for Sandra.'

'I think it's a disgrace,' Irene said.

'They're doing the best they can, dear,' her

306

husband said, even in his misery giving Hugh a glance of complicity as he had done on many occasions in the past when his wife had been unreasonable. 'Can we see her?'

'Of course. She's in an oxygen tent, and she's very ill, you know. You may not...' his eyes met Ted's, and they both looked at Irene doubtfully. She settled matters for them. 'You go and see her,' she said to Ted. 'Then come and tell me.' She folded her hands firmly over the bag in her lap.

Hugh and Ted went out.

'It upsets her, you know,' Ted said apologetically. 'She never could stand illness.'

'It upsets you too,' Hugh said.

'Oh, me.' He shrugged.

A small, reliable figure, he stayed with Sandra until she died. He made no fuss, he moved when they asked him to, he stood aside for them to carry out procedures that hurt him much more than the unconscious Sandra, he acted with great commonsense and held anything that seemed to him to need holding. Occasionally he frowned and licked his lips. But he stuck it out to the end.

Irene had gone home, on his instructions. At four in the morning Sandra died.

'I'm sorry,' Hugh said. 'That's it. There's nothing more to be done.'

'It can't be helped,' Ted said. His eyes, which had been dry and red-rimmed, suddenly filled with tears, and he blew his nose. 'My poor darling,' he muttered indistinctly. He frowned and swallowed, and patted the iron hospital bed. 'There it is. Got to go and tell the wife. Come in, later on this morning, and sign forms, eh?'

Hugh took him by the arm and walked him to the door of the room. 'Try and get some sleep first,' he suggested.

'Dare say I will,' Ted agreed equably, but neither of them believed it. 'You get some sleep too,' he added. 'Need it as much as I do.'

Hugh looked at his watch. It had been a long day. In an hour and a half, though, he was due to fetch Clare from Lavender Cottage to drive her to the station for the first London train.

'Hang on a bit,' he said to Ted, 'and I'll run you home.'

Ted began to protest.

'Nonsense. I've got to go to the station anyway. You sit down here, and I'll be back for you in ten minutes.'

He ran up to his room, telephoned Clare, who said she was putting the kettle on for tea, and that he had better join her. He told her about Sandra.

'Oh, that's the girl you and Max were telling me about at the party. You both said she was dying. Oh dear, I am sorry. Have you been up all night?'

He realised that he had. 'Yes, they rang me

soon after I got back here. Oh, and Ben rang first. Nyganda's off.'

'Oh.'

'We'll talk about it later. I'm more or less on my way out to you now, but I wanted to warn you, I'll have Ted Clifford in the car with me. I'm running him home.'

'You'd better both have a cup of tea, then,' Clare said briskly.

'Well–'

'I expect you need it. And coming in here will give Sandra's poor father something to think about. You'd better have some scrambled eggs. I'll make them.' She rang off.

Hugh grinned to himself. He always enjoyed Clare in a managing mood. He splashed his face with water, then went down and collected Ted from the ward. They went out into the fresh air of the early morning, and drove out across the marshes. Another day had begun.

CHAPTER SEVENTEEN

'I dread meeting this girl,' Annabel said throbbingly to Simon, not for the first time.

'I wish you could make up your mind to like her,' Simon said unhappily. Since Hugh's letter announcing his engagement to Clare had arrived, Annabel had been hell to live with. If there was one thing she could not stand, it was being crossed. She had made up her mind that Hugh was going to marry that nice pianist with the glorious hair and the responsive manner, and now, a bolt from the blue, came this letter. Annabel had not been far off demanding, 'How dare you disobey me, you naughty boy?' But cunning – and Simon – had prevailed. She had written instead what she considered to be an understanding letter to her misguided elder son.

As her understanding took the form of suggesting that Hugh need not despair, since she was sure some way out of his predicament could be found, if he would only take the next plane to Zurich and discuss the whole subject *calmly* with his devoted mother, it was not received with appreciation by Hugh. His predicament, clearly, was what his mother evidently envisaged to be the unfortunate necessity to marry Clare within three months.

Hovering between rage and amusement, he wrote back telling her categorically that he was marrying Clare because this was what he wanted most in the world, and adding, lying, that he was sure she would love Clare when she met her.

Nothing, of course, could be more un-likely.

Now the meeting was upon them. Simon and Annabel had flown over for the wedding on Saturday, and were in London for two nights before going down to Brookhampton. Hugh and Clare were to dine with them.

'I positively *dread* it,' Annabel repeated. 'I'm sure he's simply throwing himself away on some chit of a secretary from that awful town.'

As Hugh and Clare were expected to arrive within minutes, Simon found the omens distinctly unpromising.

'I think we'd better have a drink,' he suggested, 'and not wait for them.'

'I couldn't dream of it,' Annabel retorted sharply. 'No one can say I failed in common courtesy the first time I met my – ugh – daughter-in-law.'

Before the atmosphere could deteriorate further, Simon was relieved to spot Hugh, escorting a girl who astonished him. He had expected nothing like this. Perhaps he had been over-influenced by Annabel's wails of 'some ordinary little girl he's picked up in Brookhampton, of all places. A doctor's daughter, of course. Who goes sailing with him. Another of these hearty athletic types like poor Jean, I haven't a doubt. When he could have married that beautiful chestnut-haired pianist.'

This girl was not beautiful. But she had distinction, and, Simon discovered, apparently unshakeable poise, since she appeared neither angered nor frightened by Annabel's *grande dame* hauteur and disapprobation. She took it in her stride and remained polite but entirely calm.

Hugh knew how to pick them, Simon thought. A pity Annabel wouldn't take to the girl, though she softened a little when she found the creature at least knew how to dress.

Clare was wearing her silver tunic and tights, and over them she had a short black cloak – short cloaks were newly in – fastening high at the throat. She had painted her eyelids silver, and her fingernails (the reason that she was not wearing silver lipstick, too, was simply that Hugh objected to it). Her only jewellery was her engagement ring, a square-cut diamond in a modern setting that Annabel valued instantly as costing at least as much as the Alfa-Romeo of which he had once been so proud.

'I'm glad to see,' she remarked in her voice that was tinkling like the ice in their martinis, 'that you've not fobbed – er – *Clare* off with one of those cheap and nasty little rings.'

Clare spread her hand and turned it about, saying nothing.

'Diamonds are forever,' Hugh commented. 'According to the advertising men, anyway. So they had better be good.'

He looked at Clare, and she looked back at him. It was obvious to Simon that the word that held the two of them was not diamonds, but forever. He watched them pledging one another in silence under Annabel's nose, and envied Hugh.

Simon and Annabel went to Brookhampton, and stayed at the Rose and Crown, that hostelry so despised by Hugh. The Calderwoods had staunchly offered to put them up, but Hugh had firmly declined their offer. He knew how tiresome Annabel could be as a guest, suddenly throwing the house into uproar by demanding hot lemon, black coffee, egg flip, breakfast in bed, her suit pressed, or a telephone call to Zurich. Then, of course, she detested Jean Ravelston, who would be staying there. 'It simply isn't viable,' he told Jock. 'They can stay at the Rose and Crown, and like it. Let her turn that dump upside down. Do the place good. By the way, don't forget, on Friday, I'm relying on you to come to my dinner there.'

He was having the traditional stag party on the eve of his wedding, and had invited the entire resident medical staff at the hospital.

'I should only put a damper on the proceedings,' Jock protested.

Hugh grinned. 'That's the idea,' he said cheerfully. 'Stop them getting out of hand. Save me the trouble. One of the reasons I'm asking you.'

'Are you serious?'

'Couldn't be more so. I don't want the affair to degenerate into the equivalent of a bump supper, with a lot of riotous horseplay and everyone getting sloshed. I'm too old for that sort of high jinks, thanks very much. Besides, I don't intend to have a hangover on my wedding day. So I should be most appreciative of your presence. Apart from that, I'd like you to be there.'

'Right, then, that's settled. Thanks very much, Hugh, I'll look forward to it. The girls had better have a get-together at March Farm that evening, don't you think? Emma's arriving with her brood and her *au pair* girl in the afternoon. Foretaste of real family life for Clare. She'll like that.'

'It seems a dreadful imposition,' Hugh said. 'All my family dumped on you, complete with nappies and *au pair* girls.'

'Nothing we like better than a full house, you know that. In any case, we don't seem to have netted your *entire* family. Don and Nicola aren't arriving until the actual ceremony, I gather?'

Their eyes met, Jock's highly amused. Hugh reddened. 'As far as I know,' he said.

'Clare hasn't met her, has she?' Jock probed. He wanted to discover if Hugh had told Clare about his previous girl-friend.

'No.' Hugh grimaced. He had nerved himself to tell Clare all about Nicola, their love and its ending, only to find he had been forestalled by the indefatigable Ben. 'She appears to know all about her,' he said wryly. 'Ben apparently related my love life to her in considerable detail when she can hardly have been more than seventeen. Educative, he had the astonishing nerve to inform her. And what he left out, Emma has filled in. They yakked away together for hours in the kitchen the other night.'

Emma and Clare had in fact taken to each other at once. Clare was not at all what Emma had expected. All Hugh's girls were sophisticated, of course, and this one was no exception. Emma had loyally entertained them over the years, had found them hard to handle, and had prayed that he would not find himself tied to one for life. After ten years of marriage to Rodney, Emma

315

thought she knew the qualities required for marriage to a Ravelston. Clearly Clare had them. This was a relief.

Over drinks in the untidy sitting-room, where a teddy sat on the windowsill and the desk was covered with a pile of wooden bricks, a pack of Happy Families, a roll of cotton wool and a hairbrush, they began to know each other. The *au pair* girl had finished putting the children to bed (Emma and Rodney had two girls and two boys, the youngest eighteen months and the eldest eight) and was now in the kitchen seeing to the vegetables, while the casserole Emma had prepared the previous evening simmered in the oven. Emma relaxed thankfully from what had, not unusually, been a strenuous day. She had been dreading this evening, but it was going to be all right.

Hugh relaxed equally. He was very fond of Emma, and to him the evening ahead presented no demands. He looked at Emma, plump-cheeked, her nose a little shiny, her gleaming brown hair flopping untidily about, since she had washed it herself that morning, and at Clare, tonight wearing a striped polo-necked dress with shoes and stockings matching the brilliant purple of the dress, and suddenly thought 'at home with the women in my family'. The thought delighted him, and the feeling of security it brought. These were the two women of his

316

family, and he loved both of them. His life was knitting together. For years it had been split. First there was the gap between himself as Annabel desired him and as his grandfather saw him. Then the break in his development when disaster struck and he left the Central and everything that had until that time mattered to him. He had tried in his years at Brookhampton to solve the dilemma of who he was, irrespective of what others wanted him to be, what sort of personality he owned, what he himself wanted to make of his life. He had begun to solve it, but there remained a gap between Hugh Ravelston, working in the wards and clinics, and Hugh Ravelston dithering about in his private life, in a muddle first about Nicola and then about Judith, trying to be with them both what he was not. Now he had Clare, and at last it was all beginning to make sense. The past and the present were flowing together. He was beginning to be a whole person, integrated and secure.

Emma and Clare were talking busily about *Sea Goose* and sailing in her. A typical Ravelston conversation, of the sort Annabel deplored.

'When Rodney's at home, and you have *Sea Goose* at East Callant,' Clare had asked, 'do you do much sailing?'

'Last time he was home, hardly any,' Emma admitted. 'I was pregnant, for one thing. And

317

the children need such a lot of feeding, and they so very quickly get bored and fractious on board. You have to keep taking them ashore for paddling and sand castles and ice cream. I left them behind with Anne-Marie once or twice, but then that was rather a strain for her. As soon as they're a little older, we shall take them with us.'

'It must be difficult, though,' Clare agreed. 'Hugh and I were wondering, weren't we? Because we'd like to have a boat we could cruise in, but then we want to start a family too. And Hugh has this cottage at East Callant – you know it, of course – and I wondered if we mightn't do better to use that as a holiday cottage, and keep Hugh's Flying Fifteen. Not so satisfying as long cruises, but exciting, and probably more practical, at least until the children are out of nappies.'

Hugh grinned. 'She always says "the children" as though we have half a dozen stashed away in the boot of the car,' he told Emma. 'I keep pointing out to her, it's a long slow haul having them.'

'You aren't really thinking of six?' Emma asked, blinking.

'Clare is. I'd settle for three.'

'I always longed to be part of an enormous family,' Clare explained. 'So I'd simply love to bring up a brood of children.'

'I tell you what,' Emma interrupted.

'About sailing. Why don't we join forces?'

'Um?'

'You know how Rodney and Hugh have practically shared *Sea Goose* for years now. When Rodney's home, of course, we keep her at East Callant. Why don't we all share *Sea Goose* and Harbour Cottage, and the cooking and nappie washing and minding the horrid brats and everything?'

'What a wonderful plan,' Clare said, her eyes shining.

'You've got something there,' Hugh agreed.

'Then you and I,' Emma pointed out to Clare, 'could take it in turns to look after the children, and the other could go sailing.'

This theme occupied them throughout dinner. Afterwards Clare went with Emma to see to the washing-up. She admired the kitchen, which, unlike the rest of the house, was streamlined with modern stainless steel and gadgets, brilliant with clear colour and shining with functional efficiency.

'If you're really going to have six kids,' Emma replied, 'make sure of a good kitchen before you reach number two, or it'll be too late, and you'll end in chaos.' She laughed and began filling the dishwasher. 'Have all the mechanical aids,' she added, 'otherwise you're completely bogged down.'

'Do the saucepans go in that thing?' Clare demanded.

'No.'

'I'll wash them up, then, while you do the dishwasher.'

Emma chuckled happily. 'I can see you'll be a much more congenial member of the family than Nicola,' she remarked. 'Washing up saucepans is not at all Nicola's line.'

'No?'

'Emphatically not. Lazy little slut.'

'What is she really like? I know Ben loathed her.'

'She's a bitch. But, let's face it, a damned attractive one. Don't kid yourself about that. Rodney always says–' Emma paused, frowning.

'What?'

'It's difficult to express. That – that Hugh is muddled about girls because of Annabel. That Annabel is awful, but he loves her, so he looks for a girl in her image. Now, personally, I think Annabel's a dead loss.'

'Me, too.' Clare dried her hands and hung up the tea towel.

'But she's very attractive, and she has great charm. In a way, you can't help falling for her when you're with her.'

'I can,' Clare said grimly, sitting down at the kitchen table.

'So can I, as a matter of fact, but I can understand it when other people can't. Especially men.'

'I suppose you're right.'

'Anyway, Rodney says Hugh has always looked for another Annabel, to love him as she hasn't done. And of course the search always ended in failure. They didn't. Because they were as superficial as she is. The wrong sort of person for him altogether. That's why Nicola let him down at the crucial moment.'

'How she *could*. I've never been able to understand it.'

'Nor me. But then we're neither of us like that. We're different.'

They looked at one another. 'We love our men,' Clare began.

'More than ourselves,' Emma ended. 'Well, it's true,' she added, flushing.

'You're right,' Clare agreed.

'Rodney says,' Emma continued, 'that Annabel has interfered a lot with Hugh. Not just over girl-friends, but over the life he leads, and the person he's tried to become. He's tried to be what Annabel wanted, which is a great mistake, because he isn't naturally like that at all. He's a typical Ravelston, only more so. He's more like his grandfather than any of them. Take this determination to stay in clinical medicine, to his own disadvantage. That's old Sir Donald. He was a great clinician. Not Archie, and not Rodney or Don. They're lab workers. Investigators. But Rodney admits now he was probably wrong when he tried to persuade Hugh to go into the research laboratories and do biochemistry instead of clinical research. He thought it was for his own good, but Hugh's too like the old man. It wouldn't have suited him. Fortunately, he knew it. He was right, Rodney thinks now, to settle for nonentity at Brookhampton. I'm sorry,' she added. 'That's very tactless of me, and perhaps Rodney is wrong about his future as a clinician. I don't see why it should be as dreary as he makes out.'

'Hugh would agree with him, though. He says he chose with his eyes open. Of course, I don't understand all this about nonentity, myself. My grandfather wasn't Sir Donald Ravelston, F.R.C.P., though. He was plain Charles Seabrook, M.D., a general practitioner in Fordham, like his father before him. But there was nothing wrong with his life that I could see. It gave him satisfaction. And there's nothing wrong with Brookhampton that I can see either. It's a great improvement on Fordham, for instance. I didn't know Hugh at the Central, where everybody was so grand. I only knew him at the Brookhampton General, which strikes me as a good hospital doing a lot of useful work and staffed with some outstandingly nice and capable people. All right, so it's not the Central. So what? Not everyone has to be born and raised and die at the Central. A dead bore it must be, I should have thought.

My father was at Bart's, and my grandfather at Guy's.'

'Attagirl. That's the stuff,' Emma said appreciatively. 'You instil that point of view into Hugh. And keep on about your father at Bart's and your grandfather at Guy's. I like the sound of that, in this family.'

They sat in silence in the gleaming kitchen for a minute or two. Emma was composing a letter to Rodney in her head, all about how excellent Clare was going to be both as a wife for Hugh and as an addition to the family.

'Then there was Judith,' Clare said exploratively.

'She wouldn't have done,' Emma said at once. 'Too tense. Very lovely, of course. But an egotist. I'm perhaps not being at all fair to her, because I know she was very unhappy at the time I first met her. But Hugh was the one Rodney and I cared about, and she was no good to him at all. Of course, Hugh's dreadfully vulnerable.'

Clare smiled tenderly. 'Yes,' she said. 'He is.'

'Rodney is too, though he doesn't let people realise it if he can help it. But of course,' she frowned and sighed, 'it's not all gas and gaiters being married to a Ravelston.'

'In what way especially?'

'You have to fend for yourself.'

'Oh yes,' Clare agreed at once, memories of many occasions on *Sea Goose* flooding in.

'Rodney's absolutely sweet to me when he remembers about me, and when he's not engrossed elsewhere. But when he's pre-occupied I'm expected to look after myself, as well as after anything of his he happens to have temporarily overlooked. And just when you need him most, there he isn't. It's not my idea to bring up my children by myself. But he wants a family, and he wants to go to the Antarctic, and so I'm expected to cope. You'll be expected to cope, too.'

'I don't think I'll mind,' Clare said confidently.

'You wait,' Emma retorted ominously. 'You just wait.' She curled her lip, still full and soft like a child's. 'You're like me,' she announced. 'You don't want to be the little woman. You'll be an equal partner, you think, and do your stint. Right?'

Clare nodded. This was how she saw her marriage.'

'That's what I thought. But by equal partnership I didn't mean Rodney in the Antarctic and me here with an *au pair* girl and four holy terrors. O.K., so you don't see Hugh going off to the Antarctic for a couple of years at a time. Nor do I. But he'll do something you haven't bargained for. Because that's how the Ravelstons are. They need us terribly, and they make great

324

demands on us. But when we need them, where are they? They're not selfish, or callous. They just happen to be fully committed somewhere else at that particular moment. So you have to look after yourself. And you have to cling on grimly to the fact that you love them – though at times like that you more likely loathe them – and remember to stay the same, and welcome them with open arms when they decide to come home, and not be fractious and complaining.'

'It's worth it,' Clare suggested. She was sure of this.'

'Oh yes, it's worth it.' Emma sighed, and exchanged a look with Clare. 'It sometimes seems to me,' she remarked, 'that women are either bitches, like Annabel and Nicola, and their men dance round them in dutiful and agitated circles. Or they're mugs, like me, and probably you, too. Don takes Nicola her breakfast in bed before he goes to the hospital every morning. Don, of all people. Can you believe it? The only time I've ever had breakfast in bed since I married was when my legs were completely unable to support me and I was running a temperature of a hundred and two.'

'But do you want Rodney to bring you breakfast in bed?'

Emma chuckled. 'Not actually. Rather crumby and upsetting to my daily routine.

But I can't help rather caring for the idea of it.'

'Honestly, though, Emma – don't you truly prefer to be the one taking people their breakfasts? Come clean.'

'I wouldn't mind a day off now and again.'

'No, but basically you want to look after Rodney and the children, to be the one they turn to, rather than have them all thinking they've got to look after you? I mean, what do we get married for? Not to have an easy time. I don't want an easy time.'

'You won't get it, duckie.'

CHAPTER EIGHTEEN

The four of them, Hugh and Ben, Jock and Archie, dinner-jacketed and mellow, returned decorously to Marsh Farm just before midnight on the evening before the wedding, coming into the big hall with the Persian rugs and the steadily ticking grandfather clock to find the house simmering round them with stifled laughs, hushed conversations and glimpses of pyjamaed figures on the landing above. The house was full, to Margaret's delight. She was in the drawing-room with Jean Ravelston, both of them wearing dark woollen dresses with narrow sleeves and draped bodices, and their best court shoes, their hair newly set, back-combed and bouffant. They were drinking brandy in front of the fire and reliving their student days. Jock and Archie joined them.

In the big gingham-hung kitchen with the big table and the wheelback chairs, Emma and Clare, in slacks and polo-necked sweaters, were drinking cocoa and replanning Harbour Cottage to sleep fifteen. Anne-Marie, fresh from the bath in an enveloping scarlet dressing-gown and with

327

her hair in short pigtails, her chubby face pink and shining, was with them, on her way to the study, where a bed had been made up for her. Hugh and Ben joined them.

'Behold my tomorrow's wife.' Hugh kissed Clare.

'You're not meant to be seeing me this evening. I was told I had to leave before you came back.' Clare grimaced. 'It's supposed to be bad luck or something. Mother would be livid.'

'Too bad.' He kissed her again. 'I'm glad you waited.'

'How was your dinner?'

'All right. Not bad at all.'

'You look extremely handsome – and rather red in the face. Both of you, in fact.'

'Brandy.'

'H'm.'

'We are drinking cocoa,' Emma said pointedly.

'They're drinking cocoa, Ben.'

'Why?' Ben asked simply. 'The house will run to something more potent, you know. Or do you like the stuff?'

'We gave it to the children when we put them to bed, and then–' Emma broke off, and looked round. 'Where's Anne-Marie gone? I promised her cocoa too.'

'She scooted smartly out as we came in, panic-stricken in a scarlet dressing-gown,' Ben told her.

'I must take her cocoa to her then.'

'I'd better go home,' Clare said, drifting towards the door. 'Got to get up in the morning, I suppose. Ought to be punctual, perhaps.' She gave Hugh a sidelong glance.

He smacked her on the bottom and said, 'I'll drive you.' They went out together.

When Hugh returned, he found Ben alone in the kitchen. 'They've all gone to bed,' he announced. 'We might as well follow them – unless you want me to make you a cup of cocoa? That's not a very nice noise to make,' he added reprovingly.

'Not meant to be a nice noise. Meant to indicate considerable disgust.'

'Emma will probably teach Clare to give it to you every night,' Ben said unkindly.

'Then I shall quickly teach her not to,' Hugh retorted. He leant against the kitchen table and regarded Ben, who, sitting in the comfortable old basket chair near the Aga, showed no disposition to move.

'A nice crowd tonight,' he remarked lazily. 'I liked that fellow Gibson. And Max is very sound.'

'Sound,' Hugh repeated. 'Sound. You're middle-aged already, summing up people as sound.'

'The taint of the teaching hospital,' Ben agreed. 'You can't escape it in the end. Petrifying. I've had ten years of it now, and it's marked me. As a matter of fact–' he broke off and eyed Hugh thoughtfully.

'As a matter of fact what?'

'I don't know how you'll feel about it – I didn't intend to tell you until you came back from your honeymoon, you see, and–'

'Cut the cackle and come to the 'osses. What are you up to that you think I shan't like?'

'You may not mind,' Ben began doubtfully, and paused.

'Cough it up, for God's sake. This suspense is wearing me down.'

'Well, I'm going to Nyganda. In your place, so to speak.'

'Going to Nyganda?' Hugh was amazed. 'Are you, you old so-and-so. Isn't that a bit rash?'

'Career-wise?'

'Yep.'

'Possibly.'

'In fact not a very *sound* plan, old boy, at this juncture.'

'I shall have to make my way again when I come back, and work pretty hard to regain the position I have now, if that's what you're thinking. But I may not want to be where I am now.'

'The youngest consultant at the Central.'

'Peter Pan in person,' Ben said caustically. 'And that's what I shall be, if I stay on. I tell you honestly, the idea of spending the next thirty years walking the wards at the Central frightens me horribly.'

Hugh looked at him. Some people, he was thinking, have all the luck. And then throw it away.

'You're not as unlucky as you may think,' Ben continued, apparently having read his expression. 'You were forced to get out, I know, and you had a rough time. But the result was you made a life for yourself. It's time I did the same, not stood around accepting what the pundits hand out.'

'I find it difficult to understand,' Hugh said mildly. 'What's wrong with the Central?'

'You think you'd like a chance to spend the next thirty years there? You wouldn't, not if you tried it. Look what it's done to Vanstone, for instance.'

'What?'

'You worked for him, you know what he's like.'

'Clever, a bit hard.'

'Supercilious, and shallow. Oh what a clever boy am I, and don't anybody dare step out of line.'

'Perhaps. But you'd never end up like Vanstone.'

'Rodney got out. My father got out.'

'Yes.' Ben was only repeating Jock's action of a generation earlier, of course, Hugh realised. 'Your father will be pleased,' he remarked.

'Think so? I wasn't sure what he'd feel.'

'Oh yes. He's been muttering about were you doing too well (of all things) and where would it lead? I told him you'd be all right. Which you would be. You don't want to be frightened off by looking at people like Vanstone. That would never happen to you.'

'Well, I hope not. But the truth is, I'm bored. It's an old man's world, the Central. I enjoyed it while I was on the way up, and I was completely blown up with pride when I got on the staff. But I don't want to stay there for the rest of my life. I want to go out and do something. Barham agrees with me. He told me if he hadn't been offered the Chair he was going to do a spell in Nyganda himself. Worthwhile, he said. So you see, he wasn't exactly offering you some post he despised.'

'I didn't know he'd thought of staying out there himself.'

'He tells me it'll do me all the good in the world. His generation, he says, had a war to go to, but our lot missed that. We ought to do a spell in a developing country instead, if only to develop ourselves, he thinks. All I was uneasy about, was whether you'd feel I was snapping the opportunity up too quickly. Before it was decent, in fact.'

'I shan't get it. There's no chance of that.'

'Well, no. I made sure of that before I decided. Barham said he hadn't a hope in hell of getting your appointment past the old men. There was a lot of talk, he says, about the press publicity. Gossipy old hens.'

'You take it, if you want it. I don't mind. I'd just as soon stay here, as a matter of fact.'

'Tell that to the marines.'

'No, it's true,' Hugh said slowly. It was, though he had not known it until he was actually saying it. 'I haven't your wander-lust, you know. I was sorry to be leaving here, even while I wanted to go to Nyganda. As you say, they're a nice lot in this place. I'd just as soon stay.' He thought about it. It was the truth. 'I feel at home. I'm ready to settle down and raise a family, put down some roots.' He smiled and raised his eyebrows in self-mockery. 'Hark at me. How I should have scoffed a few years ago if I'd heard someone else say that. But I mean it. I feel entirely comfortable about it.'

'You should be just about ready to settle down,' Ben admitted. 'Unlike me, I'm about ready to take off. But you've been pushed around a lot in the last five years. Now you can do with a period of consolidation. As long as you don't mind about Nyganda.'

'Take the job and good luck to you. Clare and I will come and visit you there. I'd like that. Interesting. M'm, yes,' he began to visualise a month in Africa by way of holi-day, seeing the work at the Ikerobe Hospital under Ben's aegis. 'Excellent plan,' he said with enthusiasm. 'You go ahead.'

'Don't get puffed up,' Ben said, 'but you have a very generous nature, did you know?'

'Eh? Why do you say that?'

'You don't grudge your friends much.'

Hugh laughed with genuine amusement. 'Thanks very much,' he said. 'I honestly thought for a moment you were going to tell me something really splendid about my character, and all you mean is that I don't grudge you a job I can't have. Terrific. Congratulations, Ravelston, what a tremendous fellow you are.'

'Plenty would grudge it. Don, for instance.'

'Oh, Don. He'd grudge a meal to a starving Indian.'

'Of course he's always been jealous of you.'

'Of me? Don?' Hugh was amazed. 'Not much to be jealous about, I should think even Don could see that – and does, clearly.'

'As far as he's concerned, you're the younger one who came along and threatened his position in the family.'

'Do you know, it never crossed my mind.'

'It often crossed mine. At Garside, for instance, and in the holidays much more. He used to watch you and Rodney together, with hatred and envy written all over his face. You stole Rodney's affections from him, he thought. In a sense he was right. Rodney is much more fond of you than of Don (well, who wouldn't be? Poor old

334

Don). There was nothing he could do about it, the situation existed, and he had to learn to live with it. But he never has learnt.'

'If my father hadn't died, and I had been the eldest of a separate family, perhaps Don would have been an entirely different person,' Hugh suggested.

'Oh no, he wouldn't,' Ben said with certainty. 'You weren't the real cause, simply the occasion. If you had never been born, Rodney would have had some interest or friendship that would have made Don jealous. It's in Don that the trouble lies, not in his environment. He's jealous and vindictive, and that's it.'

'Poor Don, I almost begin to be sorry for him. Then I remember how he's behaved, all my life, and I stop.'

'One day you'll be sorry for him. He only married Nicola to get even with you. You'll watch his marriage fail, and you'll pity him.'

Hugh remembered these words the next day as he and Clare greeted Don and Nicola at the wedding reception. The prediction seemed unlikely to be fulfilled, if he were to judge by superficial appearances – they made a sleek and self-assured couple. Don was handsome and confident in morning dress and buttonhole. Nicola lacquered and breathtaking in an orange Bernat Klein tweed coat, an orange sombrero tied over the dark mist of her hair, orange shoes, bag and gloves, with a yellow silk scarf and yellow stockings. A radiant and head-turning presence, whom Annabel, unfortunately wearing Bernat Klein tweed herself, found infuriating. 'Who is she?' she demanded. 'Don's wife? She looks common.'

Slim and perfectly proportioned, Nicola walked delicately as ever by Don's side, smiling and agreeable. Only the two of them knew how they had bickered all the way down in the car over the cost of her outfit. Now, as they met Hugh and Clare, she took Don's arm. He would never be Hugh, of course, but he could give her what she wanted – the entrée, for instance, to occasions like this, and the Bernat Klein coat, however much he grumbled. Annabel, in fact, was right when she labelled Nicola as common. It was the clue to much of her behaviour. The reason why she had dropped Hugh when he had to leave the Central and go to Brookhampton. She had loved him more genuinely than any other man she had ever known. Yet, when she had visited the cheap lodging in the back street, she had been terrified. She had sprung from mean streets like this herself. She was never going to return to them. This was not what she wanted from life. She could not give up her days at the Central, her flat in London, all the young men waiting to take her out, in order to bring up babies in a back street in

Brookhampton. Even for Hugh Ravelston she could not face this.

So she had left him. It had hurt her to do so, been far more painful than she had expected. There had been another miscalculation, too. She had not allowed for the fact that Hugh Ravelston was not going to sink into obscurity in a nameless street of ugly terraced houses. Obscurity by Central standards, by Ravelston standards, was not anything like the existence Nicola had known as a child, and to which she had dreaded returning. She could have brought up her babies in a comfortable house with a view over the estuary, with two cars in the garage and an *au pair* in the kitchen with her. She had panicked too soon.

She had tried to drop Don and regain Hugh. But it had been too late. She had been forced to realise this, and she had settled for second best. She smiled charmingly at Don now, for effect, and then at Hugh.

He experienced a pang, as he remembered their days together and how he had once loved her. But then nostalgia was past. She was beautiful as ever, but she had left her precarious youth behind in the last few years, and he could see the iron hand behind the velvet – or, strictly, orange suede – glove. She was poised and dangerous, out for what she could get. Lethal, as he had told Clare, and he thanked his stars that she had Don in her clutches and not himself.

Clare was looking poised but not dangerous. After long and protracted argument with Hermione – who saw her daughter in a medieval dress with a train – Clare had compromised. She wore an ivory velvet caftan, branded with gold embroidery at neck and cuffs, with a brief gold pillbox set straight on her short cropped head, gold stockings and shoes. She had refused a bouquet. ('Oh, darling, I thought lovely white carnations would be such heaven'), and carried a slim gold bag. She had been followed up the aisle by one bridesmaid, Emma's eldest daughter, Sally, aged six. Hermione had wanted pages too, but Clare had scoffed and Emma had refused to be responsible for her sons' behaviour. Sally's dress had been made by Hermione, delighted at last to get her hands on some wedding apparel, and was a replica of Clare's caftan, except that it ended half-way up her fat thighs. There had been moments when Hermione had been convinced that this was where Clare, also, intended her wedding dress to end, and she had not felt entirely safe until she saw Clare advancing up the aisle on Jock's arm, her dress safely covering her to her ankles. Sally wore white tights with her caftan, and white shoes with gold buckles, which to her were the high spot of the day. She carried snowdrops, her pudgy face brimming with careful solicitude.

Now, at the reception, Clare's dark eyes were huge under the gold pillbox and her lips curved gently. Her hand lay easily on Hugh's arm as she surveyed Nicola with intense interest. This was the first time they had met.

They chatted for a moment or two, and then Nicola asked, 'And where are you off to for your honeymoon? *We* went to North Africa, didn't we, darling? It was absolute heaven. Are you going somewhere exciting?'

'East Callant,' Clare said in her most downright tones. 'Harbour Cottage,' she added flatly.

Nicola gave a little scream. 'You *can't* be. When there's Paris, Rome, or Prague. We went to Prague last summer. And Warsaw. And then on to the Black Sea.'

Hugh snorted. 'Doing a preliminary reconnaissance, Don? Thinking of defecting behind the Iron Curtain?'

'Don't be ridiculous. I agree with Nicky, there are so many places to see, why on earth you have to stick around in East Callant in mid-winter...? Especially when you're going to be stuck down in this dreary hole for the rest of the year. I take it you are staying? Very unfortunate, all that publicity.' He looked triumphant.

'Yes, I'm staying,' Hugh agreed briefly.

'Oh, it's not at all bad here, darling, you mustn't exaggerate,' Nicola said kindly. 'I thought the church was quite interesting, and the drive out here was pleasant, wasn't it? But I do think you are making a mistake not to go abroad for your honeymoon. I mean, East Callant at the best of times isn't exactly one's cup of tea, and in winter–' she shivered expressively.

'We shan't notice,' Clare said simply. 'Or I shan't anyway.'

'Nor shall I,' Hugh said firmly. 'We shall have other things to think about than the climate.' He smiled at Clare, and wondered how long it would be before they could get away.

She smiled back at him radiantly, and then threw casually at Nicola, before they moved off, her final remark. 'You see, I find it rather overwhelming to be in love with Hugh. I don't particularly want to be overwhelmed by Paris and Prague and Rome and Warsaw as well. Too complicated for me. I like life simple.'

Hugh was delighted. He looked down his nose at Don, who returned the look.

It had been Clare's suggestion that they should spend their honeymoon at the cottage. Hugh had put forward Paris, and had talked about hotels. Clare had remembered at once how he had taken her conscientiously to dinner at the Rose and

340

Crown, like a kind uncle, because he knew she was young enough to enjoy dinner at a hotel.

'Hotels,' she muttered disparagingly. 'I know you still think I'm a child and have to be doled out treats. But I'm growing up and I want different things. Can't we be alone together? No four-star hotels.'

'Even I don't expect to spend my honeymoon on *Sea Goose* in mid-December,' Hugh said, his lips twitching.

'I know – the cottage.'

'Would you like that?' he asked doubtfully.

'We can light great fires, cook huge meals for ourselves at whatever time we feel like, and go for walks – even a sail a little, if the weather turns fine. We can go into Cambridge for meals and shopping and to look around the colleges. A nice domestic routine, all by ourselves.' She put her arms round him.

He sighed with satisfaction. 'Sure you won't be bored?'

'Bored?' she repeated. 'Bored?' She sank into gales of laughter.

After the reception, Daniel took Hermione for a drive, and then to dinner at a country hotel where the food was outstandingly good. Hermione visibly relaxed.

'A very straightforward meal I thought we'd have,' Daniel suggested. 'After all these funny oddments you've been having.'

Daniel considered Hermione had been existing on weeks – except when he himself took her out and fed her – on tea and toast, interspersed with sherry and biscuits. Now he ordered steak and kidney pudding followed by apple charlotte, of both of which he was inordinately fond.

Afterwards, drinking coffee in a quiet corner of the lounge, he said firmly, 'Well, Hermione, one wedding is always said to lead to another, you know,' and proposed to her.

'Oh Daniel, how terribly nice of you,' Hermione fluttered. 'I ought to say I'm surprised–'

'Why?'

'Only of course I'm not, naturally I've thought about it. But–' she frowned, and pleated her handkerchief into minute and regular folds.

'But what?'

'I don't – you must know, Daniel, I'm not – I'm not at all like Margaret.'

'Of course you're not. Don't need to tell me that. Eyes in my head, my dear.'

'No, but I mean – I mean – I don't make at all a good wife. This – this is terribly difficult for me to say, because I only half-understand it myself. But I know I shan't suddenly change. I don't even want to change, not at my age. I haven't the energy for it. I – I didn't manage to change, when I

342

was younger. When I must have been much more adaptable. So it's no good thinking I'll change now.'

'My dear girl, what makes you think I want you to change?'

'Oh, but I ought to. If I decided to marry again. I didn't realise until recently. I've been very stupid, I'm afraid. I've been watching Clare and Hugh, you know, and it's all so different from when I married Tom. Of course, Clare is older and far more sophisticated than I was when I married, but – but she's so much more sensible than me, Daniel.' She ended on a note of agitation.

'I know she is, my dear. You're quite right. But I'm a very sensible fellow, you know. Sensible enough for two.'

'But – but you see, I must tell you, I have to tell you before it's too late, I may make a *dreadful* wife. Tom and I – it's wasn't all his fault, you know, that our marriage broke up. A lot of it was mine. I did none of the things that wives are supposed to do.' She spoke in faint wonderment, and might from her tone have been saying 'none of the things that unicorns are supposed to do' from all the bewilderment she evidently retained still as to those mythical duties.

'Not to worry, Hermione.'

'But – but Daniel, it's no good being *kind*. You must understand. I don't think I'd be any better this time. I – you are so kind, I couldn't bear you to marry me and be disappointed. You've got to understand. I'm not domesticated. I can't run a house. Woodie has always done it for me, and I – oh, Daniel, I haven't had any sex life since Tom went to Malaya.' She blushed scarlet. 'That was over twenty years ago. I haven't missed it, and I don't think I want one now.' She raised agonised eyes to his.

Daniel had immense self-confidence. He wanted at this moment only to comfort Hermione, who had worked herself into a terrible state. He could see she was ready to marry him, and needed only a little reassurance and some firmness. 'It'll be quite all right, my dear,' he said solidly. 'Just trust me, and we shall do very nicely together.'

So it was settled. They would be married in the New Year, they decided, and Woodie would move with Hermione to the Warren, Daniel's house outside Brookhampton. Daniel had few doubts. Hermione was the type of woman he had always liked, he had one successful marriage behind him, and he was tired of solitude. There would be problems, of course, but none that he could not handle. Hermione was only too glad to be managed, she assured him. He gave her a wonderful feeling of security. She would be glad, she added mischievously, to be rid of Mary Farquharson at last, and all her inter-

344

minable chat about dreary old St Ursula's.

'Poor Mary, I should have broken away from her years ago, Clare was quite right. I'm afraid I've been very feeble.'

'You hadn't a man to manage for you,' Daniel said.

Their own future settled, Hermione began to mull over the wedding. Daniel looked amused, and ordered brandy.

'I must say,' Hermione began, 'I thought it was all in excellent taste. Hugh's mother – who is very charming, don't you think, though frightening – I thought looked a little ostentatious, didn't you? All that orange fox.' Hermione herself had been elegant in smooth oyster kid with mink collar and hat, and beneath it an oyster velvet suit and her pearls. 'But at least she had some style. I'm very fond of Margaret, but she simply does *not* know how to dress.'

'Salt of the earth, Hermione.'

'Oh, I daresay, but truly she and Hugh's aunt were a pair of frumps. Both of them in their old musquashes and those awful felt hats. They looked as if they were out doing meals on wheels, not attending a wedding.'

Daniel had to laugh.

'Fortunately they didn't get into many of the photographs,' Hermione added smugly.

The photographers had been there in force, and pictures appeared in the London papers.

Hospital Colour Bar Row – Doctor Weds. Dr Hugh Ravelston and his bride, formerly Miss Clare Dunn, leaving Brookhampton Parish Church after their wedding today. Below this, since their readers might have shorter memories than their own, they printed a small version of the earlier photograph of Max and Hugh. The caption pleased no one, but the photograph was good, and Clare in her beauty sent the sale of caftans soaring, while at the Brookhampton Hospital the patients were as delighted as Hermione.

At the Central they were anything but delighted. They regarded the publicity sourly. 'Young Ravelston's in the news again, I see.'

'Can't seem to keep out of it. Don't understand it at all.'

'Handsome couple, you'll admit.'

'H'mph.'

'Extraordinarily good-looking family, the Ravelstons.'

'H'mph.'

'I've never been able to understand, you know, how he managed to find himself in that position.'

'What position? Chap gets himself into the papers – get himself into anything, if you ask me.'

'Yes, but the G.M.C. and all that trouble. Made the place too hot to hold him, didn't he? Eh?'

'Pity, really. Capable young devil.'

'Can't keep himself out of the *papers*, though. Don't call that very capable. H'mph.'

'Pretty girl, eh?'

'Dunn, the virologist's daughter, I'm told.'

'Really? Bart's man. Done quite well for himself, though.'

Hermione, at least, was pleased with the photographs, and showed them to Daniel with pride. He took a different attitude. 'Poor chap,' he said. 'They can't leave him alone, can they?' He mentioned the publicity to Jock on the next occasion they met.

'I don't think he minds now,' Jock said. 'He has other things in his life, at last. With any luck he'll never even see this lot, in any case. All forgotten by the time he comes back on duty.'

'Hope so,' Daniel agreed. 'I must warn Hermione not to brandish them at him. And the publicity, however unfortunate it was from his point of view, served our purpose, if nothing else. We can keep him here now.'

'No need to go looking for a consultant to run the intensive care unit after all,' Jock said. Their eyes met.

Daniel nodded. 'Very satisfactory,' he said.

EPILOGUE

Down at East Callant, Harbour Cottage was warm and welcoming. Jean had been down there, to air the place, and lay in stocks of food for them. She had found a local woman to come in daily, and Hugh and Clare were greeted by a roaring fire in the sitting-room, hot water in the tank and roasting beef in the oven. The curtains were drawn against the early November dusk, and the firelight flickered on bookshelves and comfortable armchairs, while there was a tang in the air from great bowls of tawny chrysanthemums left by Jean.

Clare stretched, and yawned. She was wearing a grey Cossack coat, collared and cuffed with chinchilla, a high chinchilla hat, and tall grey boots. 'I feel dead,' she remarked. 'I think I'll have a bath. The water's hot, and I've told Mrs Baxter not to wait, that I'll dish up the meal myself. You have a drink while I have a bath,' she suggested.

'All right,' Hugh agreed. She went upstairs, and he heard her footsteps overhead.

Suddenly he realised, I'm married to the girl, he thought. He shot upstairs and erupted into the bedroom. Clare was sitting in front of the dressing table. She had taken off her coat and the fur hat, and sat in a brief grey tunic with a white polo-necked sweater, taking off her boots.

Her glance met his in the mirror. 'A long day,' she said. 'This morning seems about three months ago.'

'Let me pull,' he suggested, and removed her boots. 'Now I'll unzip you,' he said, and did so.

'Oh,' she expostulated. 'Oh, but–'

'But nothing.'

'My bath – the oven – the joint–'

He pressed his mouth on hers, and carried her over to the bed. She mumbled a faint protest.

'It'll be all right,' he said.

It was.

'It was very nice,' she said.

'You sound surprised.' He turned his head lazily and looked at her. She was lying on her back, staring at the ceiling.

'Not at all what I expected,' she explained.

'Oh? What did you expect?'

'I don't know. Well, for one thing, I thought you weren't supposed to enjoy it for the first time.'

'It's not inevitable. You liked it, did you?'

'You know I did.' She smiled at him joyfully.

'What else was different from your expectations?'

'Oh – it's difficult to say. I don't quite know. I thought it would be more mysterious, I suppose. Out of this world.'

'Wasn't it out of this world?' he asked, faintly disappointed, but settling her comfortably against him and treasuring her soft warmth. She immediately curled herself round him and fitted herself into his angles like a second skin. She was right, he thought. Nothing between the two of them could be described as out of this world. Very much the contrary.

'No,' she said definitely. 'Like this. This is delicious. Cosy and delicious. The feel of you. Making love was delicious, too. I thought it would be poetic. Or something like that. But it wasn't, it was simply delicious, and like doing something you've loved all your life. I can't imagine how anything so marvellous – how this can be the first time I've ever – so absolutely *meant* ... what a gorgeous thing to do.' She mumbled incoherently for a moment longer, then yawned briefly. Suddenly he realised she was asleep.

He settled her head conveniently against his shoulder, and went to sleep himself.

The publishers hope that this book has given you enjoyable reading. Large Print Books are especially designed to be as easy to see and hold as possible. If you wish a complete list of our books please ask at your local library or write directly to:

Dales Large Print Books
Magna House, Long Preston,
Skipton, North Yorkshire.
BD23 4ND

This Large Print Book, for people
who cannot read normal print,
is published under the auspices of

THE ULVERSCROFT FOUNDATION